O9-BUD-387

SNOW, FIRE, SWORD

SNOW, FIRE, SWORD

By SOPHIE MASSON

An Imprint of HarperCollinsPublishers

Quotation on page v from "What It Takes" by Peter Kocan, published in *Fighting in the Shade*, Hale and Iremonger, 2000. Reproduced by kind permission of the author.

Eos is an imprint of HarperCollins Publishers.

Snow, Fire, Sword

 Printed in the United States of America. For information address HarperCollins Children's Books, a division of HarperCollins Publishers, 1350 Avenue of the Americas, New York, NY 10019.
www.harpereos.com

Library of Congress Cataloging-in-Publication Data
Masson, Sophie, 1959–
Snow, fire, sword / by Sophie Masson.— 1st American ed.
p. cm.
Summary: In the mythical, Indonesia-like country of Jayangan, a village girl and an apprentice sword-maker embark on a magical journey to defeat a hidden evil that threatens their land.
ISBN-10: 0-06-079091-1 (trade bdg.)
ISBN-13: 978-0-06-079091-2 (trade bdg.)
ISBN-10: 0-06-079092-X (lib. bdg.)
ISBN-13: 978-0-06-079092-9 (lib. bdg.)
[1. Magic—Fiction. 2. Spirits—Fiction. 3. Fantasy.]
I. Title.
PZ7.M42386Sn 2006 2005018149
[Fic]—dc22 CIP
AC

Typography by Hilary Zarycky
2 3 4 5 6 7 8 9 10
❖
First published by Random House Australia 2004
First U.S. Edition 2006

It's one thing to see such heroism
Through the simplifying haze of the years,
Another to perform it at the time
Amid darkness and confusion and tears.

PETER KOCAN

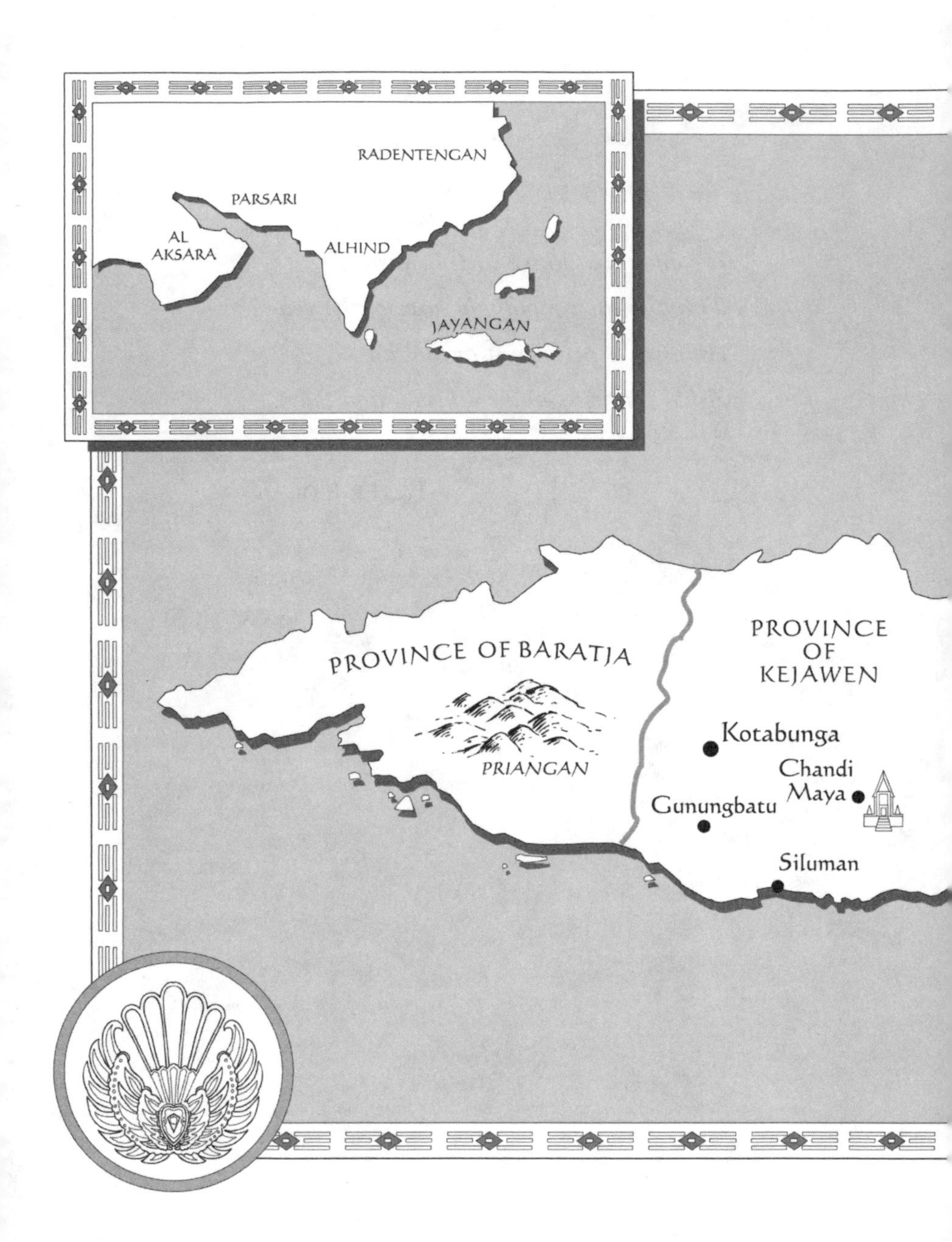
RADENTENGAN
PARSARI
AL AKSARA
ALHIND
JAYANGAN
PROVINCE OF BARATJA
PRIANGAN
PROVINCE OF KEJAWEN
Kotabunga
Chandi Maya
Gunungbatu
Siluman

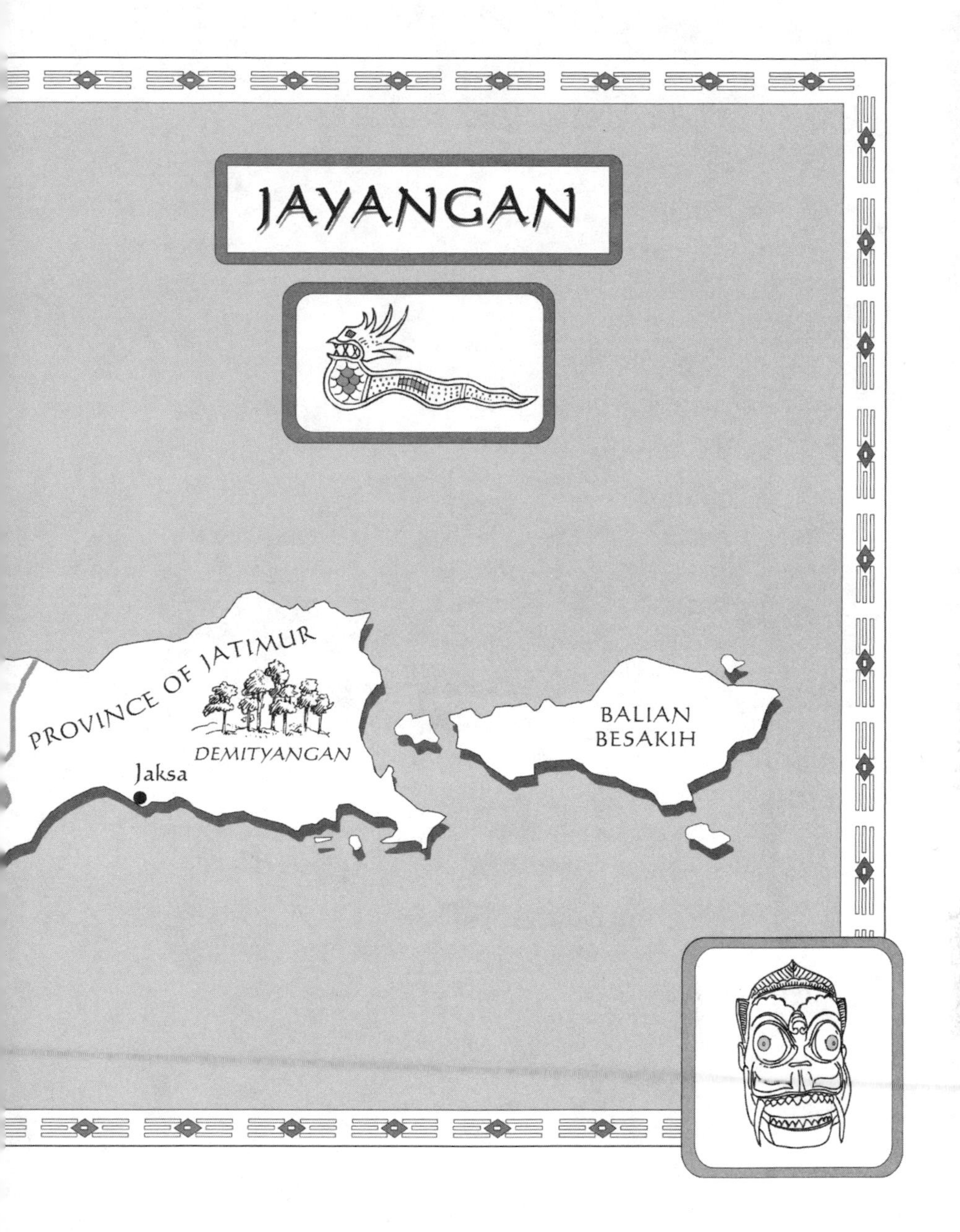
JAYANGAN
PROVINCE OF JATIMUR
DEMITYANGAN
Jaksa
BALIAN
BESAKIH

SNOW, FIRE, SWORD

ONE

HOW TIRING THIS journey was! Why did they have to walk, rather than go by car or bus? Why go around the long way rather than use the main roads? Why, oh why, spend uncomfortable nights sleeping in forests and ditches instead of comfortable guesthouses? Grumbling to himself, Adi trudged along the muddy dirt track behind his master. Before they'd left, he'd been so excited at the prospect of his first visit to Kotabunga, the great capital city of Jayangan. It was more than excitement at the prospect of seeing the city, seat of the Sultan of Jayangan. It was also because this was a great moment in Adi's life.

After two years in Empu Wesiagi's workshop, working at all kinds of tasks, Adi had been allowed to help his master create an important new kris, from beginning to almost the end: carefully shaping and tempering the curved skystone blade, decorating the metal and leather scabbard with delicate tracework. Only right at the end did Empu Wesiagi take over, for that was the time when the sacred, magic formulae were said over the weapon to dedicate its spirit to its new owner, who was to be none other than the Sultan himself!

Adi's joy at this honor had been tempered by the kris-smith's strange insistence that he not tell anyone where they were going. If he must tell his family something, he should tell them they were going over the sea to Balian Besakih, to consult with a kris-smith over there. Adi could not understand this deceit but he trusted his master so did as he was told. After all, Empu Wesiagi had given him the coveted apprenticeship in his workshop, and had over the last couple of years proven to be a good and kind master. Yes, Empu Wesiagi must have his reasons.

As he must have his reasons for choosing to go to Kotabunga by these winding and out-of-the-way paths. It didn't help, though, when you felt tired and dirty and uncomfortable, when the road seemed to stretch interminably in front of—

"Stop!" Empu Wesiagi's voice jolted Adi out of his rebellious thoughts. "Adi, can you hear anything?"

Adi stared at his master, who had stopped stock-still in the middle of the path. The old man's face was pinched and drawn. He looked unwell, thought Adi, dismayed.

"Hear anything, sir?" he said carefully. There was nothing of note to be heard, just the usual sounds of the countryside—the breeze swishing in the paddy fields to either side of the road, the shushing sound of wind in the forest beyond, bird calls, distant engine noises. He looked around. Night was beginning to fall, shadows were creeping in over the fields, it would soon be time to stop and— In the next instant, Adi got the shock of his life, for his beloved master sprang on him with such ferocity that he fell over backward onto the muddy road. Before he had time to react, Empu Wesiagi pulled him with extraordinary force deep into the paddy. "Stay here!" he ordered. Dazed, baffled, Adi tried to scramble to his feet. With a swift movement, the kris maker unsheathed the kris—the beautiful new weapon that was a gift to the Sultan—and pointed it threateningly at his apprentice, who fell back. "Stay here. Don't even try to argue. Whatever you see, whatever you hear, whatever happens, don't move, or you will die."

Adi could well believe it. His master's eyes shone with a red light; the kris's beautifully made, sinuous, wickedly sharp blade was pointed right at Adi's throat.

"Do you understand me, Adi?"

Adi swallowed. He nodded. Empu Wesiagi's eyes narrowed. He reached into his clothes and took out two lengths of rope and a large handkerchief. "I have to do this, Adi. You cannot follow me." Kneeling down, he swiftly tied Adi's hands together, and then his feet. But before he could gag the boy with the cloth, Adi suddenly found his voice. "Master, why are you doing this? What have I done wrong?"

"Forgive me," said Empu Wesiagi, tying the gag around Adi's mouth. "It is for your own safety. The hantumu must not know you are with me."

The engine noise was getting louder. No, not one engine, but several motorbike engines. An ordinary sound—so why did the hair rise on the back of Adi's head, why did his spine feel like ice? He could not speak, but he could still think, and in his mind, two words spoken by the kris maker echoed. The hantumu. He shot a look at his master. Was the great Empu Wesiagi in league with the hantumu?

Empu Wesiagi whispered, "Adi, there is no time. But do not forget this. I brought you with me because you are the very best apprentice I have ever had. And that is why I cannot afford to let the hantumu know you are with me, Adi. You must get to Kotabunga."

Adi closed his eyes. His heart pounded, his bound hands were clammy. He was in a dream. A nightmare.

None of this was happening. When he opened his eyes again, his master had vanished. He heard the swishing sounds the paddy grass made as the old kris maker ran swiftly back to the road. The motorbike engines got louder and louder. Sweat ran down his face, trickled down his neck, soaked his clothes. Images filled his mind, images cobbled together from overheard stories. The hantumu. Dark forces, figures of whispered legend, of bad dreams, and yet now roaming the land once more. The hantumu were eyeless, some said; they dressed all in black and were mounted on black motorbikes, huge swords by their sides. They were assassins, but no one knew where they came from, why they did what they did—murders, kidnappings, the torching of houses, of sacred places. So many things like that had happened in Jayangan in the last few years. No one had been able to catch them, for they always vanished as mysteriously as they had come.

The noise of their engines was so loud now, Adi knew they must be only a short distance away; they must be nearly at the spot where he and his master . . . Then, suddenly, Empu Wesiagi shouted, "I am here, you scum. Here, if you can take me! Ah, you thought I would be afraid!"

The motorbikes revved, then were quiet. A cold voice that sent shivers down Adi's spine answered, "It is nothing to us if you are afraid or not, old man. You come to our master alive or you come to him dead—that is of little importance."

Adi's heart swelled. His master was most definitely not a traitor.

"You won't take me easily, scum of the devil!" Empu Wesiagi's voice rang out, then a clash of steel. Adi could imagine the old man standing on guard, surrounded by the evil hantumu. He could imagine him whirling around, attacking them with the new kris he'd made. Empu Wesiagi was a good fighter as well as a good smith. He would not give up easily.

The battle raged for longer than one would have thought possible knowing that an old man, though strong and broad and big and wily, was gravely outnumbered by evil assassins armed to the teeth. Clash of steel, shouts, screams, bloodcurdling shrieks filled the air for quite some minutes. Bound, gagged, Adi raged against his helplessness, wishing with all his heart he could break his bonds and go and help his master, no matter what he had said. But the rope was tied tightly, the gag too. There was nothing he could do but listen helplessly. His eyes filled with angry tears. Finally came the sound of a motorbike starting up, and another, and another, and another. Four of them. There had been four of them. Adi could hear nothing now except the roar of the machines. An icy hand gripped his heart. Was his master dead, or wounded? Would they come looking for him? No, they did not know he was here. His master had sacrificed himself so they would not know.

The engines rose to a crescendo, then began to fade. Night had fallen. There was no moon. Adi could see nothing. The paddy grass closed in around him, prison and refuge. He had to do as Empu Wesiagi wanted and get to Kotabunga. Yet he was bound and gagged. His master had taken the kris; he could not even cut his bonds. How could he get away?

TWO

DAWN WAS ALWAYS a busy time. Up quickly from her sleeping mat, splashing a little water on her face, brushing and plaiting her long hair, rushing to get all her chores done before she would have to hurry to school, Dewi had no idea that this day her life would change forever.

Her older sister, Ayu, and older brothers, Wisnu and Jafar, were up, too, but not her father, Bapar Wiriyanto, who had had a late consultation the night before. Ayu, who since their mother's death some years earlier had looked after her siblings, was cooking breakfast, and the fragrant smell of rice and chicken stock filled the little kitchen. She barely glanced up as Dewi went out, and why should she? Dewi did the same thing every morning. She needed no supervision. She could have done it in her sleep.

Outside, the air was still cool. It would not stay that

way for long. Soon, the sun would climb into the sky and the day would really begin—a long, hot, hot day, with perhaps a short shower in the evening to cool things down again.

Dewi walked slowly, swinging a little covered plastic bucket in one hand. Without her mind being aware of it, her bare feet followed the path through the family compound toward the paddy field. She walked along thinking of the exams she'd have to take at school in just two months' time. She was not worried about them, for she was a good student and found the work quite easy. But the exams were partly to ready you for the next stage of school, and for the job you might do later. Her teacher thought she should try to become a teacher herself. Dewi had no interest in that, though she was too polite to say so. She had had a dream ever since she was a little girl, but a dream she spoke of to no one. It was of someday becoming a dukun like her father. Girls rarely became dukuns, for it was felt the work was too dangerous. Father had not yet said which of his children was to follow him in his work, and Dewi had never dared to broach the subject with him.

Dewi sighed. Her father, Bapar Wiriyanto, was one of the most important men in the village of Bumi Macan and beyond. His power as a dukun was well known. People traveled quite long distances to visit him and ask for his help. He could cure ills and heal wounds, but most of all, he could see hidden things in the spirit world.

As a young boy, already with a certain gift of his own, Wiriyanto had been taken in by the Harimauroh, the tiger-people of the forest, who sometimes appeared in the forms of tigers and sometimes of people. When he had emerged from the forest, his talents had vastly deepened and improved. He still talked and walked regularly with the tiger-people, leaving his body to enter into the spirit-tiger realm. He had a spirit guide, a very powerful tiger-man who went by the name of Bupatihutan and who was his medium when he went into a trance-journey. Dewi had seen Bupatihutan once or twice, when her father had gone into a trance. This, too, she had spoken of to no one.

She reached the paddy field and walked into a row, picking snails up and placing them in her bucket. They were for the ducks, who loved them and grew fat on them. She had to take care not to crush their shells; the ducks did not like them dead. The snails plopped in with a soft sound. They moved in and around and over each other; Dewi had to put the cover on the bucket, because otherwise they would slide out. She squelched through the wet ground, picking and dropping, her fingers sure and quick; she would soon have enough snails to fill her bucket. She would take them back, feed the ducks, change into her school uniform, have breakfast, wash the dishes, and be ready for Jafar to take her on the back of his motorbike to the little school in the next village. Her morning was ordered, precise. She knew everything that was going to happen in it. It did not worry her, on the whole. Only sometimes, sometimes, she was a little restless, wondering what it might be like to live another way. But she did not talk about that to anyone, either.

She reached the end of the row and turned into the next. The great green stalks of rice rose above her head. In the distance she could hear all the noises of the compound and the village: roosters crowing, the heavy tread of water buffaloes being readied for work, the busy shuffle of insects in the swaying grasses, the sputter of a motorbike engine, the odd shout from someone. She could smell flowers, and stagnant water, and spices, and grass, and smoke from cooking fires.

All at once, a strange unease gripped her. She stopped and looked up, toward the line of forest beyond the village. The forest had always drawn her, and yet she was afraid of it too. In it lived the tiger-people and other spirits, good and bad; in trances, her father's soul wandered there, on his quest for knowledge and healing. It was known, though rarely talked about, that in the center of the forest was the village of the tiger-people. Anyone who went too close to it would be torn to pieces, unless they happened to be someone like Bapar Wiriyanto. And even a great dukun such as he went in only on the Harimauroh's express invitation.

But the forest was just as quiet and peaceful as the paddy field. Dewi frowned a little and shrugged. There was nothing happening; all was as usual. She bent down to pick up one last snail. And almost screamed and dropped the bucket, for there, gleaming through the rice stalks, was a pair of eyes. A pair of large, dark eyes, set under a shock of silky hair, in a round, muddy, tear-stained face that was filled with fear and shock and a huge weariness.

A part of Dewi's mind hammered at her: go, go, run away! Run for help, this is not something you want to know about! But another part of her—the part that wanted adventure, that sought out mystery, that was not afraid—pushed back the rice stalks and got a good look at the face.

"You're gagged!" she said, surprised. Her eyes widened again as she saw his hands and feet. "And bound! Who did this? Who are you?" He was a couple of years older than her, she thought—sixteen, maybe? Whatever, she had lost her fear altogether. "Was it thieves?"

Above the gag, the bright dark eyes flashed. Dewi understood their expression, and flushed. "Sorry." She bent down to untie the gag.

"Thanks. My bonds, please, will you . . ." The boy's voice was hoarse. And it had an accent: the accent of the people of Jatimur, in the east of Jayangan. He was far from home.

Dewi reached inside her sarong and took out the little pocketknife she carried everywhere with her. You often had to cut string and such on a farm. She bent down at the boy's feet and sawed through the rope. He wriggled his feet. "Ow. Pins and needles." He held out his bound hands. "Please, will you cut these, too?"

As she worked, she took in more details of him. He was slight and small, rather thin, dressed in a blue T-shirt, jeans, and battered sneakers. A tiny silver heart hung on a chain around his neck, marking him as a Nashranee, a member of one of the minority religions of the island.

"Thank you," said the youth, rubbing at his wrists as the rope fell away. "Oh. Ow." He touched the red welts on his skin gingerly. "It hurts."

"My father," said Dewi, "he's a dukun, he can help to heal that for you."

"Your father's a dukun? Will he . . ." Suddenly he stopped, crouched down. "Miss, get down! Get down!"

Startled by the urgency in his voice, Dewi dropped to her haunches beside him. Instantly, she was down in the warm green world of the paddy, the grass closing in over her head. The bottom of her sarong was getting wet, but she paid no heed to it. Her heart beat fast, for his fear was infectious. After a while, she whispered, "What is it?"

He gestured at her to keep quiet. She listened, but could hear nothing except the usual sounds of morning. She shot a look at the boy. The strained expression on his face was changing, relaxing a bit. "Sorry," he said at last. "I heard a motorbike. . . . I thought . . . I thought it was them."

"Who? The people who tied you up? What happened? Who are you?"

"My name is Adi. I am from a village called Desagua, in the province of Jatimur. I am an apprentice to Empu Wesiagi, the great kris-smith. And you, miss, you are?"

"I am Dewi, youngest daughter of the great dukun Bapar Wiriyanto, of Bumi Macan."

The boy nodded. "Miss Dewi, thank you for helping me. I will not need to trouble you or your family any longer. I must get to Kotabunga. But first I must go and see if . . ." He made as if to get up and go, but as he got to his feet, his still-numb legs folded under him and he fell to the ground. Dewi rushed to help him.

"You cannot go anywhere like that," she scolded. "You are weak and hurt. You are exhausted. You are probably hungry. My father would be very angry with me if he thought I had let a stranger in need go on his way without helping him. At least come to our house for a rest."

Adi smiled faintly. He was embarrassed by his own weakness. "I will be all right once I—"

"Once you have had a rest," said Dewi firmly, "and a good bowl of chicken soup and rice."

Adi swallowed. Indeed, he was very hungry, very tired. But he couldn't go without knowing . . .

"My master," he said quickly. "The kris maker, Empu Wesiagi. I need to know . . ." He clenched his hands. "If he . . . if he is dead, or if . . ." He looked at Dewi's face and said, "My master was attacked. We were going to Kotabunga, to deliver a special new kris to Sunan Tengah, the Sultan of Jayangan." Dewi nodded without surprise. In the island of Jayangan, most men carried the long dagger called a kris, except for the Pumujisal, a small, strict sect of the majority Mujisal religion, who frowned on all such things as superstition. Krises weren't just weapons; they were also believed to carry a mystical power, each suited to the spirit of its owner. The Sultan was well known as a ollector of beautiful, powerful krises.

Dewi said, "But this is not the direct road to Kotabunga."

Adi fingered the heart around his neck. He looked at Dewi's bright, sharp face. He didn't really want to tell the girl everything. For a start, it was dangerous for her. "I'm not sure, but I think he was afraid something like this might happen. We were on the road, just back up there," he said, pointing. "And then they came . . . and . . ." He gulped. "I just want to go and see if he is . . . if there is any sign of him or if they have—"

"You keep saying 'they,'" said Dewi. "Who are they? Who attacked you and tied you up?"

"Please," he said quickly. "I need to look at the road. To know if my master . . ."

"You can't go," said Dewi. "You can hardly walk. I'll go."

"No! You don't understand."

"I'm sure your robbers are long gone," said Dewi stoutly. "It was straight through the field, where you were attacked? On the little road near the forest?"

Adi nodded. He rubbed at his legs, trying to will them to work properly. "I'll come," he began, but he was speaking to thin air. Dewi had already streaked off between the rice stalks.

She reached the edge of the field and stopped to

listen. Nothing. Cautiously, she parted the rice stalks and looked out. She half expected to see a dead body lying in the middle of the road, but there was nothing. Carefully, she crept out of the field and onto the edge of the road. The mud was churned up. Something had certainly happened here, she thought. There were tire tracks, the marks of many feet, all crossing over one another, and there . . . She crouched down, her heart thumping a little. Blood. And there . . . what was that, half trodden into the mud? She stretched out a hand for it.

"That's the picture my master always carried," said Adi behind her, making her jump. He took the little colored square from Dewi's hand and tried to wipe the mud off it. "See, it's a picture of Rajadi, the greatest kris ever made, the kris of the Sultan's family." Dewi stared at it. "He must have dropped it when they took him." Adi looked up and down the road several times, as if looking would make his master reappear.

"What can robbers want with him? Maybe they want to ransom him? Was he carrying anything of great value?"

"Only the kris," whispered Adi, swaying a little on his feet. Shame, fear, and rage boiled inside him. He should have been fighting at his master's side. He should have been allowed to. It was not right of Empu

Wesiagi to make that decision for him. "The kris he had made for the Sultan. I must go to Kotabunga and tell him."

"I think we should go first to my father," said Dewi. "He will know what to do. And perhaps we can take you to Kotabunga, after you have rested. You look terrible, Adi. You cannot go anywhere on your own just now."

Adi looked at her. A grateful tiredness washed over him. Suddenly, all he wanted to do was sleep, eat, sink gently into forgetfulness. "Thank you. You are very kind."

"Not at all," said Dewi. Not for the world would she have admitted to the frightened, weary boy before her that her pulse was beating with a weird kind of excitement.

THREE

"YOU WILL BE late for school. What were you—" Ayu began as Dewi walked in, but her words dried up when she saw Adi behind her. Ayu's glance flew to Dewi's face. She frowned a little.

"Adi needs to speak to Father, elder sister," said Dewi respectfully. "He needs his help and protection."

Ayu's face cleared. She was used to people wanting to consult Bapar Wiriyanto. It was not normal—indeed not fitting—for Dewi to bring in such clients. But she would give her sister a talking-to later. She inclined her head gracefully toward Adi. "I will take you to our father," she said. "I think he has finished his meditation and is ready to receive people."

"I would like to come with . . ." Dewi began, then flushed as her sister raised her eyebrows. "You will be late for school, little sister," said Ayu courteously.

"Eat your breakfast."

Adi glanced quickly at Dewi. His eyes were wide with shyness now, rather than fear. But Dewi did not insist. She knew it was not her place to go and petition her father on this matter; besides, though Adi might be shy, he would surely not like to be spoken for. So she nodded and turned to her breakfast bowl, while Ayu led Adi out of the kitchen.

Her stomach churned as she mechanically spooned Ayu's good rice into her mouth, not noticing its succulent fragrance as she normally did. She was filled with unease. Bumi Macan was only a small place, a village in the remote Kejawen countryside, and it had always been a good place to live. It was not hard to farm the rich and fertile soil; children were cared for well; and though of course there was conflict between villagers at various times, it was hard to remember when an attack such as the one on Adi and his master had last happened. In fact, Dewi could think of none. People said the spirits smiled on the villagers of Bumi Macan, that Bapar Wiriyanto's good relations with the Harimauroh protected them from all harm.

Ayu came back into the kitchen. Her usually serene face was puzzled. "Father wants to speak to you, Dewi," she said. "He is in the consulting room." Dewi could read the questions in her face: What have you done? Who is this stranger? Why is Father perturbed enough to send for you, the youngest child, and thus the most ignorant? Dewi got up and inclined her head to Ayu. "Thank you, elder sister, for a good breakfast," she said softly, and she slipped past without saying anything more. She knew Ayu would be looking after her, wondering, a little uneasy now too, and her heart thumped. Had she done wrong, bringing Adi here?

The dukun's consulting room was in the center of the house. It was small, dark, and hot, without windows and with only one door. It smelled of incense and lamp oil, and was bare except for a small shrine at one end of the room: a table covered with a red cloth, on which reposed several objects and small holy pictures. Like most people in the village, the dukun was a Mujisal, but he also used images from other faiths, combining them all. That was the way in most of the region of Kejawen, and had been the way for hundreds of years in the village of Bumi Macan. No one found anything strange in it; for there were no fanatical Pumujisal in Bumi Macan, with their hatred of other faiths and what they called devils.

Dewi peered into the dim room. She could see her father sitting cross-legged in front of the shrine, with Adi beside him. All was quiet. Expectant. A shiver of awe rippled over her. She had very rarely been allowed anywhere near the consulting room when her father was working. In fact, he usually kept the door tightly shut. Not today, though.

Dewi hesitated. She did not quite dare to alert her father to her presence, but he turned his head and saw her. He beckoned her into the room, still without speaking, and motioned for her to kneel a little distance from them.

"Daughter," he said, in his deep, warm voice, "Adi has told me you insisted he come here." His face was set, unreadable.

Dewi stammered, "Father . . . I hope you . . . you are not angry . . . but I thought it best to—"

"You did well, child," said Wiriyanto gently, and his face broke into one of his rare smiles. "You did very well."

Dewi felt heat rushing up to her face. Her father so seldom complimented anyone. She bent her head. "Thank you, Father."

He sighed. "Adi told me he did not tell you who attacked his master." He paused. "But I think you should know. It was the hantumu."

Dewi's hand flew involuntarily to her throat. "The hantumu, Father?" She, too, had heard the mysterious stories of the assassins' crimes and depredations. Who in Jayangan had not? But the hantumu had never been sighted close to Bumi Macan before. Did that mean the spirits' protection no longer held good?

Dewi's father was watching her reaction. "Today, Dewi, I want you to stay home. You are not to go to school, is that understood? Jafar will make your excuses to the teacher. He will tell her that you are unwell."

She raised her head, surprised. "Why, of course, Father."

After a moment the dukun said, "I want you to stay home because you are part of this. Fate decreed it was you who should find Adi. Dewi, look after our guest. He will be hungry and tired."

"Thank you, Bapar," whispered Adi. "I cannot express how—"

"Then do not," said the dukun calmly. "Eat, drink, rest, my friend, and do not think of thanking me. I have heard a great deal of your master, Empu Wesiagi. I have heard that he is the greatest kris-smith since the days of the old kingdoms. That he should be in danger is a calamity for all Jayangan. Now I must seek advice from the Harimauroh." He nodded, dismissing them, and they left the room quietly.

Once outside, Dewi said, "Why did the hantumu just tie you up and leave you in the paddy? That isn't usually their way." Her voice was a little tight. She wished Adi had told her earlier about the hantumu.

A rather shamefaced expression crept over Adi's features. "I'm sorry, Dewi. I should have told you. But you see . . ." And he plunged into the bewildering story of how his master had turned on him and tied him up. When he had finished, Dewi was silent a moment. Then she said, "But did you actually see them?"

"No," said Adi hopelessly. "I heard their motorbikes, heard the voice of one of them, heard my master's battle with them. But I did not see them." Adi's face crumpled. "You know what is most terrible to me? That I did nothing to save him, that I could not!" He grasped at the silver heart around his neck, holding it tightly as if to gain strength.

"He did not want you to," Dewi said gently. "He wanted you to survive, to be free so you could do as he wanted you to."

He looked gratefully at her. "You are right." His face fell again. "But I do not know what it is I must do. I only know I must go to Kotabunga. That I must see the Sultan."

"Father will be able to tell us more," said Dewi, hoping she was right. Deep inside her, a fear was growing, a fear born of a new and terrible knowledge: Evil had come crashing into the once-peaceful little world of Bumi Macan.

FOUR

ADI ATE RAVENOUSLY and went off to bed in the boys' room without protest. Jafar and Wisnu went to school, and Ayu worked around the house. She had only raised an eyebrow when Dewi told her that Father had said she would not go to school today. Father's decisions were not to be countermanded, but Dewi knew that Ayu must be curious.

An hour passed, then two. Adi slept on. Dewi changed into a dark skirt and white blouse and sandals, tidied her little cubbyhole of a room, and tried to study. But she could not concentrate. She tried to read, but the words kept dancing in front of her. She tried to pray, but even the familiar, comforting words of prayer seemed to slide past her restless spirit. Finally, she wandered out through the courtyard and into the small garden beyond it.

This was Jafar's domain: He had inherited their mother's love of flowers and her gift for growing them. He had made of this place a fragrant, quiet little world of beauty and contemplation, full of orchids of all kinds, palms, bamboo, bougainvillea and frangipani, and clouds of shimmering, papery butterflies. There were cool, deep-green shadows she could sit in, quietly, and watch the hidden life of ants and beetles that went on so busily under leaf and bloom and stalk, and try to put her mind at peace. Father sometimes said that in a way humans were like ants and beetles, so tiny in a big world, before God. We were given a beautiful, beautiful world, and love within it, and family, and the guidance of the spirit world. We were different from ants and from other animals, too, he said, for human beings have been given knowledge of the truth of the universe—that there is always struggle between dharma and adharma, good and evil, clear sight and blindness. It is an eternal struggle, eternally fought, in every age and every place and every human heart.

She started. A hand had come to rest on her shoulder. She turned. There was her father, looking down at her. His expression was unreadable, his face very pale. There was a strangeness about him that made her scalp crawl.

"Father," she whispered.

"Come, child! Quick! Quick! Come to me!" His voice was thin, wavering, rising to a scream. As his words died away, so his form seemed to fade too. With a beat of terror and awe, Dewi realized what had just happened. He was not standing there in the flesh, in front of her. He was "away," in the world of the tiger-people. He was in danger, and he had called on her to help him!

She ran all the way back through the courtyard and into the house, passing the startled Ayu, who was hanging clothes on the line. As Dewi raced toward her father's consulting room, Adi came out of the boys' room, rubbing his eyes. "What's up?" he said, but Dewi ignored him. She had just reached her father's door when a roar fit to burst the eardrums filled the air. Shouting, terrified, determined, Dewi pushed hard at the door. It was stuck. She threw herself at it, crying, sobbing, yelling; and there was Adi, too, pushing at the door, shoving it hard. Suddenly, it gave way, and they both fell into the room.

It was very dark. All the lights, including the one Father always kept burning in the shrine, had gone out. They could hear labored breathing and smell something—a rank, wild-animal smell. Lying on the floor as if he had been flung there was a crumpled, still figure—Bapar Wiriyanto.

"He's fainted, I think," said Dewi after a terrified half moment, listening to her father's chest. "Help me, Adi. We need to help him sit up. There, put your hands under him . . . oh!"

She nearly screamed, for there, just beyond the shrine, in the darkness yet somehow clear as day, was a face she'd seen before. A stern old man's face, with yellow eyes—the eyes of a tiger. Bupatihutan!

"Sir, what has happened . . . why is my father . . . ?" she stammered.

The yellow eyes glared into her. Though his mouth didn't move, in her mind Dewi suddenly heard a deep, resonant voice. "There is a great battle looming. Go to Kotabunga. You must find Snow, Fire, Sword."

"Honored lord," said Dewi, puzzled, "is Snow, Fire, and Sword in Kotabunga? Where do we find them? There is no snow in our country, but perhaps you mean artificial snow? Or are these names of magic talismans? How do we use them?" She waited, but the voice said nothing. She said, "Sir, my father is hurt."

"There is a great battle looming," the voice suddenly boomed in her head. "There is little time. You must find Snow, Fire, Sword."

"Please, Bupatihutan, I cannot understand if you do not—"

"Snow, Fire, Sword," said the voice, with a crackle

of impatience; and suddenly, the yellow eyes winked out and the face disappeared.

There was silence for a moment; then Adi said, with a catch in his voice, "Who were you speaking to, Dewi?"

She turned her head back toward her father, whose eyes were still closed. She swallowed and murmured, "My father's spirit guide. He is a tiger-man. From the forest."

Adi involuntarily put a hand to his heart pendant. "Lord protect us." He paused. "Did he . . . did they hurt your father? Are the spirits angry with us?"

Dewi looked at him and shook her head. "I don't know."

"What are you doing?" came Ayu's anxious voice from the doorway. "What's happened to Father?"

"He . . . he fainted," said Dewi. "He's all right, I think, though."

"Why is it so dark in here? Who blew out the lights?" Neither Adi nor Dewi said anything. Ayu groped around for the matches that were kept near the oil lamp and lit the wick. A golden glow flowered instantly behind the smoky glass. "That's better. Oh, Father!"

Bapar Wiriyanto was struggling up from the floor. He put a hand to his head. Dewi, with a thrill of fear, saw his hand was bleeding and scored with claw marks. Ayu saw it too. Her eyes widened. But she was a practical girl. "I'll get bandages, water, disinfectant." She went quickly out of the room.

"It's nothing," said the dukun quietly. "Superficial cuts. If they really wanted to hurt me, they could have."

"But Father," said Dewi, "I don't understand. Why did they hurt you at all?"

"It is nothing. Just frustration, impatience, maybe even fear." He sighed. "Yes, the spirits, too, may feel these things. You must not think it is only we humans who may be afraid. There is great turmoil in the spirit world these days, Dewi and Adi, and fear of what is coming."

"Of the great battle," Dewi whispered, and her father stiffened.

"What did you say?"

"Bupatihutan said there was a great battle coming," said Dewi. "He said we had to go to Kotabunga and find—"

"Bupatihutan told you?" interrupted her father. "You saw him?"

Dewi nodded rather uneasily.

"I see." The dukun looked into his daughter's eyes. Dewi shivered a little, for in her father's eyes was not the expression of love and firmness and gentleness she was used to, but a deep, searching light. She could not look away. "Is this the first time you have seen Bupatihutan, my child?"

She shook her head.

There was a short silence; then Bapar Wiriyanto nodded. Slowly, he said, "I understand. How could I have been so blind?" He smiled and touched Dewi gently on the shoulder. "Did he tell you any more, my dear daughter?"

His voice was full of love and pride, and it made Dewi's heart swell. She said, "He said we must find Snow, Fire, Sword."

"Snow, Fire, Sword!" exclaimed her father, but he broke off as Ayu came back with a bowl of water, bandages, and disinfectant. Carefully, she dressed his wounded hand. She asked no questions. She was used to the strangeness of the business their father was in, the gift he wielded—and its dangers. When she had finished, she said, "Father, you should rest."

"Yes, my child," he said absently. Ayu sighed and picked up the bowl. She knew her father would do just as he wanted. As she was about to leave the room, he said, "Ayu, will you please go and ask Anda Mangil if he is free to drive us three to Kotabunga today?" Anda Mangil lived two doors away from Dewi's family. Most villagers did not have cars, only motorbikes and bicycles, so as the proud possessor of a stately old car, he was by way of being the official taxi driver in the village.

"Very well, Father," she said, and was gone.

"The Harimauroh confirmed what I already suspected," Bapar Wiriyanto went on, when Ayu had gone. "The hantumu have been operating all over Jayangan, kidnapping and killing people, and not randomly. Their targets are those wise in the old ways, those who are respected for their links to the spirit world: kris makers and puppet masters and dancers, dukuns and priests, teachers and mystics and musicians. The victims have been from all the corners of Jayangan, and from all the different faiths. As well, the hantumu have attacked and desecrated many sacred places—not out of mindless vandalism, but as part of a very deliberate plan. If the links with the spirits are broken, the people of Jayangan will be left all alone to face the enemy. It is a very dangerous enemy—the most dangerous of all, because it is a hidden one. The hantumu are only its most visible shock troops. Their aim is to spread terror throughout the land of Jayangan, so the people will be demoralized and the country fall more easily to the evil ambitions of their master. The hantumu would not be what they are without the hidden power behind them. We cannot defeat them until we defeat their master."

"But who is their master? Or what?" Dewi felt a cold finger inching down her spine.

"The spirits do not know, Dewi. They cannot see him."

"But why? Why can't they see him?"

"The enemy's tactics have already begun to bite. The link between our world and the spirit world has been weakened. And as more sacred places are attacked and those wise in the old ways are killed or disappear, the spirits' power grows weaker too. They cannot see clearly. They know there is a dangerous enemy there, but they cannot make him reveal himself. That is why they are afraid."

Adi said, "Have they any idea what this thing—this power, this enemy—what exactly its plans are?"

"To take over the human and the spirit worlds of Jayangan." Adi and Dewi stared at him, their blood freezing in their veins. Dewi stammered, "B-but can't the spirits stop . . ."

Her father shook his head. "They cannot. In fact, some of the spirits would like to just block themselves off in the spirit world and leave humans to their fate. I persuaded them that would not be a good idea." He touched his hand gingerly. "One or two did not take kindly to my words.

"We must go to Kotabunga and persuade the Sultan

to act, once and for all. I have no way of getting into the palace, for I am but a village dukun, but I have a friend in Kotabunga, Bapar Suyanto, a master musician, who is greatly respected at Court, and who will understand. We will go to him, and together we can go to the palace. He has a little guesthouse where I have often stayed. It will be safe there for all of us."

"Father," Dewi said, "Father, what of Snow, Fire, Sword? Why did Bupatihutan say we must find it? What is it?"

"I think that is all he knows," said her father slowly. "The spirits cannot see fully; the enemy is too clever. Perhaps Bupatihutan can see that these things—Snow, Fire, Sword, whatever they may be in reality—are necessary to defeat this enemy. But he can see no further than that. The spirits are not infallible, but we must trust it is a clue. We should get to Kotabunga as quickly as possible." A horn sounded outside. "And here, just on time, is dear Anda Mangil! Come, my children, let us depart."

He looked happy, Dewi thought, happier than she had seen him in a long time. Could it be that her dignified, courtly, calm father was actually looking forward to danger and adventure? It did not fit with her earlier notions of her father, but then, this day had hardly been ordinary, in any way.

FIVE

ANDA MANGIL'S CAR was big and comfortable, and though it was about thirty-five years old, it looked pristine, the dark-red paintwork buffed carefully, the silver radiator gleaming, even the tires blackened regularly with special polish. Inside was just as beautiful, with the wooden dashboard and old-fashioned radio, soft, dark-brown upholstery, and chocolate-colored carpet underfoot. But it was more than that—Anda Mangil had decorated the inside of the car with little pictures of Jayangan's sacred places, cut from magazines and mounted in colorful plastic frames that had then carefully been glued to the walls. Colored foil wreaths and garlands had been positioned around each picture. A tiny silver-and-glass vial of sacred mountain-spring water hung from the rearview mirror, along with a bunch of artificial orchids. In the glove box Anda Mangil kept miniature copies of each of the three great holy books of Jayangan—the Mujisal Book of Light, the Nashranee Book of Love, and the Dharbudsu Book of Life—as protection against accidents. Anda Mangil himself was a Dharbudsu, but he said that it was a good thing to have all three books with you, as triple protection.

Anda Mangil had had this car for as long as anyone could remember, and he loved it dearly. Indeed, it was a standing joke in the village that Anda Mangil was married to his car, that she was a most exacting wife and certainly did not leave him time or money enough to look for a real human wife. Anda Mangil did not mind the joke. He was a round, cheerful, simple man with a bouncy and hopeful nature, and he laughed as heartily as anyone at his obsession with the car.

Dewi's father sat in the front with Anda Mangil, chatting equably about village affairs, and the weather, and crop prices, and other such ordinary things. Adi and Dewi sat in the back. Normally, Dewi would have enjoyed looking at the pictures of the sacred places, but today she had too many other things on her mind. Adi had looked curiously at them—and had exclaimed over the lovely little sacred books that Anda Mangil had reverently taken out of the glove box to show him—but now he was silent, staring out the window as the countryside slowly unrolled past them.

Dewi suddenly felt sorry for him. At least she was in familiar territory, and she had her wise and brave father with her. Poor Adi was alone. She leaned over to him and whispered, "Have you ever been to Kotabunga before?"

Adi shook his head. "It was to be my first visit. I was so excited. Kota Bau, the main city in our part of the country, is big but ugly, and smelly. But Kotabunga, home of the Sultans, is supposed to be so beautiful."

"And it is beautiful," said Dewi. Her face clouded. "How I wish we were just going sightseeing there!"

He nodded. They relapsed into heavy silence, each lost in their own thoughts.

Anda Mangil shot them a glance in the rearview mirror, then leaned forward and clicked the radio on. The latest hit song, "Beloved," was playing, and Anda Mangil softly sang along to its haunting melody of lost love. Everybody was crazy about that song in Jayangan that year; you heard it everywhere. It lightened the mood in the car; even Bapar Wiriyanto, no great lover of pop music, was smiling. Adi began to hum along with it, and Dewi listened with pleasure as she watched the parade of life outside the windows. Fields and villages lay on either side of the road. The day was well advanced, and people in big hats bent over their work in rice fields; a team of water buffaloes patiently pulled a plow. Cars and trucks and buses and motorbikes and bicycles filled the road like a great noisy river, and roadside stalls were doing a busy trade.

The closer they got to Kotabunga, the busier it became, and soon, as they approached the city proper, horse-drawn carts and pedal-powered betchars, a kind of rickshaw, joined the throng. Anda Mangil, still humming under his breath, was kept busy dodging in and out of all this traffic. He obviously enjoyed it; his round, cheerful face was alight with glee as he cornered and smoothly wove in and out. He played the car horn as if it were a musical instrument at a dance, announcing a new step. Through the smart new suburbs, with their white mansions behind high walls topped with broken glass and rusty iron; through the busy market district, where traffic was slowed almost to a standstill; through the rows of tiny higgledy-piggledy houses of betchar and horse-cart drivers; past stalls and food carts and busy restaurants; dodging through streets lined with hotels and guesthouses full of foreigners from all the corners of not only Jayangan but the whole world; past the huge batik market; and finally into the gold and jewelry district, with its dozens of little shops.

There, at last, was Bapar Suyanto's guesthouse, sandwiched between two gold shops. Anda Mangil stopped the car and they got out.

"I have decided to stay overnight at my cousin's place, and only go back to Bumi Macan tomorrow," said Anda Mangil, as Dewi's father thanked him and paid him for the trip. "Would you like me to come back here tomorrow?"

His eyes met Bapar Wiriyanto's. The dukun nodded. "Thank you. That would be kind."

Anda Mangil smiled. "Very well. Enjoy yourselves." He looked at Adi. "I think you'll find Kotabunga exceeds all your expectations. But then, maybe I'm biased!" He laughed, and with a wave, he maneuvered the car back up the street. They stood for a moment, looking after him. Then Bapar Wiriyanto sighed. "How I wish the world were full of people like Anda Mangil, taking pleasure in all things in life. It would be a very much better world if that were so."

In front of Bapar Suyanto's guesthouse was a little flower-filled courtyard, with cane chairs arranged invitingly around small round tables, and a fountain playing. Dewi noticed a woman sitting at one of the nearby tables, sipping a glass of iced tea. She was a foreigner, and one of the strangest-looking people Dewi had ever seen. She was tall and thin, with a long nose, blotchy red and white skin, and hair of such a bright red color that Dewi could not help staring. It was as red as flame, she thought, as unnaturally red as the tinsel garlands that decorated Dharbudsu temples on feast days. It stuck out in all directions, escaping the bright paisley scarf she had clumsily tied around her head. She was dressed in a very odd collection of clothes—loose yellow satin trousers under a yellow and red and pink embroidered tunic with long sleeves, a sequined waistcoat, a long black sleeveless coat, and a second scarf in various bright colors draped around her neck. No wonder she looked so hot and prickly! A collection of gaudy trinkets on silver chains hung down her thin, almost concave chest, and long bead and silver earrings hung to her shoulders. Around her ankles she wore thick silver chains, and her dirty feet, with long, incongruously red-painted toenails, were bare.

The woman looked up, straight at Dewi. She smiled, a curiously intimate smile, but it was not this that froze Dewi to the spot. It was the woman's gaze, which was like nothing she had ever seen before: She had large, light-brown, almost yellow, eyes, black-rimmed as a cat's, and her pupils—her narrow, vertical pupils—shone red, red as flame. Or, at least, that was how it seemed to Dewi in that horrified instant. She blinked, and saw that she must have been mistaken, for the woman's pupils were an ordinary black, and round.

The woman smiled again and looked as if she were about to speak, but Dewi had had quite enough. She hurried away to her father and Adi, who were standing at the reception desk talking to the girl there. And what the girl had to say almost made Dewi forget about the odd stranger sitting there in her chair.

"I am sorry," said the young woman. "I am sorry," she repeated, "but you have just missed Bapar Suyanto. He was called away to the palace on urgent business by the master of ceremonies, Lord Emas. Perhaps you could go there."

The dukun pulled at his lip. "Right. Thank you." He turned to Adi and Dewi. "You two stay here. Miss," he said, turning back to the receptionist, "please book us a large room. We will stay here tonight."

"Certainly, sir," said the girl.

The dukun fumbled in his pocket and brought out a roll of small banknotes, which he handed to Dewi. In an undertone, he said, "Go and buy something to eat from a stall. I will go in a betchar to the palace and return as quickly as I can. Do not go anywhere else, do you understand? And do not speak to anyone about what we are doing here. And"—here he dropped his voice even lower—"there is something else besides money in this bundle of notes, which I want you to keep on you at all times, do you understand? Don't look at it right now. But keep it, hold it safe, and it will protect you. Do you promise me that, Dewi?"

"Yes, Father," said Dewi, taking the bundle of notes and putting it in her pocket. Unease gripped her. "Please, Father, you will be careful, won't you?"

"Of course, my dear child," he said, gently touching her shoulder. "Don't be afraid. Just remember what I told you."

Dewi wanted to ask him more questions, but the dukun smiled at them both and left swiftly, heading back out into the street.

"Shall we go and find something to eat, then?" said Adi.

"I am quite hungry," admitted Dewi.

"Young ones, listen." The voice behind them made them jump. "Young ones, you must hear this."

It was the redheaded woman from the courtyard. Up close, she was overwhelming. Her voice was deep, deeper than any woman's voice Dewi had ever heard before. She moved strangely, in a motion that was both gliding and jerky, as if she were trying to remember how to walk. Her hands were long, her fingers narrow, her nails curved and burnished to a high red sheen. Her hair swung under her scarf like a living thing, while the angry red heat blotches on her skin seemed to glow brighter with every word she spoke. She smiled in a way that was meant to be reassuring.

"It was not that I, Kareen Amar, did mean to make you afeared." Her accent was odd, as was the way she used Jayanganese. "I heard what was said. Yet such cannot be true. Lord Emas is away, so it could not be he who called Bapar Suyanto to the palace. It is I, Kareen Amar, who tells you this."

Adi and Dewi stared at her. The woman came closer to them, and as she did so, a strange smell caught at Dewi's nostrils. It was a smell like . . . like . . . she couldn't quite place it, but whatever it was, it made the hair rise up on the back of her neck.

"It is I, Kareen Amar, who tells you this. Kareen Amar," she repeated with an odd eagerness, searching their faces as if they ought to know who she was, and the significance of what she was saying. Seeing they had no idea who she was, she fumbled in the pocket of her jacket and brought out a grubby business card. "You look here. It says."

They glanced at the clumsily printed card. In big, wavy letters, it announced that this was "Kareen Amar, renowned singer and songwriter."

"You see?" said the woman eagerly. "You read?"

"We read," said Dewi uncomfortably, shooting a glance at Adi, who was just as disconcerted. Kareen Amar's name meant nothing to them; they had never heard of her. Besides, she didn't look like any singer Dewi or Adi had ever seen, but a freak, a madwoman.

Kareen Amar was surveying their faces anxiously. "I know this, young ones. You must listen to me. Really listen. Lord Emas is away. He is not at the palace. Bapar Suyanto is not there either. Listen to Kareen Amar. Kareen Amar knows. This is so."

Dewi and Adi looked at each other. Then, with one accord, they rushed out of the reception area, through the outer courtyard, and into the street. They looked wildly up and down the street, then Adi gave a shout. "There, look, the betchar, just turning the corner!"

Unmistakably, it was the dukun, sitting straight-backed in the elevated carriage of the vehicle, the betchar driver pedaling slowly behind him. Usually, betchar drivers were young, but strands of coarse gray hair escaped from under this one's cap. His slow, almost clumsy gait as he pedaled along gave them hope they might catch up with him. "Bapar Wiriyanto! Bapar!" called Adi, and he ran down the street, Dewi close behind him.

The dukun did not turn around, but the betchar driver must have heard them, for he looked over his shoulder at them. He was a small, wizened man, with little, narrow eyes. He looked at them and smiled. His eyes seemed suddenly to grow, to change from brown to red, his lips to stretch wide, revealing a mouthful of sharp teeth. Dewi and Adi froze in their tracks. There was a malevolent power as deep as it was inexplicable in the betchar driver's unnatural red eyes: It mesmerized and paralyzed them so that for a few crucial seconds they were unable to move, only stare after the betchar as it went up the street and around the corner.

Not once during all this time did the dukun turn his head. By this, and what they now realized was his unnaturally stiff posture, Dewi and Adi knew he had been bewitched and could not move or speak, any more than they could. It was only when the betchar had vanished around the corner that they regained control of their bodies.

"What was that?" gasped Adi, shaking. Dewi shook her head, baffled. "Whatever it was, we've got to follow. This time, I'm not going to stand by and do nothing!" Adi suited action to words, taking off down the street, in the direction the betchar had gone. Shock and fear had numbed Dewi completely. Her father had said not to leave the guesthouse. He'd told them to stay safe. And anyway, they'd never catch up with that thing, that demonic betchar driver. She suddenly remembered something else her father had said, about the thing that would protect them. Heart pounding, she pulled out the banknotes and unrolled them carefully—there, in the middle of the roll, was a strange small, sharp, curved object the size of a fingernail. Her stomach gave a lurch. She knew at once what it was. A claw. A tiger's claw. Her father's own talisman, preciously kept. Tears filled her eyes. He had given her his own protection! The numbness drained away. She must be worthy of his trust, she must, she must!

She set off after Adi. Rounding the corner of the next street, she caught up with him; he had come to a standstill.

"Can't see it at all," he panted. "The betchar's vanished completely."

The betchar must indeed have been an otherworldly vehicle, for it wasn't easy for a normal vehicle to move in this crowded street, the main gold sellers' alley. The gold dealers had set out their wares on long wooden tables in front of their shop doorways and were doing brisk business. Most were from the Radenteng people, whose ancestors had come from the mighty empire of Radentengan, far to the north of Jayangan, centuries before.

Adi and Dewi fought their way through to a less crowded part of the street, near a rather down-at-heel little gold store called She-Po Gold Market. There was not even a counter outside this one; the dusty little shop looked closed, a bamboo blind drawn across its smeared window. Panting and disheveled, from the vantage point of the shop's doorstep they looked out over the milling masses. But of course there was nothing to be seen.

"What can we do now?" Adi wailed.

"I don't know." Dewi took out the tiger's claw. "Father gave me this," she said.

Adi stared at it. "Oh," he said blankly.

"It is my father's talisman. He said it would protect us."

"I see," said Adi gently. Their eyes met. Like Adi's master, Dewi's father had sacrificed his own safety to protect them. It was up to Adi and Dewi not to let them down.

Dewi's mind was slowly clearing after the shock of what had happened. She said, "That thing—the betchar driver—that wasn't a hantumu, was it?"

Adi shook his head. "It certainly didn't look like anything I've heard about. Though it had eyes like those of ogres or demons in puppet plays." Jayangan was famous for its puppet plays, in which the forces of good—princes, gods, animals of various sorts—battled the forces of evil, like ogres, giants, demons, and witches. "It certainly was not human," he added firmly.

Dewi shivered. "No. It was not. But if it's a demon,

it must be a shape-shifter. Father would never have got into the betchar if he had seen the eyes of that thing."

"So how did we see it?" said Adi.

"I don't know. Perhaps it chose to show itself to us like that because it wanted to frighten us, to warn us off."

"Then it's probably vanished into another world," said Adi gravely. Dewi shivered again.

"There's only one thing we can do now," said Adi. "We have to do as my master and your father wanted. We have to go and see the Sultan."

"You can't just walk in there! You have to make an appointment through a Court official. And how are we going to do that? We don't know anyone there. We are young and unimportant."

"We will find an official," said Adi, squaring his shoulders. "We will ask for an audience. You will see." He fumbled in his pocket. "I have my master's card here. Everyone at the palace knows Empu Wesiagi. He is an honored visitor. They will let us in with this."

Dewi looked doubtfully at the crumpled business card. "Are you sure?"

"Well, we can try," said Adi with a sudden, darting smile. Dewi's spirits lifted. He was so positive, so determined not to let obstacles stand in his way. She smiled back. "Yes, we can," she said. "We . . ."

Suddenly, Adi's face changed. He was staring at something up the street. Dewi turned. Coming straight at them through the crowded street, scattering people right and left, were four black-clad men riding on motorbikes. The hantumu! She turned to run, as did Adi, but before they could take a step, they felt hands grabbing them, propelling them back through the dark doorway of the gold shop. Slam went the door, and they were in a hot, close, dimly lit room. A woman's voice said sharply, "Get down, there. Don't move. Don't make a sound."

Hardly daring to breathe, Adi and Dewi did as they were told. Crouching in the darkness, heads down, they couldn't make out the features or form of the person who had spoken to them. They could see only a pair of very small, indeed tiny, feet in beaded slippers. "Stay there. Do not move, understood?"

They nodded, without saying a word or looking up. They saw the feet move off, heard the shop door swing shut, something rattling. Then silence.

SIX

MINUTES PASSED. All was quiet and dark and peaceful. Adi's and Dewi's pulse rates gradually returned to normal. Their eyes became accustomed to the dim light, and they began to make out their surroundings.

They were in what looked to be a storage room. Boxes and baskets and parcels of various kinds filled the shelves. There were a couple of trunks in a corner of the room, and a big old carved chest in another. The other two corners were curtained-off alcoves. A dusty Nashranee holy picture, of the Lord's heart surrounded by flames and roses, hung on one wall. Otherwise the room was bare of ornament. There was a not-unpleasant smell in the room, of spices mixed with sandalwood and incense. Light came in only faintly through a half-open door at one end of the room, but the door out to the street was firmly closed.

Adi whispered, "Dewi, why would a Radenteng gold dealer save us from the hantumu?"

Dewi shrugged. Before she could reply, a voice, the same voice as before, spoke. "It is safe now. Come out, my son and daughter."

They could see the woman clearly now, for she held an oil lamp in one hand. They stared in amazement—their savior was an extraordinary sight. She was indeed a Radenteng, and old, very old, with skin like wrinkled, crushed golden silk. But despite her age, she was dazzlingly beautiful, with deep-set dark eyes that had strange blue glints in their depths. Her silvery hair was in a soft bun clipped with a lovely blue and silver barrette in the shape of a star, with a transparent veil over that. She was dressed in an embroidered long-sleeved blue and green tunic of heavy silk, under which were trousers of the same color, and her tiny feet were perched in the beaded slippers they had first seen. Her hands were very fine, of the same crushed-silk texture as her face, and on her fingers glittered a great many rings. Her nails were long and pointed, and painted a luminescent shade of pearly blue, like mist on water.

Overcome by this vision, Adi and Dewi could only stare at her for an instant. Adi was the first to speak. "Oh, lady," he breathed, "you look like the picture of the Lady of Grace in our church in Desagua."

The lady smiled. "No, dear Adi, I am not she," she said in a sweet voice, with the singsong accent of the Radenteng. "I am a wanderer from the spirit world of the Radenteng who has made a modest home here. My name is Kwanyin. Now, you can begin by telling me everything that happened out there. Where is your father, Dewi? I was expecting him too. The Harimauroh sent a message that you were coming together."

Dewi and Adi looked at each other, then Dewi rapidly poured out the story. She finished by exclaiming, "But Lady Kwanyin, we did not know you were expecting us. What is our purpose here?"

Lady Kwanyin smiled. "Is that not a strange question, my child? You have come to Kotabunga to meet me, have you not?"

Both of them stared at her. She shook her head ruefully. "Oh, dear. I thought you must know. But perhaps the Harimauroh thought it was best this way; that it would protect you. The important thing is that you are here. I am to send you on the first stage of your quest, to find Snow, Fire, Sword."

"But we thought . . . the Sultan . . ." cried Adi, who couldn't take his eyes off the beautiful old woman.

"That must wait. He is not yet willing to believe the full truth. There are more important things to do first, things that will absolutely convince him to act," said Kwanyin.

"Lady Kwanyin, my father . . ." began Dewi.

"Ah, sadly, my dear, that must wait too."

"But, please, where is he? Where did they take him? Will he be safe?"

"My child, I wish I could tell you for sure, but this is a strange and difficult enemy we face. We cannot see into his motives or ways. That is why we need you to find Snow, Fire, and Sword. Only thus will his true nature be revealed, and we can see ways of defeating him. Only then will the shadow of the hantumu and their master be lifted from the land of Jayangan."

"But Lady Kwanyin," said Adi breathlessly, "why us? Why do you need us to find these things? We do not know what they are, or where to begin to look for them."

"My poor children," said Kwanyin very kindly, "it is indeed a difficult quest you are on. You see, even we spirits do not know precisely what these are. We need you because you are brave and good human beings, like your father, Dewi, and your master, Adi. They have been taken by the dark power, and now it is up to you to step into their shoes. Are you ready to do that?"

Dewi and Adi looked at each other. Dewi said, "What is it we must do now, Lady Kwanyin?"

"You will prepare yourselves for the first stage of your quest. You are to go on a journey to the beach of Siluman."

"Siluman!" breathed Adi, eyes wide. "But that is the portal to the land of the Queen of the Southern Sea, Rorokidul!"

"That is correct," said Kwanyin. "It is the portal to the land of my sister water-spirit, Rorokidul, whose power is much greater than mine in Jayangan. The ocean realm is a place of great knowledge and power, being the element that links the many different lands of the world. That is the reason you should go there. It may be that Rorokidul has more knowledge than other spirits as to the true nature of the things you must find—Snow, Fire, Sword."

Dewi said urgently, "But Lady Kwanyin, everybody knows that the realm of Rorokidul is a place where one must exercise great care, that it is dangerous, and that without permission—"

"You will go to Siluman and see Tuan Gelombang, who guards the portal to Rorokidul's realm," said Kwanyin briskly. "You will give him my name and explain that you are under my protection. Like Rorokidul, I am a water-spirit, and she understands my ways. She will honor that protection, and Gelombang will vouch for you. Do not be afraid of that."

Adi and Dewi looked at each other. Kwanyin smiled. "I know, my dears, it's not very much to go on. I wish I could tell you what Snow, Fire, and Sword are, but I can't—not because I don't want to, but because I really don't know. These things must be discovered by humans—we cannot see what they are. Are you ready to take on this quest? Are you ready to trust us, and to help us? We spirits cannot defeat this enemy on our own—and you humans equally cannot defeat him on your own. We are in this together. Will you help, my dears, to find Snow, Fire, Sword and defeat the shadow that threatens to destroy Jayangan?"

A lump came into Dewi's throat, and one to Adi's. They looked deep into Kwanyin's kind, dark eyes. Together they whispered, "Yes. Oh, yes."

Kwanyin beamed and clapped her hands. "Now then, my dears, let's get you prepared to go to Siluman. There is much to do."

She led them to one of the shelves. She opened a box and lifted out from it another box, then another from within it, and another, till she got to two small, hard cases. She snapped one open, and inside lay a ring. It had a golden band, which glistened like sunlight, and in the middle of the band was a ruby as red as blood. "This one is for you, Dewi," said Kwanyin, and she slipped the ring on the girl's finger. She snapped open the other little case. There was another ring: a rather heavy one, made of ivory and crystal, inlaid with silver. "This is yours, Adi." And she slipped the ring on the boy's finger.

Marveling, Adi and Dewi looked at the beautiful things sparkling on their fingers. "Oh, Lady Kwanyin," breathed Dewi, "these are so fine."

"From these, and Tuan Gelombang's words, Rorokidul will know I have sent you." She surveyed Dewi and Adi critically. "Now, you cannot go dressed as you are, in these flimsy modern things. It does not look serious. Rorokidul is not a modern girl, and of all the Jayangan spirits, she is the one who likes ceremony the most. I fancy you need new clothes."

She glided over to one of the baskets and opened it. From it rippled what looked at first like a wave of living red and gold, but as Kwanyin seized hold of it, it resolved itself into a shimmering silk sarong suit of a style Dewi had never seen before. More things came out of the basket then: a coat of red silk overlaid with a gauzy, shimmering golden material; a headdress of gilded leather set with glittering shards of crystal; bracelets of the same gilded and decorated leather; finely worked, flat golden sandals. It was a costume fit for a queen. Dewi's eyes and heart were full of it, her blood beating fit to burst in her veins. "Am I to wear this?" she whispered.

Kwanyin smiled. "Who else?" she answered. She turned to Adi. "Now you, my son." She opened another basket. "I think you will find this to be in the right size."

Adi's clothes were magnificent too—a sarong in a darkly gleaming, thick, rich blue fabric, shot through with strands of gold and silver. It went with a coat made of the same deep, rich stuff, but with golden cuffs and a silver collar. To wear under it was a shirt made of the finest, softest, whitest material, and there was a gorgeous close-fitting silk headdress, of a midnight blue with strands of the same colors as were in the rest of the clothes. Adi gasped when he saw them. He could not keep his eyes off them. Kwanyin smiled and pointed at the curtained-off alcoves. "Go and refresh, and change."

As if in a dream, they obeyed her, their arms full of the beautiful things they had been given. The alcoves had not looked big from outside, but they discovered two bathrooms beyond them. In each bathroom was a tall marble tub filled with fragrant cool water that had been strewn with flower petals, and cakes of sweet-smelling soap, and ivory dippers to ladle water over yourself. Beside each bath were lotions, and great soft towels with which to dry, and a mirror, to watch one's transformation.

Dewi stood in her bath, ladling sweet water over herself, feeling all the dust and heat and worry of the day wash off her. Even her fear for her father had left her, for Kwanyin had spoken of him as if he were still alive and had suggested that he might yet be saved. Excitement was grabbing hold of her again; she was filled with a sense that she was in a most wonderful adventure.

"That is good." Kwanyin nodded her satisfaction as they both stood before her, resplendent in their finery, hardly daring to look at each other. They felt almost shy. Dewi no longer looked like a neat schoolgirl but as beautiful and shimmering as a goddess in an old painting, or a princess of long ago, with her long hair rippling down over her gorgeous clothes, and the fine bones of her face accentuated by the golden headdress. And Adi was so straight and tall and handsome in his princely costume, all puppyish awkwardness gone, like a dashing prince in an old story.

"Are you ready, my children?" Kwanyin's deep-set eyes were full of a wise, kind laughter, as if she could read their thoughts and understand their feelings.

"Oh, we are, thank you, Lady Kwanyin," Adi said, eyes shining like stars. Dewi could not speak. She just nodded solemnly, her heart full of joy.

"That is good. Now, remember, my dears—not all the spirits you meet will be as direct as I. Most are far greater in power than I am in Jayangan, and are very conscious of the right way in which they must communicate with the human world. You must take care." She looked deep into their eyes. "Do you understand, my dears?" When they nodded, she went on, "Well then, you must set off for Siluman."

They looked at each other, puzzled. Kwanyin smiled. "Don't look so surprised. It will be an easy journey, for my dear Anda Mangil will take you."

"Anda Mangil?" Dewi's eyes widened in surprise.

Kwanyin nodded. "Anda Mangil is a good man. I have known him a long time. And he knows the way to the beach of Siluman, as well as Tuan Gelombang."

"Oh," said Dewi weakly. Adi gulped; Dewi could see the Adam's apple bob in his throat. Kwanyin said, "Now let us summon Anda Mangil," and she clapped her hands twice, gently, and made a curious little trilling sound in her throat. And suddenly, from somewhere outside, came the familiar sound of Anda Mangil's car horn.

SEVEN

ANDA MANGIL WAS parked not in the street in front of the She-Po Gold Market but behind it, in a narrow alleyway that ran along the back of the gold dealers' shops. Not only did he not look surprised to see them, but he was dressed in quite different clothes from the neatly pressed white shirt and dark trousers that they had seen him in earlier that day. He was in the dress of a Kotabunga courtier: a magnificent white, dark-blue, and brown flower-patterned sarong; a high-necked dark-blue jacket of the finest cotton, bordered with gilt; with a pure white shirt underneath. Around his waist, he wore a cloth belt, and at this belt, he wore a lovely bronze-scabbarded kris. On his head was a silk headdress like Adi's. The simple man Anda Mangil had become someone almost unrecognizable. The only thing that was the same about him was the pendant he always wore on a chain around his neck—a charm in the shape of a mandala. Even his manner had changed. It had become solemn, courtly, dignified.

"Lady Kwanyin," he said, getting out of the car and bowing, "it is an honor to see you."

"It is a pleasure to see you, dear Anda Mangil." Kwanyin smiled. She put a hand on the car's hood. "And your dear friend the car. How well she looks! I am not one for machines, Anda Mangil—but for this one, I make an exception."

Was it her imagination, Dewi thought, or did the car shift slightly on its wheels, as if giving a little squirm of pleasure under Kwanyin's hand?

Anda Mangil beamed. "You do us both much honor, Lady Kwanyin."

"Now, you know what has to be done, my dear friend. Take care of them—and of yourself. Remember, Anda Mangil, that this is a dangerous enemy. The more protection you have, the better."

"I had thought of stopping at Chandi Maya, Lady Kwanyin," said Anda Mangil. He gestured to a basket on the seat beside him. "For that very purpose I have brought gifts to offer in the Temple of the Great Mother."

"Excellent," said Kwanyin. She turned to Adi and Dewi. "Farewell, my dear children. Farewell, and all my blessings go with you."

They chorused their thanks and got into the car. They waved to Kwanyin as they pulled away from the curb.

"She was so kind," murmured Adi. "Kind and friendly."

"The Lady Kwanyin understands many things," said Anda Mangil. "She is a spirit of unusual distinction, perhaps because she is still lonely and a little lost in Jayangan, and understands human uncertainties better than many of our own spirits who have never left the world of Jayangan."

How strange it is to be here in the familiar, friendly interior of the big car, thought Dewi, to sit looking at the back of Anda Mangil's head as he drove, and know she was looking at someone she thought she knew but didn't really.

"Anda Mangil," she asked uncertainly, "did you know we were supposed to go and see the Lady Kwanyin in Kotabunga?"

He shook his head. "No. I knew nothing of any of this until the Lady Kwanyin sent for me." He paused. "I knew then I could not stand by. Not while the hantumu took my good friend, your father, Dewi. Oh, child, we live in dark and troubled times." He looked at Dewi in the rearview mirror, and she saw his eyes were full of a sadness she had never seen in them before. "Of course I knew about what had happened in other parts of Jayangan, but I hoped, like your father, that our little world of Bumi Macan might be spared. Now I know that was an unworthy hope. None of us will be spared. We must fight. Whatever we do may fail. But it is our only chance, or evil will overtake our land. The Demon King grows hungry for power again, and all of us who love Jayangan must fight him if he is not to destroy everything."

Adi and Dewi both shivered. The Demon King went by different names in Jayangan, according to your religion: Mujisals called him Iblis, Nashranees called him the Dragon, and Dharbudsus called him Rawana. But whatever name he was called by, the lord of evil—and his demon allies and human accomplices—wreaked havoc and chaos and destruction in both human and spirit worlds. Good needed champions if it was to defeat evil. But it was a hard thing to face, knowing it was you who had been chosen for this difficult and frightening task. How could you know if you would ever be up to it?

Adi spoke the thought aloud. "Why us? Kwanyin said it was because we were good and brave, but I do not feel myself to be either. Besides, my master was good and brave, and he was taken."

"Perhaps it is this. The evil we have to face wears a different mask from in the past. You are children of modern Jayangan, so it is up to you, as much as your elders. For it is not just the past we are defending, but our present and our future." He smiled, and the light of it transformed his face, so that he looked once more like the old, cheerful Anda Mangil. "I am nothing special, either, you see. I am an elderly fool who is too mad about his dear friend, an elderly car. But you see, perhaps that is why I am here now. I know this car so well, I understand all its workings—more, I understand its soul. This is no ordinary car. It can sometimes do things that . . . that seem impossible to everyday eyes. This is a new magic, and it, too, can be used, as well as the old things. Perhaps you and Dewi have, or will find, other such magics."

Adi and Dewi looked swiftly at each other. "What magics?" said Dewi.

"You will have to discover them, I think. But this I know—though I am afraid of what lies ahead, I know we are doing the right thing. I know I was born to be of help in this task. And I am glad that the Lady Kwanyin called me." He smiled suddenly, a darting, mischievous smile. "And of course, I am delighted that it includes the opportunity to drive my dear girl farther than I have done for some time. I hope you're up to the task, dear one," he said, with a little tap on the wheel. Both Adi and Dewi jumped when the car horn—no doubt pressed by Anda Mangil—gave a loud and seemingly indignant blast. Anda Mangil laughed. "There, there," he said gently, "no need to take on so, dear friend."

Adi and Dewi smiled at each other. "He really is mad about it," whispered Adi, and Dewi whispered back, "He's always been teased about it, back home." All of a sudden, the atmosphere, which had been so grave, lightened.

An hour passed. They had left the city far behind now and were out in the countryside, on the far southern side of Kotabunga. The landscape had quite changed. The green paddy fields and pleasant little villages to the north of Kotabunga had been replaced by dryer, harsher land and the air was more dusty. This was the way to Chandi Maya, vast temple complex of the ancient Dharbudsu kings, and one of Jayangan's sacred places. Dewi had never been this far from her home territory before.

She looked down at her lap and the rustling golden stuff of her clothes; the thrill that was half excitement and half fear filled her again. She looked at her finger, at the ruby glowing like a miniature fire in its golden setting.

Fire! It was like fire! The thought made her glance over at Adi's finger, and the ring he wore. Its design seemed familiar to her. Surely it was just like . . . like . . .

"Adi!" she hissed. "Do you still have that picture, you know, of Rajadi, the famous kris? The one that was left behind on the road?"

Adi stared at her, then nodded. He put a hand inside his jacket, slid out the little square of muddy colored paper, and handed it to Dewi. It was said that the kris Rajadi had been made centuries ago for King Senopati, the legendary ruler who was supposed to have built the huge temples of Chandi Maya in a single day. The kris had a finely incised black skystone blade made of thousands of layers, a blade that had never, in hundreds of years, shown the slightest sign of rust. Magical words were written on the blade, words of such potency that it was believed they held the very heart of the power of the Sultans of Jayangan. They had inherited Rajadi from their Dharbudsu ancestors and kept it safe in the palace in Kotabunga. Rajadi's scabbard was made of pure gold, worked through with filaments of silver and set with precious stones. And its hilt was made of ivory, with crystal and silver in it. It looked just like Adi's ring. . . .

Adi saw the similarity too. He went pale. "What does it mean?" he whispered.

Dewi said, "I think it means I have Fire and you have Sword, Adi."

"A kris is a dagger, not a sword," objected Adi.

"But perhaps it's symbolic of a sword. Maybe these rings aren't just for protection. Maybe we'll be shown how to use them in Siluman."

Adi took back the picture of Rajadi and put it away. "How can that be?" he muttered.

"Lady Kwanyin said we had to discover them!" said Dewi excitedly. "Remember? Adi, perhaps we only have to find Snow." A dizzying thought, born of what Anda Mangil had said, suddenly pumped in her head. If she had Fire, and Adi had Sword, then Anda Mangil must have Snow. "Anda Mangil!" she cried.

Anda Mangil gave a start, and the car wobbled a little. "What is wrong, Dewi?"

"Your hands, Anda Mangil, your hands. Are you wearing a ring?"

"A ring?" said Anda Mangil, puzzled.

"Yes!"

"No, I'm not wearing a ring," he said, glancing at her in the rearview mirror. "What's wrong?"

Crestfallen, Dewi said, "It . . . well, I hoped you might have Snow, because I think Adi and I have Fire and Sword."

Now Anda Mangil looked completely baffled. "I don't understand."

"Did the Lady Kwanyin tell you we had to find Snow, Fire, Sword?" said Dewi.

He nodded. "Yes. But she said you were going on a quest to find them. She did not say that you already had them."

"Yes, but she said we had to discover them. Maybe that means we have to deduce what they are. I thought perhaps the rings we were given for protection . . ." She lifted up her hand to show him. "And Adi's got one too. They could be Fire and Sword! The power of those things could lie in these rings. Magic often lies in rings, doesn't it? That's why I asked if you had been given a ring, because it could have been Snow."

Anda Mangil shook his head. "No. The Lady Kwanyin did not give me a ring of protection, because I do not need it. I am just taking you to Siluman, and waiting there till you come back from the realm of the Queen of the Southern Sea."

"It seems a little too easy to me, anyway, Dewi," said Adi gloomily. "We didn't have to look for them or discover them—the Lady gave them to us. Besides, she said she didn't know what they were."

Anda Mangil broke in. "We are almost at Chandi Maya. We will ask for the guidance of Lord Senopati in this matter, as well as protection. He will know at least if this ring you wear, Adi, truly has the spirit of Sword, if it is based on his own kris. Agreed?"

"Agreed," they echoed, and leaned back in their seats, heads whirling with excited thoughts and questions.

EIGHT

THE GREAT CARVED stone towers and spires and stupas of Chandi Maya rose from the flat plain like ancient giants slowly rising to their feet. Built in the old days when the Dharbudsu Kings had ruled over Jayangan, before the coming of the Mujisals from Al Aksara, the Great Desert, Chandi Maya had fallen into disrepair over the centuries but was still an impressive, awe-inspiring place.

There were at least thirty temples in Chandi Maya, linked by a maze of stone avenues. The biggest temple of all stood in the middle of the maze, and this is where Anda Mangil was leading them. Not another soul walked along the great avenues of broken stone; not a sound, except for that of their own footsteps, broke the eerie silence. Dewi and Adi felt uneasy. The silence was almost like a living thing, a waiting thing. They kept close to Anda Mangil. Sometimes he would pause and give a little nod, or a bow, this way and that, in respect to the ancient spirits and Dharbudsu gods whose holy place this was.

They reached the huge central temple, the Temple of the Great Mother. Towering above them, it was a truly splendid sight: Every square centimeter of its surface was carved with scenes from the ancient stories; its yellow-white stone glittered in the sun as if it were made of gold. There were no windows, only a dark doorway. A long, steep flight of stone steps led up to the doorway, and Anda Mangil started up these without hesitation. Dewi followed suit, but Adi, struck with a sudden fright, stared up at the doorway, which looked for all the world like a giant's open mouth. He had never set eyes on a place like Chandi Maya. The Dharbudsu temples he'd seen back home were cheerful little wooden open-air pavilions, with flags fluttering, and flowers, and incense.

Anda Mangil turned. "Come, Adi," he said gently. "There is nothing to be afraid of. This is a good place. I can vouch for it."

Adi felt for the tiny silver heart he wore under his finery. "I hope you are right," he said with an effort at a light tone, starting up the steps.

As Dewi came closer to the yawning darkness of the doorway, she could sense a presence more and more strongly. There was someone—something—there, she was sure of it. She wanted to talk to Anda Mangil about it, to be reassured, but she could not open her mouth. Her feet just kept moving of their own accord, drawing her up, and up. Anda Mangil reached the doorway, stepped through it, and disappeared, as if a hand had reached out from inside and whipped him in. The hair rose stiffly on the back of her neck; a cold sweat broke out on her brow. She stopped and waited till Adi reached her on the steps. She whispered, "Are you all right?"

"Perfectly," said Adi, though he looked pale. "Are you?"

"Oh, I'm fine. I was just waiting for you to catch up."

Their eyes met. Adi quietly extended a hand to Dewi. "Shall we go in together?" he whispered. Dewi swallowed, nodded. Shyly, she put a hand in his. So, together, they crossed the threshold. Instantly, they were enveloped in darkness. As their eyes began to adjust, they saw Anda Mangil bowing before an altar of plain stone, chanting quietly. He had taken the gifts out of his basket—flowers, fruits, beeswax candles—and laid them on the stone.

In front of him was a beautiful golden statue of the Great Mother, a woman with a fierce but lovely face and many arms. Her many hands held, among other things, fruits and flowers, and skulls and bones. To one side of the altar was another figure, of stone this time: a massive and extraordinarily lifelike statue of a warrior. It had a handsome face under a coiled, tall headdress, armor on much of its body, and a large kris clasped to its breast with both hands. Suddenly it moved, sending flickers of light throughout the temple. So sudden was the movement, so bright the flashes of light in the darkness, that Adi and Dewi had no chance to move or even cry out; they just watched in petrified terror as the stone figure, unclasping its hands, stretched its arms out to either side of it. In one hand, it still grasped the kris. It was the blade that was making those flickers of light.

Dewi and Adi were so frightened that they felt as if they had been turned to stone themselves. The splendid folds of their clothes lay stiff and cold on them; their hearts seemed to have stopped beating. Only their still-joined hands felt even slightly warm.

"Why do you disturb the peace of the Temple of the Great Mother? I am the guardian of the temple, Senopati." The voice was huge, booming. The face was human and yet not. It stayed within its carapace of stone, and yet the carved cheeks and nose and forehead rippled slightly, the way stone and earth ripple in a quake. The eyes stayed fixed, the expression eternally frozen.

Anda Mangil spoke, calmy, courteously. "Great Lord Senopati, warrior of renown, destroyer of the wicked, we bring gifts for the Great Mother, in the hope she may grant us protection. And we would like your guidance, O Senopati. We are Anda Mangil, Adi, and Dewi, and we seek Snow, Fire, and Sword, to defeat the forces of evil that once more threaten Jayangan."

The kris flashed once, twice, three times; then Lord Senopati's great hands brought the dagger down, with great delicacy, onto the altar. The great voice rumbled, "It was right you came here, for I have a warning. Snow, Fire, Sword you seek. These must be found, and held. Without them, you are in very great danger indeed. Your enemy knows of your existence, and of what you seek, and he will search to find you before you can accomplish your task."

There was a dismayed silence. Then Anda Mangil said, "Our enemy knows what we seek, O Lord?"

"Yes. He will try to find them before you do. And he will try to use them for his own ends. He will try to stop you getting to them."

"But Lord Senopati, does he know, then, what Snow, Fire, Sword are?"

"No. He does not. But that is even more dangerous. Beware! He will have you followed to see if you find them—and then take them himself."

"Great Lord," said Dewi, daring to break in, "how do you know these things that even the spirits do not?"

The great stone warrior turned his head stiffly to face her. "I am not a spirit like the others. They were never human, but I was. I was once a man, and now I live only in this form, for my body has gone to the land of the dead. I am neither fully human nor fully spirit, but a dweller in the shadowlands between, and so I see things neither spirits nor humans see. I meet the ghosts of those who have passed like me into the shadowlands. And from some of these, who have been murdered by the enemy who hunts you, I have learned certain things."

"O Lord Senopati," Dewi said, "were any of those who spoke to you named Bapar Wiriyanto or Empu Wesiagi?"

"No," said Senopati.

"Lord Senopati, are any bearing those names in the shadowlands? If . . . if they are there, they would just have arrived."

There was silence; then Senopati said, "There is no one of those names newly arrived in the shadowlands."

Hope flared in Adi's and Dewi's faces. Adi said, "Lord Senopati, did you hear—can you see—can you tell us the nature of what we seek? Are they rings? Are they talismans, or instruments of power?"

"No," said Senopati. "Snow, Fire, and Sword are to be your companions in this fight, and not just instruments of power. I do not know exactly what or who these companions are. I know the enemy seeks the same things, but I do not know who he is. I can tell you this. When I was alive, I fought the hordes of the Demon King, and living eternally in Chandi Maya was my reward. I have known many wicked men who have fought under the banner of the Demon King. Some chose evil because of their greed, their lust for power, their hunger to destroy. This one shares some of these things. But something else drives him too—something I cannot understand, something that makes him different from the evil men I have known before. This enemy has veiled his face."

"He is a man, then," whispered Adi. "He is not a demon."

"There are worse things even than demons," boomed Senopati. "Demons are what they are because it is their nature. Men who become demonic through their deliberate embrace of evil are worse still, and far more dangerous."

"Great Lord Senopati," said Anda Mangil quietly, after a short silence. "We need your guidance in one more matter—could it be possible that the spirit of Kris Rajadi is bound up with the ring that Adi wears?"

"Kris Rajadi's spirit is bound to the sky-iron," growled Senopati. "It does not wander the earth but stays in Kotabunga. It is a different Sword you seek. You must not be fixed in your thoughts."

"Then, great Lord Senopati, the ring on the hand of my other friend does not bear the spirit of Fire either?"

"It does not bear the spirit of Fire," rumbled Senopati, "but it may call fire, if the right words are used and there is no other way. As indeed may the other ring. Both are rings of protection, and because you seek protection in the water realms, their power is bound up with the opposite of water, which is fire. Yet they are not, in themselves, what you seek."

Anda Mangil bowed deeply. "We thank you, O great Lord Senopati."

"There is nothing to thank me for, Anda Mangil. I am only pleased that I am not altogether forgotten in this world."

Why, thought Adi suddenly, there is a wistful sadness in Senopati's voice. "O Lord Senopati, I was afraid to enter this place, but now I am glad," he said.

"Yes," said Dewi. "You have been very kind to

us, Lord Senopati."

Senopati let out a strange, scratchy kind of laugh. "Kind! It is a long time since anyone used that word of me. Even in life I was not given that name very often. But it is a good one. I will cherish it, in the long darkness of my stony sleep. Thank you."

"O Lord Senopati," cried Dewi, "was it difficult to fight the Demon King when you were alive? Did you know what to do? We are so confused and uncertain, my Lord."

When Senopati's voice came again, it was not big and booming, but soft, and touched with memory. "Yes, child, it was difficult indeed. We often did not know what to do. We were afraid, and confused, and sometimes despairing, for the Demon King was strong, and at first we were not. He was full of tricks and made us lose our way a number of times, but we fought because we could not bear to see everything destroyed. We fought because we could not live, otherwise. We could not be slaves." The voice was fading, fading. They strained to hear it as it became softer and softer. "Do not forget that light and darkness are mixed, that the child comes out from the watery darkness of the mother's belly into the light, that the sun's heat can burn all in its path, yet without its distant light, all would die." The voice had quite faded now, and Senopati was once again a strangely lifelike statue, stone eyes fixed eternally on some point behind those who knelt at the altar, massive hands clasped around the kris on its chest.

They spoke little in the car as they pulled away from Chandi Maya and resumed the journey to Siluman. The gods and heroes of the ancient stories had once seemed so different to them. Yet now, both Adi and Dewi knew that was not the case. Senopati had become a great legend, a great hero, and eventually the guardian of the Temple of the Great Mother, but he had once been a young, confused person. He had not known from the beginning the outcome of his fight with the forces of the Demon King; he had suffered and been afraid, like them. The thought gave them immense comfort.

NINE

DEWI HAD SEEN the sea only in pictures, and even the best of them did not prepare you for the reality—and certainly not the reality of Siluman. As Anda Mangil cautiously crept the car down the narrow cliff road that led to the beach, Dewi's heart beat fast and her scalp prickled with nervous anticipation.

Siluman beach, of jet-black sand, lay at the foot of great gray cliffs honeycombed with caves. Makeshift shrines and tents huddled down one end of the beach, protected from the wind by a jut of cliff. The cold southern ocean that prowled at the edges of the sand was known throughout Jayangan for its massive waves and dangerous currents, but it was the sheer expanse of it that took Dewi's breath away. She had never imagined that it could really be as big as this, stretching into the infinity of the horizon, abruptly cutting off the earth. She had always lived surrounded by land and sky, in a world bounded by green fields, with the quiet forest at its edge. She had always lived surrounded by people, gardens, houses, and the soft smells of incense and food cooking. The sea was big and wild, and not a track creased its surface, no road made by man could touch its wilderness. How could they ever think of going into such a place? The beach of Siluman was only the portal into Rorokidul's realm, and even it looked mighty inhospitable to human beings.

"Wah," said Adi softly, beside her. "An amazing sight!"

Dewi nodded. She was about to speak when he wound down the window of the car and put his head out, sniffing delightedly at the air. "This does me good!"

Dewi stared blankly at him. He saw her expression. "My parents' village is near the sea," he explained, smiling. "My father is a fisherman, and I helped him on the boat before I got the apprenticeship with my master."

"You went on the sea?" It made her feel queasy just thinking of it. You would be so small on that vastness, a speck hanging from the jaws of a great, blind, greedy beast.

"Of course! Not only on it, but in it. I even learned

to swim," he said gently. "The sea can be good to those who respect her and understand she is not to be treated lightly."

"It must be different in Jatimur," said Dewi. "Maybe the sea is a tame thing there, and not enchanted. The southern ocean is not like your ordinary fisherman's quiet sea, is it, Anda Mangil?"

Thus appealed to, Anda Mangil smiled. "I do not know the sea at Jatimur, and so I cannot be sure," he said diplomatically, "but the southern ocean is indeed a place of great renown, and its mistress a great queen."

The car bumped down the last few bits of road, onto the beach. Here, Anda Mangil paused, the engine still running. "Look over there," he said, pointing to the cliffs at the far end of the beach. "Over there is a cave, which is the entrance to Rorokidul's realm. Tuan Gelombang guards it. We will go there together." He opened his door, and Dewi felt her throat flutter with apprehension. For a moment, she wished he would just close the door, turn the car around, and head back up the cliff road, away from this place. But she said nothing of it, only opened her own door and followed Adi and Anda Mangil as they climbed out of the car, carefully locked the windows and doors, and set off across the beach to the cliff.

Despite the makeshift shrines and tents, which meant people must live here at least part of the time, or at least visit on pilgrimages, there seemed to be no one about. This could be explained by the fact it was the middle of the working week, but also because the weather down here on the beach was so unpleasant, with a vicious little wind whipping up stinging scurries of hot black sand. If there was anyone at home, they were staying inside their tents out of the wind and not bothering to come out and look at them. And why should they? Pilgrims often came to this spot to ask for the Queen of the Southern Sea's help or blessings. They would be a common sight here.

Dewi found the sand very uncomfortable to walk on. Hot and clinging, it slipped into her sandals. She had an unpleasant image of it as a thin coating over the entrance to hell. In her tight clothes, she stumbled more than once. The blustery wind blew the gritty stuff into her face and down her neck, adding to her discomfort. What made it worse was that Adi and Anda Mangil were surging on ahead, seemingly quite at ease on this unstable ground. Once, Adi turned to help her, but she gave him a glare, saying stiffly that she could manage perfectly well. She couldn't, but she was never going to tell him that. She was the daughter of a great dukun, not some simpering little girl.

She concentrated on her annoyance in order to stop thinking about the great beast ocean that prowled and growled just a few meters away. She found it all very disturbing: the way the waves reached like the flickering tongues of frogs or snakes to catch at the sand; the way humpbacked billows of foam and glassy water rushed and roared from a great distance, to expire on the beach, then gather themselves up again and retreat; the way the black sand at the edge of the water, sheened by the endless passage of waves, acquired a weird mirrored translucence that seemed bottomless, and that she could imagine falling into, endlessly, like a hole in deep space. The briny smells and wild shouting of the sea set her teeth on edge; looking ahead at Adi and Anda Mangil trudging confidently, she knew that even if she shouted at them to wait, the noise of the wind and the waves would carry her words away.

A picture of her home, of the garden, of her sister and brothers and her father came into her mind. O Lord of all creation, she prayed, dear Lord, please let us get home safely, back to our village, back to the smells of home, the routines of every day. I will never be dissatisfied and bored again.

"Is all well, little lady?" The harshly accented voice at her elbow made her jump, and she turned hastily to see a curious-looking man regarding her. He had just come out of one of the tents she had passed, and stood there eyeing her with frank interest. He was very tall and powerfully built, dressed in flowing black robes, waisted with a thick bronze belt, and there was a black-and-white cloth wrapped around his head. His face was very wrinkled, with light-brown hawk's eyes deeply set into strong, hard features. What could be seen of his hair under the headcloth was iron gray, but he wore a thick black mustache and a forked beard, both of which had been hennaed so that their blackness shone with reddish lights.

Dewi lowered her eyes. The man's foreign appearance and his direct gaze made her feel very uneasy, but she did not want to appear impolite, so she whispered, "Thank you, sir. All is well. I go to join my companions over at the cliff there."

The man shaded his eyes and looked across the sand. "Ah. You go to the cave, to visit Tuan Gelombang." He looked down at Dewi. "You will not find him there. He had to leave this morning on most urgent business. He must have been in a hurry, for men on motorbikes came to fetch him."

Dewi's breath caught. She stared at the man. "Men on motorbikes?"

"Yes. I only caught sight of them from the back, mind. They took him up the other side of the cliff—

there's another road up there— What!"

They had both jumped, for the deafening blast of a car horn had ripped at the air. Whirling around, Dewi saw four men all in black, mounted on motorbikes, right beside Anda Mangil's car. They wore masks that covered the top halves of their faces. And at the front of one bike crouched a thing like a twisted monkey in shape—but whose eyes glowed red as fire.

"The hantumu! The demon!" she shrieked. "Adi! Anda Mangil! They're coming! They're coming!" Her words were carried away by the wind and drowned out by the screaming of the car horn. She began to run toward her friends, shrieking warnings as she went. Before she could get very far, she fell over, sinking into the sand. She scrambled up, covered in sand, sobbing; and all at once, she was gripped around the waist and whirled into a black storm, disappearing into stifling folds of cloth. A fierce voice hissed in her ear, "Keep quiet. Very quiet." Half dead with fear, Dewi did exactly as she was told. She felt her captor taking a step back, then another, then another, and another. Wrapped in suffocating, wind-rough cloth, she could see nothing at all, but she could hear sounds very well: someone else's heart just above her ear, beating regularly and calmly; shouts; the car horn blasting on and on, like a scream for help; the roar of motorbike engines; and the hiss and sputter of sand thrown up by motorbike wheels racing past. . . .

Then silence. She felt herself being put down. "You can come out now." The man's voice startled her so much, she gasped. "But you still stay quiet, do you hear?"

The cloak was taken off her. She blinked and discovered she was in a large, rather dark tent made of black woolen fabric. The owner of the tent sat cross-legged near her, on a carpet. He had a glass of something in his hand. "Here," he said, handing it to her. "It's mint tea. Good for shock. Drink it," he ordered when she showed no sign of doing so.

She hesitated, then drank down the tea. "Thank you. It was very kind of you to—"

"Don't mention it," said the man. He was looking curiously at her, and she felt rather uncomfortable under his scrutiny. She got to her feet. "I had better go. My friends . . ."

"You can't go out there just now, little heart," said the man, also rising. "Wait a little while. They might come back, and you'll be a goner if they do. They can't see you in here. They can't even see my tent."

"How can that be?"

"My tent has been sprinkled with zummiyah water," said the man, "and I have written 'Adhubilah' at the entrance." He misinterpeted Dewi's baffled look. "Zummiyah is holy water from the sacred well near the House of Light in Al Aksara, the Great Desert," he explained, "and 'Adhubilah' . . ."

"I know, it's the sacred formula that keeps evil spirits at bay, but only spirits from—"

"From the world of the Jinns, that's right," finished the man. "Why do you look surprised? I had a few adventures in my time, in the world of the Jinns, and not all of them remember me fondly. Lucky I was so armed this time, for out there, with those wicked men who hide their faces, was an afreet, of that I am sure."

Dewi knew the stories of the Jinn. They were the Hidden People of the original Mujisal of Al Aksara, the Great Desert and, like the otherworlders of Jayangan, were of many and different kinds, living in different realms. Some were good, some bad, some in between. The worst ones of all, those who came from the demonic realm of Jehannem, ruled over by the dread Lord Iblis, were the afreet—shape-shifters with hearts of pure evil.

"Oh, sir," she cried, on the verge of tears. "Are you sure it was an afreet with those hantumu?"

The man nodded. "I can smell an afreet from a long way away. It was good they did not find you."

Dewi whispered, "I thank you for—"

"For nothing. What else would you have had me do?" He put his face to the tent flap and carefully looked out. "They are gone."

"I will go, then," Dewi said. "Thank you very much, and may God be with you."

"No," said the man. "You must not go from here on your own. It is not safe."

"My friends—"

"Are not out there anymore. That is all I know, though we must hope they escaped," he said.

"I must go and look for them," she cried, her lips trembling a little.

"You will not go alone," said the man sharply. "So you were going to the realm of Queen Rorokidul," he continued.

"How did you know?" she asked warily. He had saved her from her enemies, but could she really trust this strange foreigner?

"It's obvious," said the man. "I know what Tuan Gelombang does, and you were going to see him. You are dressed like a princess. Strange creatures, including a bad Jinn, are after you. You are not at Siluman for no reason. And what better reason is there than to ask for the help of the powerful Queen of the Southern Sea in some matter?"

"Oh," said Dewi, rather blankly.

"What is your name, little heart?"

"Dewi. I am the daughter of the great dukun Bapar Wiriyanto, of—"

"A dukun's daughter!" The man stroked his mustache, smiling. "Ha! Well, well, that is well!" He rubbed his hands in a gesture Dewi found rather alarming. "Why were you going to Rorokidul's realm? To find out why those hantumu and that damned afreet are after you, little girl?"

"I am not a little girl," said Dewi, stung. "I am almost fourteen." She took a deep breath and said, rather haughtily, "And what of you, sir? Are you not going to tell me your name?"

"Ha! The dukun's daughter has teeth. Excellent!" said the man, smiling. "But you may not like it, when I tell you my name."

"I believe I need to know it, sir," said Dewi.

"Very well, then. Long ago, I left my homeland of Al Aksara as an exile. I have been in Jayangan a long, long time now. And here, people call me Tuan Kematian."

Dewi stared at him. Lord Death! His name was Lord Death!

Kematian smiled, reminiscing. "I worked for a long time at the Court of Kotabunga. I was the Sultan's Chief Executioner. For many, many years, no great judgment was complete without me. I sent many traitors and murderers and villains to their deaths—and well deserved too."

Dewi took an involuntary step back, feeling cold all over. The man sighed. "People think I like nothing better than to cut off heads, and that I will seek any opportunity to do so. Not a bit of it. I worked for justice and was bound by its rules. In any case, I am no longer an executioner, merely an old fisherman who has finally found peace and reflection by the sea." He saw Dewi's expression. "You may as well trust me. I am the only one who can help you right now."

Dewi had never met anyone like this before. He had few manners, no graces; he looked fearsome and his past was fearful. In a play, he would have been cast as an ogre. And yet she remembered Anda Mangil's words—he'd said new ways of seeing were needed, to face this new threat.

This man had certainly saved her from the hantumu. Besides, he obviously understood something of the world of the Jinns, the desert spirits. If it really was an afreet with the hantumu, she would need his specialized knowledge, for she knew very little about Jinns, having never seen one before. She did not have her father, or Anda Mangil, or even Adi, to advise her on the proper course of action. She would have to make her own decision. "Very well," she said, at last. "I thank you, Tuan Kematian."

"Do not thank me till I have properly helped you." He went over to a chest in the corner of the tent. "I think it is as well we should be armed." So saying, he lifted out a large, curved sword sheathed in a metal scabbard. He attached it to his belt. "This may not do much to the afreet, but it is sharp, as men's flesh is soft. Many's the wicked head it sent rolling in its day. If I catch up with those hantumu . . ." He grinned and drew the sword slowly from its sheath. Its blade, obviously still well oiled and polished, gleamed. Dewi shivered. Then a sudden, dazzling thought made her gasp. Senopati had said Snow, Fire, and Sword were not mere instruments of power, but companions. Here in Siluman she had found a man who lived by the sword, who, in a sense, was the essence of Sword. Yes. She was sure of it. She had found the first companion—she had found Sword!

"What is it?" said Kematian, concerned, quickly sheathing the sword. "You look as though you've just seen a ghost, little heart. Don't worry. My sword obeys me. It will not jump out of its own accord."

"Oh, Tuan Kematian, there is something I must tell you!" And without pausing for breath, she told him all about her quest for Snow, Fire, Sword. When she had finished, there was a long silence as the old executioner rocked on his heels for a moment, deep in thought. Then he looked at Dewi, his eyes shining with tears. "I want to tell you something few people know. And that is my true name, the name I was known by in my homeland of Al Aksara. That name is Husam al-Din. It means 'Sword of the Faith' in the tongue of my people."

Dewi's heart thumped. "Oh," she whispered, "may I call you that, instead of . . . the other name?"

He looked at her for a long moment, and nodded. "I would be honored, little heart. I do not know if it is truly my sword and my service that you seek, but I hope it is. What a great and noble task has been entrusted to you—and how privileged I am to be able to help you. Let me pledge the sword and the heart of Husam al-Din to this most glorious quest!" And so saying, he knelt down before her, drew his sword, and laid it at her feet. "With this sword, I promise to protect and to preserve. I promise that I will not rest until the wrongdoers are found and punished."

Dewi could hardly find the words to speak at first, so moved was she. At last, she whispered, "Rise, O Husam al-Din, for you, who have much skill and wisdom, do me too much honor. I am nothing special, but I must fulfill the task I was given, or my father and my friends can never return home, and our beautiful land of Jayangan will never be freed from the threat of the Demon King."

"Ah, little heart," said Husam al-Din, getting to his feet again, "it is not for nothing you were chosen. You are not only a dukun's daughter but truly one of God's true and kind children, and I am only glad I can be your companion in this task." He rummaged around in the chest and pulled out a leather bottle and a smaller glass bottle. Carefully, he decanted a tiny stream of bright water from the leather one into the glass one, stowed it carefully in his clothes, and put the leather bottle back in the chest. "This little bit of zummiyah water will protect us against the afreet, and the rest I have left here to stop it and the hantumu from entering and knowing you've been sheltered here. Now, let us go first to Tuan Gelombang's cave and see if we can find a trace of your friends."

TEN

ADI AND ANDA Mangil were almost at the mouth of the cave when they heard the car horn blasting, turned, and saw the motorbikes roaring over the sand toward them. Adi just had time to see Dewi snatched by a tall man in black—a hantumu?—when Anda Mangil grabbed him by the arm and edged back with him toward the cave. "We've got to get in there!" he shouted. "You have Rorokidul's ring of protection."

Adi tried to say something, but he fell into the mouth of the cave and instinctively put out a hand to break his fall. His beringed finger touched the rocky wall. There was a blinding flash, and Adi was flung far into the cave, sliding along its sandy floor. Ears ringing, seeing sparks before his eyes, he scrambled to his feet and ran back to the cave entrance.

Anda Mangil was still out there. The hantumu had

almost reached him. Adi shouted, "Anda Mangil! Come in! Come in!"

Anda Mangil looked over his shoulder at Adi. He shook his head. He tried to smile. "I cannot," he said.

"Why not? Come in." Adi made to go through the cave's mouth, to grab Anda Mangil and bring him inside. But he bounced back, as if he'd just hit an invisible wall. He tried again, flinging himself at the entrance. Still he fell back. He screamed, "Let me through! Let me through!" and threw himself desperately at the entrance again. In vain. Panting, gasping, his head in a whirl, his stomach in knots, he could only stand and watch as the hantumu gained inexorably on Anda Mangil. He understood now. Try as he might, struggle and scream and pound at the invisible force field with all his strength, he could not push past it. He was trapped in safety in the cave, as trapped as he'd been in the paddy field when his master was kidnapped, as helpless to prevent or change what happened next.

Anda Mangil turned and ran. Not toward the hantumu, but toward the water. The hantumu redoubled their pace and, as Adi watched in helpless fury and sorrow, three of them jumped off their bikes and ran straight at him, crash-tackling him to the ground and dragging him back up the beach. The other rider sat on his bike, some distance away from the sea. Was he the leader? Now Adi could see the thing that crouched on his bike, a thing that filled him with a creeping horror: a twisted little monkey with blazing, unearthly eyes that were fixed on the driver.

The hantumu brought out some ropes, but as they bent over Anda Mangil to tie him up, he managed to free himself and dived for his fallen kris. Taken by surprise, the hantumu fell back momentarily, giving Anda Mangil enough time to jump to his feet, kris whirling like lightning in his hand. One of the hantumu gave a howl and reeled away as the kris drove right into his arm. Still the leader of the hantumu sat on his bike, but the monkey thing had jumped onto his shoulder and was dancing and chittering there, as if in unbearable excitement. Anda Mangil fought the other two hantumu, twisting and turning desperately, going toward the water, regaining the ground he'd lost. Still the leader of the hantumu did nothing but watch, the monkey jumping with glee. For a moment Adi's spirits rose, as it seemed to him that Anda Mangil might at least escape into the sea. Oh, if only, if only he could be there with him. Two of them might succeed in beating the hantumu back. "Let me out! Let me out!" he yelled to the invisible force field that barred him from getting out, but to no avail.

The three hantumu were all around Anda Mangil

now, including the wounded one, whose mouth was twisted in rage and pain. Yet still Anda Mangil fought on, backing away down the beach. He was tiring; the hantumu's whirling swords had caught him more than once, on the shoulder, on the leg, across the chest. Adi, tears of rage pouring down his cheeks, could see that the driver's face was beaded with sweat and getting paler by the second; blood stained his beautiful clothes. If he could only reach the waves, surely Rorokidul would help him. Surely . . .

The leader of the hantumu got off his bike. Adi saw him touch the monkey on his shoulder. And then Adi saw something he would never forget, as long as he lived. The monkey flew through the air—not like an animal, but like a leaping ghost, like a nightmare come to life—straight for Anda Mangil's throat. But it did not bare its teeth or try to bite him; it gripped with horrible little hands the driver's chest and stared him full in the face, its eyes shining like twin furnaces.

Anda Mangil gave a great cry. He staggered, dropped his kris, and put his hand up to free himself, but the monkey clung tightly, squealing in mad ecstasy, staring into his eyes as if it would consume his soul. And in that moment, the hantumu moved swiftly. Raising their swords high, they fell on Anda Mangil with savage cries of triumph, striking again and again.

The monkey leaped from his chest, capering and gibbering on the loose sand beside Anda Mangil's head. In a few seconds, it was all over.

Now the leader of the hantumu made a gesture toward his friends and they fell back, revealing the broken, bloody corpse of Anda Mangil. "Leave it there for the scavengers," the leader said, and the hantumu walked back to their bikes, the monkey chittering at their feet. They headed back up the beach, engines roaring, sand spinning under their wheels. They reached the cliff road and vanished from sight.

For an instant, Adi could not move, think, or feel. He heard the melancholy sound of the car horn, which sounded once or twice more, faintly, before fading away.

He put up a hand toward the entrance. The force field was still there. "Let me out, please," he whispered brokenly. "Let me out, I must go to my—"

Then he gasped and fell silent, for as he spoke, a massive wave reared up out of the sea and came rolling swiftly toward the beach. The instant it reached Anda Mangil's body, it tossed him up into its massive arms and Adi, gripped by terror, horror, and awe, saw that the driver's body had been washed clean of wounds. Then he saw creatures emerging from the water, surrounding Anda Mangil's body—beautiful creatures of dream, white as sea foam, with translucent hair the color of waves. Each creature held in its arms a basket full of flowers that glowed with an unearthly radiance. The wave, with Anda Mangil resting on top of it as if on a great princely bed, stayed poised there for a second as the sea creatures spread flowers all over his body, and around it. And then someone else emerged from the water: a tall, queenly woman with silver hair and dark eyes, dressed in sea blue, green, and silver. In her hand, she carried a wreath of the most beautiful flowers ever seen, entwined with what looked like the most lovely jewels imaginable. Gently, she bent over Anda Mangil's body, placed the wreath on his brow, and softly touched a finger to his lips. Then she turned and looked straight at Adi. For an instant, their eyes met, and Adi found himself incapable of speech. Then the woman turned back to the sea and raised her arms, and in an instant, wave, sea creatures, queen, and the body of Anda Mangil vanished completely from sight. All that was left was the sea, restlessly prowling up and down the beach, and Adi, alone in the cave.

Burning tears rolled down Adi's cheeks, unchecked, unheeded. He supposed that the woman had been Rorokidul, and that she had taken Anda Mangil to her palace in the Southern Sea. He knew that she had shown him this so he would be reconciled to what had happened. But awesome as it had been, Adi could not be reconciled. Anda Mangil might be honored in death, but he was dead. Rorokidul had done nothing for him while he was alive. And by forcing Adi to stay behind the force field of her protection, she had turned him into little better than a coward. Once again, he had been of no use in the fight against the hantumu. Once again, he had had to stand by helplessly while friends were kidnapped or butchered.

The rebellion in him welled up and exploded. "Rorokidul!" he ground out. "I don't need your protection. Let me be!"

Silence. But as his hands tightened around each other in his distress, the ring bit into his flesh. His skin burned from the contact. His hair stood up on end. Still he shouted, "Queen Rorokidul! Queen Rorokidul, let me be!"

Silence and darkness. But now there was a tremor under his feet, a vibration that made his teeth chatter and cold sweat pour down his neck. An uncontrolled panic gripped him then, and hardly knowing what he was doing, he pulled the ring from his finger. "Leave me alone, let me go, let me go!"

As soon as the ring left his finger, he felt the force field diminish, so quickly that he staggered and fell to the ground, tumbling out of the cave. He gasped. The sea was wild, agitated. Huge waves crashed onto the sand, washing in at the mouth of the cave. Adi clung to the rough wall, pushing against the force of the water. As it receded, he leaped out of the cave, not looking back, running with all his might up the sand.

Neither Dewi nor Husam heard Adi's light footsteps as he ran past the back of Husam's tent. As he ran, Adi took a solemn vow: He would allow no one to make his decisions ever again. He would fight. He would discover things for himself. He would not rely on the talismans or protection of spirits. He would find the strength within himself and either save or avenge his friends. Clutching his heart symbol, he offered up a prayer to God, solemnizing his vow and asking for the repose of the soul of poor Anda Mangil.

His breath whistling in his throat, he reached Anda Mangil's car. He tried the driver's door. It was locked. He tried the other doors. All locked too. He touched the gleaming dark-red hood—and sprang back, as a strange, hot vibration whooshed out under his hand. He felt a sharp sting at the ends of his fingers, like a burn. He looked at the car. He put out a cautious finger toward it, and as soon as he touched it, heat flared out again, making him jump back. He stood there, sucking at his fingers and staring at the car, heart pounding. Had the hantumu bewitched it?

A sudden movement caught his eye. There was someone by that black tent. A man all in black! Adi ducked down behind the car, his palms clammy. He must get away. He must get back to Kotabunga and go and see the Sultan. It was the only thing to do. How could you rely on spirits who either didn't have the full knowledge of what was needed or got murderously angry just because you questioned them? He would walk back up the road. He might get a lift back to Kotabunga with someone if he was lucky. He was certainly not going to stay here, in this horrible place. And so Adi turned his back on the car and raced as fast as he could up the cliff road, stumbling a little over rocks and loose gravel. He reached the top quickly and turned back onto the road which they had traveled on only a short time before.

Of course, distances traveled in a car—even one as sedately steady as Anda Mangil's—appear much shorter than those traveled on foot. And to Adi, the road seemed endless, going on and on and on into the distance.

When they had driven down to the beach, he had noticed, from the comfort of the car's soft seats, just how deserted this road was. Unusually for Jayangan, there were no settlements for quite some kilometers around Siluman. The soil was too poor, the conditions too harsh for farming. Adi felt the full force of first the sun and then pouring rain as black clouds gathered and burst. For an hour, and then two, he walked in growing discomfort. His fear and horror and sorrow receded somewhat, but he was beginning to feel hungry and thirsty. He opened his mouth to the raindrops pelting down and so obtained some relief, but so much of it was falling, it threatened to drown him before his thirst was properly quenched. Not one car passed, not one bike, not one cart.

Then, just as the rain was easing, when he had almost despaired of ever meeting another traveler, he heard a rattle and thump in the distance. A short while later, on the road behind Adi emerged a battered, elderly, small car, wheezing and gasping its way along. It drew up beside Adi and stopped. Adi stopped too.

The driver leaned an elbow out of the car and called, "My friend, you look very tired. Where are you going? Can I offer you a lift?" He was about Adi's age or a little older, and had a round, bright face, sparkling eyes, and a head of unruly wavy hair. And his accent was pure Jatimur! Adi felt his heart lighten a little. "Oh, yes, please. I am going to Kotabunga."

"Well, I'm not going as far as that, only to Gunungbatu, halfway there. But even just a little way along might help you, no? Perhaps you might be able to rest at my master's. I will ask him, anyway. Jump in."

Adi gratefully did as he was told. He tried to smile at his rescuer. "It is very kind of you to stop for a stranger."

"Think nothing of it," said the young man breezily. "It's just normal to help a fellow traveler." After a little pause, he asked curiously, "You are from my part of the world too, are you not?"

Adi named his village.

"Why, Desagua is only a short distance from the village I came from! My father—God rest his soul—was a well-known fisherman. He used to own two boats." A sadness came into his bright face. "But that was long ago, and now I—" He broke off what he was going to say, and went on, instead, "I am glad to have met you. My name is Sadik."

Adi made an effort at politeness, though his mind kept filling with what he'd seen on the beach. "Hello, Sadik. My name is Adi."

"What has happened to you, Adi? Why are you on this road, alone?"

"I . . ." Adi looked quickly at Sadik. Should he trust this young man? He decided to play it safe. "I . . . I intended to meet some other companions," he said, stumbling a little over the words. "But they were . . .

were late, and then I obtained word that they had gone back to Kotabunga."

"You are dressed very finely," said Sadik, looking with frank interest at Adi's clothes, "yet you say you are a villager like me. Are you employed at the Court?"

"Oh no," said Adi quickly. "I was . . . er . . . given these clothes by my master, who wished me to be in fine shape for a ceremony that was to be held soon." I'm gabbling, he thought. What will Sadik think? But he seemed to accept Adi's explanation without demur.

"I cannot take you to Kotabunga myself, you understand," said Sadik. "But there will be someone else to take you on. You will come with me to Gunungbatu, to the community where I live. It is a good place, of learning and quietness and kindness. You will stay and rest. I will introduce you to my master. He will like you, I know. You can—"

"I have to get to Kotabunga," said Adi, rather alarmed by all this. He couldn't afford to wait. "I am really in a very great hurry. I cannot stay for long. Though it is indeed kind of you to propose it," he added hastily, not wanting to offend his new friend in any way.

"Of course. That is understood. We will get you to Kotabunga quickly; many go there all the time," said Sadik cheerfully, leaning forward to grind at the gears.

As he did so, something swung around his neck, catching the light. It was a little silver medallion with words engraved on it, words Adi recognized at once, as no one who lived in Jayangan could fail to do: "The Light Shines." They were written in the ancient script of Al Aksara, the Great Desert, where the Mujisal religion had originally come from. They were sacred to all Mujisals but even more so to the Pumujisal, the strict ones, for whom they were almost considered a powerful talisman.

Adi looked cautiously at Sadik; the Pumujisal didn't like the Nashranees much, and the favor was often returned. It might be best not to mention he himself was a Nashranee, especially as he'd had one or two unpleasant experiences in the past. Anyway, his heart symbol was well hidden under his clothes, next to his skin.

Sadik caught Adi's eye. "You were down on the beach, friend Adi. Was the ceremony to be held there? Was it to do with the Queen of the Southern Sea?"

Adi gulped. Before he could speak, Sadik said, "You believe in the stories of Queen Rorokidul, then?"

Adi looked away There was a hollow feeling in the pit of his stomach as he remembered what he'd seen. He said, "It is not for me to believe or disbelieve."

"Mmm." Sadik's glance flickered over him again. "I

think they are just stories. I think the sea is dangerous, though. My father met his death on it. And my mother's heart broke because of it. I hate the sea. It is the realm of madness and death."

Adi certainly did not want to be dragged into a discussion of such things. Making an effort to be calm, he said, "I am sorry to hear of such sadness, friend. I know the sea can indeed be harsh. In any case, it is not where I wish to be. I have to get back to Kotabunga, where my friends will be waiting." He added the last instinctively, and Sadik nodded.

"You have become separated from friends. That is a great sadness. We will try to make sure you are soon reunited."

"Thank you," said Adi. An obscure unease was gnawing at him, battling with his relief at being in the car. He wrestled with his thoughts, coming to a firm decision. He would rest a short while in Gunungbatu, to please Sadik, but he would leave that very day for Kotabunga. Yes. That was what he would do.

ELEVEN

"I DON'T LIKE THE look of that sea," said Husam al-Din, as he and Dewi hurried toward the cave. She didn't like the look of it either—the huge, angry waves that were crashing menacingly onto the sand, eating up more and more of it. But then, she hadn't liked the look of it from the beginning.

Husam stopped when they were a few meters away from the cave. "It's under water," he said. "We can't go in there."

Dewi said faintly, "I have the ring of protection Kwanyin gave me, and my father's talisman, which he got from the Harimauroh. Queen Rorokidul will respect them. Maybe she will help us."

"Doesn't look to me like the Queen's in a mood to listen," said Husam, "but you can try."

"She's probably just angry because her sacred place has been violated by the hantumu and the afreet," said

Dewi. "She has probably helped Adi and Anda Mangil. That's why they're not here. I'll have to go closer to the water's edge."

"Let me go first," said Husam. Drawing his sword and holding it high before him, he stepped in front of Dewi, covering her as she reluctantly walked closer to the edge of the sea. She was oddly comforted by it, though steel and bravery were surely no match for the awesome power of the Queen of the Southern Sea.

She stopped a little way from the edge. She could not bear to go any closer. The sea was dark, ferocious, terrifying. It looked as if it might devour the whole beach, the whole world. She thought she could see, flickering in and out of the wild waves, a woman's face—beautiful, but twisted in fury. Dewi raised her hands. In one, she held her father's talisman; in the other, Kwanyin's ring.

"Queen Rorokidul," she cried faintly, then louder. "Queen Rorokidul! I beg audience with you. I beg—"

The sea roared. A huge wave rose up and came rushing toward them, so swiftly that they did not even have time to move or cry out. But just as the wave reached their feet, it vanished, and in its place a fountain of water spurted up from the black sand. It was crystal clear and hung in the air like a shimmering bead curtain. Behind the curtain of water was the tall and graceful Queen Rorokidul. Her face was lovely, but her eyes were bright with anger.

"You have audience with me. What do you want, child who is protected by two spirits?"

"Your Ma-Majesty," stammered Dewi, "we . . . I and my friends came here to this place to seek your help in our quest to find Snow, Fire, and Sword and defeat the evil that stalks our land."

"I know that," said the Queen sharply, her eyes narrowing.

Dewi said, "Your Majesty, I believe I have found Sword. He stands here before you."

The Queen looked at Husam. "You think you have found Sword. Are you sure, Dewi?"

"Yes," said Dewi, her courage rising. "Queen Rorokidul, it was on Siluman, at the doorway to your realm, that I found Sword, and I wish to thank you for that."

The Queen stared at her, silent for a little while. Then she said, "Child, you surprise me. And I am not often surprised. I accept your thanks." She turned her dark glance on the impassive Husam, who still stood at guard with his sword held out. "He is not an unworthy man," she said at last. "He could well be Sword."

Dewi saw a faint smile dart fleetingly from under Husam's mustache. Emboldened, she said, "Your

Majesty, we need your help. The hantumu were here, and—"

A terrifying spasm of rage crossed the sea-spirit's face. "Don't say that accursed name! How is it that such creatures are allowed to desecrate this place with their evil presence? What sort of a world are you people creating up there on the land? Why are so many forgetting their sacred duties, their ancient obligations? Why doesn't the Sultan of Jayangan—he whose family has always been guarded by me—why does he not act?"

Dewi quailed. "Your Majesty, I cannot answer for the Sultan, but I know there are many, many people who still remember the debt they owe you. Many people who hold to the old ways, who fight to preserve what is good in Jayangan. But we are facing a dangerous and powerful enemy. We cannot defeat him easily."

The Queen snapped, "And there are many others who join the enemy, or do nothing about him. Ha! We should just turn our backs on the whole of this accursed human world."

"But there are also those like my father and the kris maker, who have put their own safety last. There are those who have paid the ultimate price," said Dewi, white to the lips.

"That is so," said Rorokidul sharply, "but they pay

it willingly, and we honor them for it."

Dewi swallowed. "Queen Rorokidul . . . my friends . . . might you tell us . . ."

Rorokidul's eyes bored into Dewi's. She made a gesture with her hand, and a little wave detached itself from the sea and came rolling down to sink and die at Dewi's feet. When it receded, it left a little, glittering object behind. Dewi bent down to seize it with a cry. It was Adi's ring!

Horror gripped at her throat. "Then Adi is . . . he is . . ."

Rorokidul raised an eyebrow. "Dead? No. He escaped the hantumu. But he is without any link to the spirits, for he threw the ring away." Her lips set in a thin line. "He said he did not want my protection. So I withdrew it from him."

"Where is he, then?" cried Dewi.

"I do not know," said Rorokidul with some asperity. "He left the beach."

"He has probably gone back to Kotabunga, then," said Husam, turning to Dewi. "To Kwanyin."

Dewi said quietly, "And . . . Queen Rorokidul . . . my other friend . . . Anda Mangil . . . where is he?"

Rorokidul's face changed. "He was a good man. A worthy man."

"Do you mean . . ."

For the first time, there was a gentleness in Rorokidul's eyes. She said, "Yes. Anda Mangil is one of those who, as you said, paid the ultimate price. Anda Mangil is dead."

Dewi sank to the sand, her hands over her eyes. Images of the man she had known all her life—kind, cheerful Anda Mangil—flashed in and out of her mind. How could he be dead? How could he be? A deep determination took root in her heart and soul. It was for the peace of the spirits of the dead and missing that she would fight; it was for their sake that she would complete the quest. Nothing would deter her now—nothing—until the diabolical man who was behind this suffering and pain and fear was comprehensively defeated. But first they must find Anda Mangil's body and lay him to rest.

"O Queen of the Southern Sea," she cried brokenly, "please tell us where my dear friend's body is to be found, so we may honor him."

"Child," came Rorokidul's voice, very gently now, "he is already in the embrace of the sea, and we will honor him, for he is a man who has richly earned all the rewards of the spirit world. His body will be laid to rest in the halls of the sea, but his spirit will still be with you, while you need it. He did not want to be at rest while you are still in danger."

Dewi, her throat thick with emotion, said, "Is there not something I can take back to his family in the village, so that they may have something to bury and mourn?"

"You can tell his family how he died, and how he will always be honored in my realm, and that of all spirits," said Rorokidul, "but I know you humans need more." A little wave rolled again at Dewi's feet, and when it receded, it left behind something she recognized—the mandala pendant Anda Mangil had always worn, for as long as she had known him. Only, when she picked it up, she saw that it shone now with the patina of pure gold, was encrusted with real jewels, and carried a scent with it, a perfume like frangipani, of such beauty and sweetness that it made tears come to her eyes. "Tell them to put that on Anda Mangil's shrine," came the voice of Rorokidul, "and to burn sweet candles to his memory, for he was one of the best men in all of Jayangan. If more were like him, we would not face what we do today."

"Thank you," said Dewi.

Husam said, "Your Majesty, I must ask what my companion may not. If I am Sword, will you be able to help us find Fire and Snow? The Lady Kwanyin thought that as the mistress of the vast realm of the sea, you might know more of the nature of these companions."

"I wish it were so, but I do not know any more than she does. But you may know the other companions when you see them, for their natures will call to yours. Only be careful—they may not know it themselves, and think you to be an enemy. Remember this: If you are in trouble and you cannot reach Kwanyin, there is one place where you might find me in Kotabunga, and that is in the Water Gardens. There is an atrium, below the gardens, that is sacred to me."

Dewi had a dozen questions. "Your Majesty . . ."

But she was speaking to empty air. The Queen had vanished. The sky was blue; the sea was flat and calm once more. And floating on it, on little rippling waves that uncoiled at their feet, were a host of beautiful frangipani flowers, some yellow, some pink, the sweetness of their perfume filling the air, just like the mandala Dewi held in her hand. She bent down to pick some up as they came riding in on the sea, and said a few prayers for the dearly beloved soul of Anda Mangil, who had given his life for his friends.

They turned their backs on the sea, then, and trudged back up the sand to Anda Mangil's car. The sight of it brought tears to Dewi's eyes again. Poor Anda Mangil—how much he'd loved this car. And now he'd never ride in it again.

A sudden blast of the car horn made her, and

Husam, jump. "Suffering cats!" exclaimed the old man. "What's the matter with this thing?" He broke off, eyes wide, mouth open, as the two front doors of the car slowly opened by themselves. The car horn sounded again, more softly, but still urgently, and then the engine started up. Dewi and Husam stared at each other.

"Anda Mangil said it was no ordinary car," whispered Dewi. She put a hand on the car and snatched it away when she felt a definite pulse under her hand. Gulping, she brought her hand back down again, and this time did not take it away when the car moved. She thought of Rorokidul's words, of how Anda Mangil's spirit did not want to rest while they needed him.

The car purred under her hand. A sudden smile lit her face, warming her. "Let's go," she said to Husam, who still looked very wary indeed. "The car will see us safely to Kotabunga. You'd better get in the driver's seat."

"Hmm," said Husam suspiciously, but he did as Dewi said. Dewi got into the seat beside him.

Husam stared at the wheel. "There's only one problem with this, little heart. I never learned how to drive. And there's no key. How can we control this infernal machine?"

The horn sounded indignantly. The car doors

slammed shut. The engine roared. With a little swish of tires, the big car jerked forward.

"Hey!" shouted Husam. "If you're going to do it by yourself, car, kindly remember to go along more smoothly!"

The car horn sounded again, sharply, rudely, as if it were blowing a raspberry. Then the engine got into gear, purring like a cat, and the car drove smoothly up the cliff road, just in the way Anda Mangil used to drive. Dewi smiled, bitterness and happiness mixed together. Thank you, she said, deep within herself. Thank you. Oh, I am so sad, Anda Mangil, that you are gone, yet so glad you are still with us, somehow.

The radio clicked on by itself, right at the beginning of Anda Mangil's favorite song, "Beloved." Dewi sang softly along with it, emotion sometimes causing her to choke a little on the sweet, familiar words. As for Husam, he was taking in all the wonders of the car, exclaiming over the pictures, leafing through the holy books, and generally acting just like anyone who came across this traveling wonder for the first time.

TWELVE

THE MOUNTAIN OF Gunungbatu was actually a bleak, stony hill set among other bare, rocky hills that stretched in every direction, as far as the eye could see. The town of Gunungbatu, as bleak and gray as its surroundings, sprawled at the foot of the hill that gave it its name. A dusty sign proclaimed it to be the biggest settlement in the region, but as this part of Jayangan was hardly well populated, it did not mean much. Gunungbatu's main street was a dispiriting huddle of unkempt stalls and shops, and its roads were in a state of disrepair. There was none of the brightness and color of Kotabunga, not even the sleepy charm of smaller Kejawen towns. The few people who were on the streets looked rough and suspicious; indeed, some of them looked like brigands who'd like nothing better than to rob Adi and Sadik of whatever they had. Adi's heart sank.

But Sadik did not seem to care. He drove through the town, chattering cheerfully about how much Gunungbatu had grown recently, since his master had made his headquarters near here. He would not hear of Adi getting out, saying that Gunungbatu townspeople were not very friendly toward strangers, that someone from the community where he lived would be sure to be going to Kotabunga in the next day or so, and that they would be glad to give Adi a lift. "I will take you to our community now," Sadik said, "for I think it would be discourteous of me not to give you some hospitality." He did not add "and it would be discourteous of you to refuse," but the implication was clear. There was no way out.

Adi nodded. "Thank you," he murmured. He looked out the window at Gunungbatu slipping past. After a short while, they turned onto a potholed road signposted to the "Community of Light." Yes, that definitely sounded like a Pumujisal community, thought Adi nervously.

"Are you sure no one will mind my being here?" he said. "After all, I am a stranger."

"Of course no one will mind! You know I was taken in by our great master when I was cruelly orphaned. He has done so much good, Adi!" Sadik's face shone. "You will see, Adi, my master, Shayk Rasheed al-Jabal, is the holiest, purest man in all of Jayangan, and probably the whole world! And he is so learned, it makes my head swim." He looked down at his hands. "I am afraid I am not the best student there. I cannot keep enough verses of the Book of Light in my head. I try, I really do. But then my silly thoughts scatter them, and I cannot remember."

They had arrived at a great white gate with the name of the community emblazoned on it in thick black letters. By either side of the gate stood four tall, broad, impassive-faced young men, heads swathed in black-and-white headcloths, and dressed in jeans and T-shirts. As the car drew up, Adi saw their hard gazes turn to him, minutely noting every aspect of his appearance. He shrank back into his seat, saying, "Sadik, I do not think it would be a good idea for me to come here. It is a private community, after all. I will get out and walk back to the town. I will find a bus there, or—"

"Don't be silly," said Sadik, stopping the car. "There are no buses, and the people of Gunungbatu can be unfriendly. They are superstitious and believe their mountain is haunted, and that strangers aggravate the ghosts that are there. They are fools! Besides, you're my friend. We always welcome friends." He got out and approached the guards at the gate. Adi watched as Sadik conversed earnestly with them. His hands felt clammy, his breath came fast. He thought of jumping out of the car and running away down the road, but did not dare to think what might happen then.

Adi could certainly see no welcome shining out from the guards' faces—only a watchfulness, a suspicion that made him feel very nervous. But in a short while, Sadik came back to the car, wreathed in smiles. "No problem," he said, jumping back in. "They will just call up to the main house." And indeed, one of the guards pulled out what looked like a walkie-talkie from a pocket of his jeans and talked quietly into it.

"No problem at all," said Sadik again, cheerfully. "You will see."

The guard finished his conversation, looked at them, smiled, and waved them on. Another guard opened the gate, and they rattled through, Adi trying to look relaxed and comfortable as they passed the guards.

"Those boys," said Sadik as they bumped along, "they are good boys, but they do not always know how to behave. Never mind—we must be careful in these days, as there may well be tricksters of the Demons' Army trying to get in."

"The Demons' Army?"

"Our master has told us there is a great struggle for the cosmos," said Sadik gravely. "The Demons are trying to control the world again. We are with the Army of Light and fight against them."

"Oh," said Adi, and a great relief filled him. Somehow, he must have come to the right place. These people obviously knew something about what was going on. They might well be able to help him.

A few men and women walking along the track paused to look at them, and Sadik greeted them, introducing Adi as his good friend. Adi smiled and greeted them a little nervously but felt himself relaxing. He looked curiously at his surroundings. To one side of the track were rice fields where people were working, and to the other were vegetable fields.

Sadik, noticing Adi's glance, said proudly that the community was almost self-sufficient in vegetables, though not yet rice or meat. "But we are getting there," he proclaimed, as they passed a herdsboy pushing along a bright-eyed contingent of goats. He waved and smiled at them, his interested gaze on Adi, who grinned back.

Now the track wound through a cover of trees and emerged into a clearing. Here was a cluster of large houses and huts, set around an open-air, pillared pavilion. The pavilion was white, decorated with bright, geometric patterns, and featured the words "The Light Shines" on its concrete pillars.

"That's our meeting place," said Sadik proudly. "We built it ourselves."

Some distance from the pavilion was an elegant building whose golden roof and white towers proclaimed it to be a Mujisal house of worship. Farther still was what looked like a high wall, perhaps the entrance to an inner compound.

The houses clustered around the pavilion were carefully whitewashed, their tin roofs glittering, and around the houses was arranged a series of little gardens. Neat pebble paths edged with white rocks linked the pavilion, the houses, and the house of worship. It was quite a sight out in this back block, and a welcome one after the dust and ugly straggle of Gunungbatu.

"So," said Sadik, drawing the car up with a flourish outside one of the houses, "how do you like my home, Adi?"

"It is very fine," said Adi truthfully. "Much has been done here."

"We have worked hard. The land was all rocks and weeds when my master first got here, five years ago."

"Wah!" said Adi, impressed. "That is a short time to accomplish all this."

Sadik beamed. "It certainly is! It is proof of the

shining nature of our master's goodness, and how it inspires people. Now, my friend, I will take you to the washhouse, so you may refresh yourself. I will ask if you may be presented to the master so that—"

"Please forgive me," interrupted Adi rapidly, "but would it be possible for you to ask your friends if any of them are going to Kotabunga soon?"

Sadik nodded. "I will ask, indeed."

As they got out of the car, Adi noticed that they were being watched by a small group of unsmiling youths. He bent his head and smiled, but their gaze did not waver, nor their expressions change. He wondered if they thought he was too finely dressed, here in this hardworking place, and unease roiled up inside him again.

THIRTEEN

DEWI AND HUSAM AL-DIN had hoped they might catch up with Adi, walking along the road to Kotabunga, but they saw no trace of him. They reached Kotabunga just before dark, in time for the daily rush in and out of the city. The crush of cars, bikes, and people made it hard for them to go along at more than a snail's pace. They were heading back to Kwanyin's place, but the gold district was all the way across town from them, and at this rate it would take an hour or more to reach the She-Po.

Dewi desperately wanted to get back to Kwanyin and see if Adi was there. She tried to keep calm, but she couldn't help thinking that, caught in this traffic jam, they would be sitting ducks for the hantumu.

"Maybe I should get out and walk there, warn Kwanyin we're coming."

"No," said Husam firmly. "Don't leave the car.

You're safer in here, I think. You'll just have to be patient."

Dewi said nothing, but her thoughts were rebellious. She looked unseeingly out the window, twisting her hands together. As she did so, she felt the red stone on the ring of protection cutting into her skin. She looked down at her hand, at the ring glowing there so brightly. Her thoughts whirled. What was it Senopati had said, back at Chandi Maya? That the ring could call fire . . . If that was the case, then this was the time to do it, when they needed speed and protection. Wildly, she raised her beringed hand and shouted, "Fire, fire, come to me! We need you, now!"

"No!" yelled Husam al-Din. "It's dangerous to call Fire like that, unmediated! You never know what—"

Whoosh! Heat instantly filled the car—an intense, searing heat—and a ghastly roaring. There was a loud crack as the vial of sacred water hanging from the rearview mirror exploded; then the little bottle Husam had stowed in his clothes also burst. The heat in the car instantly vaporized the zummiyah water. Scorch marks appeared inside the car, devouring the pictures, attacking the holy books as well. Dewi felt her throat burning, her eyebrows sizzling. Yet there was no smoke, no flame, just this hideous heat.

Husam al-Din was shouting words in a language

Dewi had never heard, words that sounded strangely like the crackling of flames. And suddenly, it was all over. The heat vanished as quickly as it had arrived, leaving a smell of burning, and scorched walls, books, and pictures. Dewi could not move, though she was not hurt. Her heart ached bitterly as she looked at the ruin of Anda Mangil's wonders. Her finger, where the ring had been, throbbed and stung like mad. The ring itself, an almost unrecognizable lump of twisted metal, its stone shattered into a thousand pieces, lay on the floor of the car.

"God be praised," said Husam al-Din. "God be praised, I remembered the right words, and we are still alive."

Dewi did not dare to look at the old man. She whispered, "Forgive me, forgive me. I'm such a fool, such a fool."

He looked down at the twisted ring. "Well, it's finished now." He bent down to pick up the shattered pieces of glass from the bottles. "Pity. We lost our protective water—still, it did protect us from the worst of it, or you and I would be up in flames right now." He sighed. "Well, fire can be a tricky thing." The car's horn began to blow, loud and long and shrill, as if in protest, or pain.

Cars in front of and behind them hooted in reply.

There was a cacophony of noise all around them; then, suddenly, it seemed the traffic jam was clearing, for they were moving along much more freely. They turned a corner, into a quieter street. And then . . .

Someone stepped right in front of their car, gesturing at them to stop. Someone familiar. Someone who filled Dewi with sudden, irrational dread. Kareen Amar, the redheaded woman from the guesthouse. She looked crazier than ever, smiling and smiling, her smile ghastly, showing her sharp, crooked teeth, her eyes full of a strange, burning light.

"Step on the accelerator!" shouted Dewi. "Don't stop, Husam!"

But the car had already skidded to a halt by the side of the road. Kareen Amar knocked at the window, shouting, "I am Kareen Amar. Let me in, young one. Let me in!"

Dewi glanced over at Husam—and got a terrible shock, for he was staring at Kareen Amar, a spellbound expression on his face. Dewi's pulse raced with terror. The old man was bewitched! She gave a strangled little cry. There had been the betchar driver, the red-eyed monkey, and now this creature. Dewi leaped into the backseat and wrenched at the door, but it wouldn't budge. "The shape-shifter's trapped us, Husam!" she cried. "Look, it's bewitched the car, it's trapping us."

Husam did not answer, just kept staring at Kareen Amar. The driver's door suddenly opened. Kareen Amar's deep voice filled the car. "Listen to me, young one, for you must. I am Kareen Amar, and you must listen to me." Husam al-Din moved over so she could sit behind the wheel.

She put a hand on it, and obediently the motor turned over. She touched the ceiling, and all at once the scorch marks on the car's walls, and on the pictures and books, vanished. The car still smelled of burning, but otherwise it was as good as new. Dewi thought, desperately, She's got immense powers; we are lost! She will take us to her afreet's lair and I will never, never see my poor father and home again.

"You must listen to Kareen Amar," said the woman, as the car began to pull away from the curb. "Stop being so afeared, young one."

Dewi suddenly found her voice. "This is Anda Mangil's car," she shouted. "It's not for creatures like you. Leave it alone, leave it alone!"

"Anda Mangil is dead," said the woman, with a terrible smile. "He is dead, and it is Kareen Amar who is now here."

Wild grief and anger surged through Dewi, and she flung herself at Kareen Amar, pounding her with her fists, yelling, "No! No!"

"Stop that, young one," said Kareen Amar, and she raised her hand, easily pushing Dewi back. She tried to throw herself again at the woman, to make her stop the car, but it was as if a wall kept pushing her back, some force that would not allow her to come near.

"Husam!" Dewi screamed. But Husam did not move. Dewi grabbed again at the door handle, breathing a desperate prayer to God in the highest Heaven as she did so. This time it opened easily, and she tumbled out into the street. She got swiftly to her feet, not looking behind her, knowing she must not allow Kareen Amar's eyes to hold her in a trance as they had Husam al-Din. She ran as fast as she could into a very narrow street, hoping that they would not be able to follow her there in the car, and even if they got out, she might have enough of a head start on them to get away. She ran with her breath whistling in her chest; she fell over once, got up, ran on, heard her beautiful clothes straining and ripping, but knew only that she must get away, as far as possible from that shape-changing thing. She and the hantumu had killed Anda Mangil, and now she was taking over his car.

Dewi groaned inside herself. Oh, if only, if only she'd known properly how to use the ring of protection! Why had she uttered those rash words? Now she was without Rorokidul's protection, without Sword, without her father, one of her companions dead, the other vanished. She was in a desperate, desperate state, and there was no telling how she would escape.

Dewi had run into an area she did not know at all. It was a place of mean little hovels tumbling over one another, of narrow, dirty, slippery streets, with open drains running down the middle of them, and of mean-faced, pinched-cheeked people looking warily at her as she sped past. The name Kotabunga meant City of Flowers, but in this part of the city, you did not feel any flowers would ever grow, only the rankest weeds. She began to feel more and more anxious as she kept going and the streets kept on getting narrower, darker, dingier, the houses closer and closer together, crowding one another above her head. Where was she? What could she do? Where could she run to?

Rorokidul's words came to her. She must get to the Water Gardens. But where were they? The picture of the gardens that hung in Anda Mangil's car—was there anything that showed where they were? She strained, trying to remember.

Suddenly, behind her, she heard a familiar, frightening sound: motorbike engines. She did not stop to turn and look but ran straight ahead, racing as fast as she could, weaving in and out of alleyways, tripping over loose stones, getting up, running on under the flat, incurious stares of passersby. She stopped and called out to a passing woman, "The Water Gardens? Where are they?"

The woman smiled at her, showing broken teeth. She opened her mouth, touched her fingers to her throat, and shook her head. The woman was mute—but not deaf, for she pointed up the street and made a gesture with her right hand to indicate a turn. Dewi cried, "Thank you, thank you!" and ran in the direction the woman had indicated. But just as she turned the corner, she tripped and sprawled headlong into a slick of mud in the middle of the street. As she scrambled up, she heard the motorbikes getting louder. They were almost on her. She couldn't run fast enough in this costume. She tore her skirt and sandals off, discarded them in the middle of the street, and ran in her bare feet and knee-length jacket as fast as her legs could carry her. The breath screamed in her chest and her throat as she spotted the great white pillared gate down the far end of the street. She recognized it from Anda Mangil's picture. The Water Gardens! She would be safe there.

Summoning up the last reserves of her strength, she sped toward the gates, the hantumu so close behind her, she could smell the hot engines of their bikes. She heard the whistle of a sword and felt a sharp sting in her shoulder, and knew she was hurt. But she was there, she was there! She literally fell through the gates of the gardens, landing heavily on slick paving stones, sliding a few meters, then whacking her head so hard that she fainted.

She came to slowly. She was lying on her back. All around her was green, as if she were enclosed in a cocoon of plants. She tried to lift an arm but could not. She attempted to move a foot but could not. She was tied down somehow. There was a throbbing pain in her left shoulder. She listened hard and heard nothing but the distant sound of water.

"Please, Queen Rorokidul, are you there?" she called softly. "I can't move. Will you . . . ?"

"Silence! This garden is my realm, not Rorokidul's!" came a woman's voice, full of petulance.

Dewi's heart fluttered wildly. "I was told this was a safe place. I was told to come here."

The voice snapped, "Ha! Safe, eh? Look what your kind has done!" And suddenly, Dewi found herself being dragged, scraped along the ground until she came to a complete and painful stop. A chink opened in the green cocoon, and she could see out. And she saw a picture of devastated beauty: bushes had been uprooted, flowers pulled out; boughs and branches littered the ground. And now she could see that she was indeed in a green cocoon, for she was wrapped, like a bundle, in strong vines. She was completely helpless.

"Look, there's more, there's more!" The vines twisted around her, making her head swivel. And she saw that some distance away was what would once have been a lovely stone garden, leading to a little pool. Someone had broken the pots, shattered the masonry, thrown rubbish in the pool, so that the whole thing looked like a pitiful ruin.

Dewi said quickly, "I am truly sorry. It was a dreadful thing to do, whoever did it. This should be a place of beauty and peace."

"It should be! But it is no longer." The voice had risen to a scream. "You are human. It is your kind did this!"

Dewi found her courage. "It may have been my kind, but we are not all alike. Please, listen. I have come to find Snow, Fire, and Sword, and heal the damaged land. I found Sword, but have lost it; tried to call Fire, but it burned me. I had two companions when I started; one of them is dead. Please, if you want to punish those responsible for this horrible thing, you will help me. For if you do not, he whose influence is behind this will win; and if he wins, not only will the gardens be desecrated, but they will be destroyed."

The vines slackened suddenly, then fell away, melting from Dewi's limbs with such swiftness that it made her dizzy to watch them. The voice said, "Get up, get up, girl! Get up and let me look into your eyes and see if you tell the truth." Suddenly there was a strange being standing before Dewi: a tall woman with green skin and green hair, with eyes the color of water and hands that were more like talons. Teeth as sharp as knives glittered in her thin-lipped mouth, and the glance she flashed at Dewi was not reassuring.

"I am Ratupohon, guardian of the First Garden," said the green woman. "So, it is you who must find Snow, Fire, and Sword? I have heard of this quest. What is your name?"

Dewi got shakily to her feet. She felt ill. Her shoulder hurt abominably. She dipped her head as politely as she could and said, "I am Dewi, Great Lady."

"You are hurt," said Ratupohon. Dewi glanced at her upper arm, where blood caked her torn jacket.

"It is a sword wound from the hantumu." Dewi winced. In the next instant, she nearly cried out loud, for Ratupohon, in one swift movement, had brought a hand down on Dewi's shoulder—and her touch was like nothing Dewi had ever felt before. It burned like fire, it stung like ice, and it seemed to penetrate through to the very marrow of her bones. But the throbbing pain went away, and when Ratupohon took her hand off, Dewi saw that the blood had vanished and the flesh under the torn jacket was completely unmarked.

"Thank you," she whispered.

"Think nothing of it," said the guardian impatiently. "It is as well for you that you called on the Queen of the Southern Sea, though. For I am in no mood to ask questions of stray humans. Revenge is strong in me."

And Dewi knew, with every breath of her body, that was indeed the case. "My Lady Ratupohon, will you not tell me what happened here?" And why you could not stop it, she thought, but did not ask.

Ratupohon's green eyes looked thoughtfully into Dewi's. "It is a good question," she said, "and deserves a good answer. Come, girl Dewi, and be my guest. Follow me." Imperiously, she turned away, her straight back slender as a whip, and as menacing. Dewi had no choice but to meekly follow her.

FOURTEEN

Adi felt a lot better after his wash. The wash-house had boasted spotlessly clean bathtubs and showers; the water was warm and comfortable; and there were good thick towels, and even a few unguents to rub on tired feet. He was still a little nervous as to what people might think of his finery, so seeing a discarded robe lying on a bench in the wash-house, he put it on over his clothes. It was very large and floated on him, but it made him feel less conspicuous. He did not put his beautiful headdress back on but squashed it into the capacious pocket at the front of the robe. He was bareheaded now, and felt a little naked without something on his head, but that would have to do. He had just thrust his feet into his sandals when Sadik reappeared, all smiles.

"The master does indeed want to see you," he said, without appearing to notice Adi's change of dress. "It is wonderful. How fortunate you are, Adi. How honored I am!"

"Mmm," mumbled Adi, not sure what to say. He followed Sadik meekly enough, resigned to the fact he wouldn't get away from here without meeting Sadik's blessed master. As they trotted down the steps of the washhouse back to the road, he said, "Sadik, did you ask anyone about Kotabunga?"

"No, not yet," said Sadik airily. "In any case, it's too late to go there now. You will have to stay tonight, and tomorrow morning someone is sure to be going there."

"But . . ." Adi broke off. What was the point of arguing? Sadik was obviously determined to show off his precious master to his new friend. It was annoying, but there was nothing he could do.

As they went along, Sadik told Adi excitedly about how the master had been exiled from his own country, thanks to the intrigues of wicked men. He had come as a humble preacher to a tiny village in Jayangan, and people had come from near and far to hear his words. Soon, news of his fame reached envious ears.

"They tried to capture him—imagine," Sadik said, eyes wide. "Those of the Demons' Army. They tried to destroy him, but an angel intervened and carried him far away, to a land where he was safe from persecution. And there, the angel protected him until such time as the Demons' Army was routed for a while in Jayangan, and then the master came back, with many followers, and began his work again, in Gunungbatu this time. Again his fame spread far and wide, and again it won him many followers. His enemies could not do much against him because the angel protected him, but they watched. They still watch, for they know he leads the Army of Light and one day he will rout them once and for all. You will see, Adi, you will see what a great and glorious and generous heart our master has. There are some who say that one day he may even become the great Lord who will bring back again the glorious reign of Truth, of God in the whole world."

His eyes were shining. Adi did not know what to say. Gunungbatu was a poor, remote little hole, he thought to himself. How could it possibly be the center of anything as grand as what Sadik was suggesting? He muttered something noncommittal.

"As an orphan, I could easily have become inveigled into bitterness and the ways of evil and ignorance," Sadik said earnestly. "It was fortunate that one day our beloved Shayk came preaching to our village and I heard his great words. For here I am, now, at last on the road to purity and kindness of heart. Truly, God is great!"

"Truly, that is so," said Adi nervously. What sort of

scary firebrand would Sadik's master be? He had heard a few Pumujisal preachers before, and they seemed to mostly concentrate on hellfire and damnation for all unbelievers. They hated everything that smelled of what they called "superstition," which meant all the beliefs other people had gathered through the centuries of life in Jayangan. They thought they could read God's mind, those proud zealots. As for himself, he wasn't even a Mujisal, let alone a Pumujisal. What would they say if they found out? He must not say he was Nashranee, or what he'd really been doing at the beach, or he'd get the most tedious earbashing.

Sadik led the way past the pavilion and around the back, to the wall Adi had noticed earlier. There was a door set in the wall, with a little barred peephole. Next to it was a bell on a pull. Sadik smiled at Adi and pulled at the bell, which rang mightily. One flashing dark eye appeared at the peephole, and a rough voice, accented with the unmistakeable tones of the Great Desert, said, "Who is this?"

"It is Sadik, Ibrahim. I have an appointment with the Shayk, with my friend, who stands beside me."

"Very well," rasped Ibrahim. "Wait."

Sadik whispered to Adi, "Do not be afraid when you see Ibrahim. He is a good man, though he looks fierce.

He has fought against the Demons' Army in far distant lands, at the master's side, and he has scars from it. But he is a good man."

At that moment, the door swung open, and an apparition filled the doorway. Despite Sadik's warning, Adi could not help falling back. Ibrahim was fearsome. Massively built, he looked like a pirate in a storybook, for he had only one good eye, the other hidden behind a black eye patch. He had a strong face, crisscrossed with old scars; and he sported a mighty mustache, and a thick pepper-and-salt beard. He wore midnight-blue robes and a turban of the same color. In one hand he held a drawn kris, the biggest Adi had ever seen in his life. "Come here," he said to the petrified Adi. And so saying, he grabbed Adi by the shoulder and pulled him roughly forward. Sadik scuttled in, and the door slammed shut behind them.

They were in a beautiful garden, quite the most lovely Adi had ever seen, but at the moment he was too scared to take in any details. The huge guard loomed over him, shaking him like a puppy. He passed a rough hand over his robe, then under it, on his clothes. With a quick jerk, he ripped the robe down, so that it fell at Adi's feet. He stood there looking at Adi in his fine Siluman clothes, a cruel smile curving the corners of his mouth. "So, why did you think to disguise yourself?" he growled.

Sadik said timidly, before Adi could speak, "It was my fault, Ibrahim sir. I lent him a robe, thinking it would be for the best if—"

"You are a presumptuous puppy!" roared Ibrahim, his mustache bristling, his eyes seeming to shoot sparks. "The master wants to see people as they are, not as they pretend to be." Turning to Adi, he said, "You are to speak the truth, do you understand? Do not even think of hiding from the master, for he can see into your heart. And we do not like lies here, for they are the weapons of wicked Iblis, whom we have to fight every second of every day."

"Yes, sir," said Adi, bowing his head. Now his heart felt as though it were melting with fear, though, ironically, the birds sang, and the flowers were so sweet and perfumed.

"Ibrahim, my dear friend, you shake the very earth with your roaring, and what is this drawn sword in the garden of peace?" said a low, gentle voice from behind them. A great change came over Ibrahim then. He dropped to one knee and put his kris on the ground. He bowed his head. "Forgive me, Master. Forgive me, Lord."

"You are very zealous, my friend. How could any evil come into this place, with you guarding it so faithfully?"

Sadik, too, had dropped to one knee, head bowed, at the first whisper of the voice. Adi turned to see an old man regarding them, a figure such as he had not at all imagined, given Sadik's story and Ibrahim's welcome.

Shayk Rasheed al-Jabal, the master—for it must be he—was a small, slight man, dressed in pure, snowy white robes and turban. He shone with whiteness, for it was not only his clothes that were white, but also his hair, delicate and wispy around his curiously unwrinkled, ivory-colored, thin face, and his equally wispy beard. Only his eyes were dark, and they shone with a soft light behind silver-rimmed glasses. He wore no ornament save a thin silver ring on one finger. Standing there in the beautiful garden, framed against the green, he looked like an apparition from another, better world. Adi felt a strange desire to bow his head and bend his knee, too, but the master walked toward him, smiled, and gracefully gestured that he must not kneel. He enjoined his followers likewise to raise themselves up.

"I think I have told you before you must not bend the knee to me," he observed. His glance at Sadik and

Ibrahim was loving and humorous. "Like you, I am merely a servant of the Light. It would be a problem if I became enraptured by such homages, my friends. Now then, this must be Adi, of whom I have heard so much from Sadik. Welcome to our home, Adi. You must be hungry. Will you not join me in a small repast? It is not much, I fear, but Sadik will fetch more if it is required."

"Of course, Master," said Sadik submissively, his eyes shining with happiness.

"Thank you, honorable sir; it is very kind of you," Adi said.

"And you must go to Kotabunga, is that not so? Well, then, we must make sure you get there as soon as possible to rejoin your friends. Let us walk in the garden, and you can tell me all about how you came to be here, and what happened on that beach, and what happened to your friends, and I will do my utmost to help you in whatever distress you find yourself. Because I see you are indeed in great distress of mind. You, Sadik, pick up that robe, and fetch the repast, and you, Ibrahim, go back to your guard duties." He smiled at Adi, who felt his heart melt under the power of those soft, kind eyes, at the purity of intent emanating from the master like a great light. I can see why he is so loved, why Sadik talked so warmly of him, Adi thought, as he followed the master of the Community of Light into the perfumed heart of the beautiful garden. And as he walked, he found himself opening up more and more to the white-haired old man, who listened benignly and did not once interrupt.

FIFTEEN

RATUPOHON LED THE way past the polluted pool and the savaged garden, down some stone steps that led to yet another water piece, which had also been disturbed, though not as badly as the first one. "I was away when it happened," she said, rather more quietly than she had spoken before. "I was on a visit to my sister-spirit in the holy forest of Demityangan, far away. I had left one of my human servants as guardian. When I returned, he had vanished, and my garden was desecrated. In the old days, I could go on such visits with no fear. Today, our power is weakened daily. Too many forget to honor us, and so our protection cannot extend very far. There are holes in it that evil can exploit." Her voice was full of sadness. "My garden is afraid now. Look, child." And she laid a finger softly against each of Dewi's eyes, in turn, and as gently took it away.

Dewi felt as if her eyes had suddenly been rinsed clean. She looked around her and saw that they were not alone. Each bush, each plant, each flower had a presence; eyes looked at her from behind every leaf, soft voices breathed unintelligible words in every rustle of leaves. She felt she truly was now in the heavenly Water Gardens of Kotabunga.

"Now look at what they did," came Ratupohon's voice. Turning to where the guardian was pointing, Dewi saw with horror the laying out of green corpses, the closing of eyes in death, the terrible wounds still bleeding green. "These are my people, whom I am sworn to protect," cried Ratupohon, "and I was not here when they needed me. Too long had my garden been sacred and peaceful; I had forgotten there were still enemies. I am ashamed—oh—I am so ashamed!"

Dewi felt the pain of it in her own soul. She whispered, "My Lady Ratupohon, I have a brother. His name is Jafar. He loves gardens. Perhaps he could . . ."

"Perhaps," said Ratupohon, and her voice was soft. "I thank you for that thought. Bring your brother here, when this is over, when you have defeated the evil ones, and we will see whether a human can heal what a human has wrought. Now—you called on Rorokidul earlier, so I suppose you must want to be taken to her sacred place. Come with me."

She was beckoning Dewi to what looked like an opening in the earth. Drawing closer, she saw that it was like a huge well, with a large spiral stone staircase descending down it, into deepest darkness. Yet right at the bottom, far below, was a pinpoint of soft light. Ratupohon started down the staircase, and motioned to Dewi to follow her.

She went down farther and farther into the bowels of the earth, down the great stone staircase that seemed to go on and on. All around her was the sound of water—water trickling down the walls, water gushing below. She was not exactly afraid, only a bit nervous. She no longer had her ring of protection. She touched her finger where it had been, remembering the twist of blackened, shattered metal that was all that was left of the ring. Oh, how she wished she had it with her.

At that moment, her foot kicked against something on the step—something that tinkled, and glittered with light. She stopped and bent down to look at the thing. It was the ring of protection Kwanyin had given her, as good as new! Greatly wondering, she bent down to pick it up and slipped it on her finger. As she did so, she felt a great jolt. Her finger burned with a cold, deep fire. She grabbed at the ring and tried to pull it off—but as soon as her finger touched it, she felt another huge jolt. "Ratupohon!" she cried then. "Ratupohon, where are you?"

"Here, here, here," came the green woman's voice, strangely distorted. "Here, here, Dewi, follow me."

She could not see anything; she could only grope forward, following the thin threads of Ratupohon's voice, the ring burning around her finger. Down, down, down she went, and the farther down she went, the lighter it became. At length, she came to a large and beautiful atrium surrounded by galleries; in the middle of the atrium was a pool of shining water. It was from this pool that the light came.

In all the galleries, faces were pressing, curiously, watching her; there were the rustlings of many presences, the whispers of many voices. But the shining pool was undisturbed and placid.

Down at the bottom, near the pool, difficult to see in the brightness but visible as a flowing of green, was Ratupohon. She called to Dewi. "You wanted to see the great Queen of the Southern Sea, Rorokidul? This is her atrium, the place where her human bridegroom, the Sultan of Jayangan, comes to pay her homage, every year, through all the centuries—or should. He has not come here for two years now, though it is the place of his family's protection, the source of much of his power. You may call on her, if you follow my instructions very carefully."

"I will follow," whispered Dewi, trying to ignore the pain in her finger.

"Stand by the pool. Look into it," said Ratupohon. "Now say, 'Great Lady of the Ocean, O Monarch of the Sea, I crave an audience with you, will you speak with me?'"

Dewi repeated the words, staring into the pool of water. The water began to boil in front of her, and clouds of steam issued into the atrium, hiding the galleries from sight, shrouding even Ratupohon in mist, so that Dewi was alone, quite alone, before the bottomless shining pool whose water boiled and churned. And then, from the great depths, something began to emerge. Just a thin pillar of mist at first, it grew and grew, and changed shape, and became a dark-eyed woman of great beauty.

"Queen Rorokidul," whispered Dewi. "Queen Rorokidul, I have done as you said and come here to your atrium because the afreet came and bewitched Sword, and I do not know what to do now."

"Sword?" The queen's voice was strangely harsh, distorted. "The afreet has bewitched Sword? You are sure?" A strange smile played over her features.

Dewi was puzzled. She repeated, uncertainly, "Yes. Please, Queen Rorokidul, will you—"

"Ha, ha, ha, ha!" boomed the Queen of the Southern Sea. As she laughed and laughed and laughed, her voice rose in tone and volume, becoming a howl. "Ha, ha, ha, ha," the voice mocked. Her face changed beyond all recognition, twisting, deforming into a hideous thing, shark mouth stretching, showing a thousand sharp, pointed teeth, throat red and throbbing, spewing out venom and flame like a vision of hell. And still the voice rose, screeching, tearing, rending at every shred of sanity left in Dewi. "You will die, Dewi! You will die! Die, like that fool driver of yours. Your death has been written—it cannot be escaped. You will die, transfixed by Sword, burned by Fire, smothered by Snow. It was your own death you came to find, Dewi! It was your death that sent you on the path to the rice field, your death that brought you to Kotabunga. Your death has brought you here!"

And suddenly, out of the water came a human figure, blinding in its whiteness, wrapped in a shroud, with icicles hanging from it. One arm was extended, and in this hand shone a great blade. "This is Snow, and Snow is your death, coming white and pure and blinding at you. Snow is ignorant of his destiny, but I know it, and can turn him into an instrument of my will. Snow, pure Snow, will sever your spirit from your body," screamed the eldritch voice. "Come forth,

Dewi, and meet your death!"

Dewi found her voice at last. "No, no!" she cried, stumbling back from the pool. But still the shrouded white figure kept coming toward her, machinelike. "No, no! Nothing is written, nothing can be, no one can know the future, in any of the worlds, save God." She fell back, groping, in panic. The mist around the pool thickened, became denser and brighter, and still the figure called Snow kept coming—human and yet not, sword in hand—while the voice screamed in wild, unholy delight. The ring on Dewi's finger burned like a bright coal, and the pain of it reached into her, consuming her.

But she did not want to die, not in this way, and so she fought. She would not die! Desperately, she scrambled away with all her will, and suddenly she could hear a voice, singing so sweetly. Softly the voice sang at first, then louder, and louder, until it felt as though the song were pulling at her, pulling, pulling. Gradually, slowly, the mist was being forced back and back and back, the shrouded figure hesitating, stopping, the arm lowered, the sword's light dimming, and all at once the ring's light winked out too, and it vanished in a puff of sulphur. Then she was falling into a blessed darkness, sweet and soft and cool; someone was holding her, rocking her; the singing went on, gentle now, soft, a wordless, blissful song. I know that voice, Dewi thought to herself, marveling, before she collapsed into the embrace of real and healing sleep.

She could not tell how long she had been unconscious, but when she awoke, afternoon sunshine was streaming in through a window. She blinked, and closed her eyes again. Her head ached. She opened her eyes, trying to work out where she was, but it hurt. She tried to think, but that hurt too much as well. She could only remember running; and then falling into a terrible nightmare. The terror began to trickle back into her, and her heart hammered uncontrollably. She closed her eyes tight, but that was a mistake, because then random images began to flood into her mind, filling her with panic. Her eyes flew open.

She looked down at herself. She was lying on a couch, dressed in the clothes she had discarded the day Kwanyin gave her the beautiful costume. She was in a quiet, small, rather dusty room, with junk piled high in every corner. She knew that place—the She-Po Gold Market! She was back in Kwanyin's place, and bending over her were Husam al-Din—and Kareen Amar.

"Now, now, young one, lie back down. Lie back down. Do not be afeared." Kareen Amar's deep voice had a pleading note, her taloned hands outstretched in entreaty, red hair flickering on her shoulders like licks of flame. "Please listen, do not be afeared of Kareen Amar."

"Yes, there's no call to be afraid of her," Husam al-Din spoke briskly. "You are safe. Never safer. Show her, Kareen, my little nightingale. Show her."

Then Kareen Amar opened her mouth, and instead of her clumsy words, the sweetest song imaginable came from between those lips. A song that filled Dewi with astonishment and delight. As the song slowly faded away, she whispered, "It was you who saved me from that thing . . . in my dream . . . in my nightmare . . . in whatever it was."

Kareen Amar smiled but said nothing. She took Dewi's hand, the hand that had worn the ring. She murmured, stroking the spot where the ring had been, "It was a false ring, you see, a false ring to lure and trap you." Dewi saw that the skin there, though pink and a little sore, was still whole.

Husam said gently, "Kareen sang you the healing song, the song of flight. She has the sweetest voice in all of her world."

Dewi remembered Kareen Amar handing her that badly printed business card back at the guesthouse—it seemed so long ago—and she blushed to remember what she had thought back then. She said, "Your song . . . it was so beautiful, so strong, it made me strong again."

"Kareen Amar knows songs, yes," said the red-headed woman with a look of satisfaction. "At least that is still the same, here in this mad world."

"I am not surprised, mind you, that you were afraid of her," said Husam with a grin, "but she is a true companion, Dewi. She has come to help us, and she has been trying to reach you and make you understand the danger you are in, and that she wishes to protect you."

"This is true," said Kareen Amar. She stood near Dewi's bed, smiling. "Young one, I am a wandering spirit of the Jinn, who travels the wide world in search of music. I am Kareen Amar, singer of the Jinn. I have seen that you require my assistance, and I wish to proffer it to you."

"I wish you wouldn't speak like that, Kareen," grumbled Husam al-Din. "That is half your trouble, speaking like some mad old book. And looking like you do, it's hardly calculated to reassure Dewi, or anybody, come to that."

"I must ask forgiveness," said Kareen Amar, looking anxious, "if I offend. This world is cold to me, though you think it deliciously warm, so I must wrap as warmly as I can. And I can hardly show myself to you in my true form, being that my nature is of smokeless fire, like all my people. If I appeared the way I do in my own land, you could not look on me at all, but be burned, instantly, to a cinder."

Dewi stared at her. Kareen Amar stared back; her pupils contracted, became vertical, turned red; and little licks of flame jumped up in them, only to die down almost immediately.

"Fire! You are of the nature of fire," Dewi repeated, staring into Kareen's eyes and smelling again that strange smell that she had noticed the first time she met her, and that she now knew to be fire.

"Why, yes, young one," said Kareen Amar, "that is the way of it: We Jinn were created of fire, and humans of clay, and angels of . . ."

But Dewi was not listening. Her heart was leaping with gladness. "So that is why you came when I called on fire," she burst out. Of course! Fire was a true companion, a living being, just as Sword was a man, and not just a weapon. She looked across at Husam al-Din, her eyes shining.

"Yes, little heart, that is so," he said gently, reading her thoughts correctly. "I only wish I could have told you straightaway what Kareen Amar was, when I first set eyes on her. But I was in a trance; so amazed, and overcome, and delighted that what Queen Rorokidul had said turned out to be true so quickly that I could not react. But you did not give me or her time to explain to you; you ran away too fast."

"I was glad you called, young one, though it did baffle me why I must be called with my nature's name, and not the name I bear, which I had told you before," said Kareen Amar seriously. "But many and varied are the words and ways of the Clay People, and I knew I was bound to you, and must find you, whatever happened."

"Well, Kareen, how about now you tell Dewi what you told me—about what your people know about the nature of the evil we face here in Jayangan, given as you're from the afreet's own world? In simple words, Kareen," said Husam. "Simple, please."

Kareen Amar shot him a reproachful look, and her mouth drew down. "You listen," she said huffily, "for it is a strange and perilous story. Know there are many different kinds of Jinns, and the wicked ones we call the afreets are under the dominion of the Demon King, wicked Iblis himself. Now there is an afreet named Hareekshaytin, who, because of a treachery he once committed against Iblis, was sold into slavery. He is in the service of a powerful human sorcerer, who has sovereignty over him. This afreet is skilled in transformation, and he can appear in many forms."

Dewi interrupted, saying, "I'm sorry. . . . I—I thought . . ."

"You thought Kareen Amar was an afreet," said the Jinn, giving a thin little smile. "That is a sadness to Kareen Amar, and in my world, that would be an insult hard to bear. But Kareen Amar understands humans in this place are like children in this regard, so she forgives," she added, gently touching one of Dewi's hands. "Now—where was I? Ah, yes. This afreet has already helped to accomplish the will of his master, the Sorcerer, through the deaths and disappearances and destruction that have happened in this land."

"So the man we seek is a sorcerer!" said Dewi, eyes wide. "Who is he?"

"We don't know," she admitted. "You see, young one, sorcerers are like slave traders in our land. To get too close to a sorcerer puts us Jinn in very great danger indeed."

"But now you are here, getting closer to the Sorcerer all the time. Why do you risk your life?"

"Kareen is an unusual Jinn," said Husam. "She is braver than any I ever met before."

Two hectic flushes appeared on Kareen Amar's cheeks. Embarrassed, she quickly said, "I am not brave. Only, it would please me if this Sorcerer was no longer a danger to any of us." She paused, then went on more steadily, "An enslaved good Jinn is one thing, but an enslaved wicked one, like an afreet, quite another, and very dangerous. Once an afreet has been enslaved to a sorcerer's will, he will do his bidding. But it is like holding a tiger: You cannot ever be sure of him. Yet a powerful sorcerer can hold an afreet for a long time, and the power of the afreet, when backed by the will of a powerful sorcerer, is such that it may even breach the protection of places that should normally be safe—especially if those places have been neglected of late by those who should know better."

"The Water Gardens are not safe anymore, if the afreet was able to get in," said Dewi.

"The spell of protection has been considerably weakened," said Kareen Amar. "Thus the Sorcerer's slave was able to slip in among the green things after you. The hantumu could not go in because they are mere human servants, not demons. They cannot break the spirits' hold, but the afreet found a momentary hole in the protective spell, and slipped in in his elemental form. Ratupohon's protection of you could never be complete while the gardens were in such a state. The afreet, under the direction of his master, sought for a tendril of your memory, something he might use to trap you."

"He read my mind?" Dewi cried.

"No, a human mind cannot be read. It is not like a book, with pages following pages, but rather like a vast storehouse, a jumble of treasure and trash, a repository of picture and thought and feeling. The afreet Hareekshaytin's great skill is in capturing some filaments of this, and twisting them to his own ends. It is what made him so feared in the world of the Jinn. It is no doubt the reason the Sorcerer was keen to acquire him as a slave. Hareekshaytin saw you put a hand to your finger as you remembered the ring of protection. That was enough."

"The feel of it," Dewi whispered. "It burned coldly, like ice."

"He found you. He entered into your soul's eye through the false ring. He held you and made you see things, yes?"

Dewi was held as if by a vice, as the images from the garden flooded back into her brain, and she saw again the semblance of Rorokidul, and the way her face changed, the eldritch voice rising, taking glory and delight in Dewi's prophesised death. "So it was not the real Rorokidul I saw? It was a vision? Just a vision?"

"It was not the real Rorokidul, no. This afreet specializes in twisting things in your mind to produce bitter dreams, harsh nightmares of great potency.

These illusions he creates can send men mad, send them to their deaths through despair and fear, or fatally weaken them so they may be killed. That was what he sought. He wanted to make you think the spirits had deserted you, tricked you, trapped you. He wanted to make you despair, to curse the spirits and God, to lose your soul. That would finally break the last shreds of protection over that place. Then you would have been the Sorcerer's. Lucky it was that Kareen Amar found you in time!"

Dewi shivered. She said, "How did you do it?"

"I did not try to follow you in this form," said Kareen Amar cheerfully, "but streaked like a flame directly to where I could feel your struggling spirit. Because the protection of the garden had been breached before, it was possible for me to slip in, in my essential form. The Sorcerer's strength may turn into a weakness—because once he has put a hole in the magic web of the spirits, he cannot control what comes through that hole any more than the spirits can. You see? In the garden, which still has some of the old protection, the Sorcerer is not strong enough yet to hold you, to break your defenses, so I could snatch you from the vision he had trapped you in. My song overcame the lying nightmare, you see. It can do so, if the nightmare has not already taken over too much of the soul."

"Thank you so much," said Dewi, impulsively laying a hand on Kareen Amar's. She tried not to wince. The feel of it was just like Ratupohon's—a mixture of fire and ice, the touch of the otherworld.

Kareen Amar looked grave and pleased, all at once. "Young one, you fought with all your might and strength of will, and that helped me greatly to draw you away. You have a strong spirit. The Sorcerer and his afreet are powerful, but you resisted them. That is a great thing indeed."

Dewi colored a little. Then she remembered what she should never have forgotten. "Adi! Is he here too? Did he make it here?"

Husam and Kareen Amar looked at each other. Slowly, Husam shook his head.

"Then where is he?"

"He may not have arrived in Kotabunga yet," said Husam. "He may still be on his way here."

"Or he may have already been captured by the Sorcerer," said Dewi harshly. Neither of the other two said anything. After a while, Dewi went on, her words tumbling over one another. "I think the Sorcerer is seeking to reel us right in to him. He needs us all before he can accomplish his entire plan."

"Yes. That is why we must not go anywhere near him until we find Snow," said Kareen Amar.

"No. That is wrong. We must go to him. We must call on his servants to take us to him," said Dewi, speaking boldly, but trembling inside at what she was saying.

"But we cannot. We have not yet found Snow," said Husam, staring at Dewi as if she had gone mad. "Fire, Snow, and Sword must be your companions, if you are to fight against the Demon King."

"We must go to the heart of this Sorcerer's power," said Dewi. "In my nightmare in the atrium, there was a shrouded figure, and he was Snow. The voice in the vision said that the afreet's master had found Snow before us, that he had made him ignorant of his true course. If we are to have any chance of succeeding, and save my father and any other captives, we must go right into the demons' lair, into the hideout of the Sorcerer, and awaken Snow."

Husam and Kareen Amar both stared at her, but before they could reply, Kwanyin came into the room. She was carrying a tray on which something hot and fragrant steamed. The smell made Dewi feel quite faint, for suddenly she realized just how hungry she was. Kwanyin walked over to her and put the tray on the table. She smiled at Dewi. "My dear Dewi, I am pleased to see you again."

"As am I! Oh, dear Lady Kwanyin, so much has

happened—and I'm so sorry that I misused the ring you gave me."

"Do not be sorry," said Kwanyin gently. "The ring served its purpose. Before you talk any further, my dear child, eat, and drink. Go on. You need all your strength."

Dewi set to gratefully. She had soon made short work of the delicious spicy fried chicken, yellow rice, and vegetables, and the long tall glass of avocado and lemon juice.

"Better now?" Kwanyin said, when Dewi had finished.

"Oh yes, it was wonderful." Dewi sighed.

"Good." Kwanyin smiled. Then her expression changed. "My dear child, I heard what you were saying, about going straight to the heart of the Sorcerer's power. You may well be right. You see why we wanted you? Your mind is an extraordinary thing. You are capable of learning and understanding so much, and acting on it. But that is also dangerous for you, as the Sorcerer, through the afreet, will have discovered that about you. And so he may well be trying to lure you in. Beware. You are brave. But I must warn you. There is no protection I can give you to do this."

"Why not?" said Dewi.

"A protective talisman works only if you know the

nature of the thing you are protecting against. We have tools of protection against common sorcerers, but this one is far from common. He refuses to accept the old ways; he does not want any of the old magical sources of power; he destroys all the sacred places. He uses the power of demons, but only when it suits him."

Husam said, "Lady Kwanyin, what of the other powers—the native Jayangan spirits? Can't they protect us in the Sorcerer's place?"

"No," said Kwanyin bleakly. "It's not just because I'm a foreign spirit that I cannot do it. None of us otherworlders can. We cannot take you there, we cannot protect you once you are there." She sighed very sadly. "Dewi, we spirits have brought you to this moment, but we can take you no farther. You will be on your own."

"Dewi, little heart, you will not be on your own. We are all of us in this," broke in Husam al-Din, his eyes shining brightly.

"Yes, all of us," echoed Kareen Amar, though the blotches in her face came and went with alarming, hectic regularity.

Kwanyin smiled wearily. "Are you sure? There is no telling what will happen once you are in the Sorcerer's power. You need the third one—you need Snow. And Snow is ignorant of his destiny."

"That is precisely why we must go," said Dewi. She remembered Senopati's words, about light coming out of darkness, and was suddenly certain. "Please, Lady Kwanyin, I understand that you, as a spirit of good, hate the notion of being near the realm of darkness and fear, but I am sure we must go there if we are to find Snow and save my father."

She felt afraid of her own words, yet she could not take them back now.

"Are you quite sure, then, child?" Kwanyin asked again.

Dewi nodded. Her hands were clammy, her voice unsteady as she whispered, "I will go out of this place of safety, Lady, into the street. The hantumu will come; perhaps even now they are there, waiting. This time I will not try to run, to escape from them. This time I will go with them."

There was a long silence. Then Kwanyin nodded. "Very well, Dewi, it is as you wish it." She looked at Husam and Kareen Amar. "And you?"

"Let us talk in private," said Husam. He led Kareen Amar aside, and they spoke together, softly, briskly.

Minutes passed and Husam returned and said, "This is what we have decided. I will go with Dewi, for I am a human man and not at such grave risk as Kareen Amar, who, because of her nature as a Jinn, could be enslaved by the Sorcerer if he catches her. It is best that Fire stays here, till we are ready and we need her particular talents. Besides, if there is one of the three left here, the Sorcerer can do nothing to the rest of us, or he will never be able to harness our full power."

Kareen Amar looked very unhappy, but she nodded her agreement. "Kareen Amar will wait with Anda Mangil's beloved, and be ready to join the great battle when it comes, for come it will, and not long from now."

Kwanyin said, very quietly, "So be it." She addressed Dewi. "Are you ready, then, child?"

"Yes." Dewi's chest muscles tightened as she thought of the waiting hantumu and the afreet's invasion of her mind. She breathed a prayer deep inside herself. "I am ready, Lady Kwanyin."

Kwanyin put a hand on Dewi's shoulder, and the girl felt the icy, burning touch of the otherworld on her skin again. It did not hurt her, only sent a shock through her, a thrill of courage. She looked at Kwanyin and knew that the otherworlder was arming her in the only way she could. Tears came to Dewi's eyes. "Thank you, Lady Kwanyin," she murmured. Kwanyin did not answer, but touched Husam's shoulder as well. Then she walked away from them and stepped to one side, with Kareen Amar.

Dewi and Husam's eyes met. "Ready?" the old man whispered. Dewi nodded. Husam walked to the door and opened it. Just as she was about to follow him, Dewi remembered the tiger's claw her father had given her. She must have it with her: It linked her to her father. But the hantumu must not find it. She slipped it under her tongue, then followed Husam out into the street.

Outside, everything was bathed in an eerie golden light. And on the opposite side of the street, sitting waiting in unnatural stillness on their motorbikes, dressed all in black, long swords in their hands, their eyes masked, were the hantumu. Dewi saw that one of them held his arm stiffly, as if he were hurt. There was no monkey with them.

She stepped toward them. "We wish for an audience with your master," she said, in a voice that sounded thick and heavy because of the tiger's claw under her tongue. She hoped they would think it was fear that distorted her voice. "We come unarmed to parley with him."

The hantumu sat staring at them for an instant; then slowly one of them got off his bike and approached them, holding his sword in his hand. Dewi could see him closely now; he had thin, pale brown skin, with deep, cruel lines under the mask that hid his eyes, and he wore a long mustache. It was hard to tell his age, but he walked like a young man, with a swaggering gait. He stopped a few paces from them, his sword held out in front of him. "Why do you wish to do this? You sound mortally afraid," he said. His voice had no inflection or expression, and it sent a shiver down Dewi's spine.

Trying to keep her voice steady, she said, "That is not for you to know. We do not give our reasons to servants."

The hantumu's hand moved imperceptibly. Instantly, the tip of his sword was under Dewi's chin. "What if I killed you right now, you scum?" he spat. "Don't think I wouldn't, just because you're a female—I've killed girls and women before now."

"I am sure you have," said Dewi, trying to sound calm, though she was so frightened she felt paralyzed, her very limbs turned to ice, her tongue over the claw heavy as a lump of wood.

By her side, Husam growled at the hantumu, "Your master would not be happy with you if you killed her or me. You know he has been seeking us."

The hantumu flicked his head toward him, like a snake. For a moment, it looked as if he would attack Husam. Then he lowered his sword and shrugged.

"You won't be talking like that soon, old man," he said, and motioned to the other three hantumu. "Check they have no concealed weapons or magic talismans."

"We told you we were unarmed," said Husam quickly.

The hantumu sneered, "You don't expect us to take your word for it, do you?"

They checked them thoroughly, but did not look in their mouths. Why should they? When the check was finished, the leading hantumu turned to his companions and said, "The girl will ride on the back of my bike, the old man on that one over there. They are to be blindfolded, gagged, and bound until we get to our master's place."

Dewi put a hand to her mouth, as if to suppress a gasp of fear, but in reality to take the tiger's claw from under her tongue and palm it into her shirt pocket. Husam, knowing this, diverted the hantumu's attention by blustering, "Don't think you can trick us . . ." but the hantumu cut him off.

"Shut up. You are going to our master's realm."

SIXTEEN

THIS IS HOW Paradise must look, thought Adi as he walked with the Shayk through the perfumed garden. There were small bright birds darting in and out of low fragrant herb bushes, and fountains playing, and a peace and quietness such as Adi had never before experienced. The Shayk had listened carefully to Adi's story but, instead of commenting directly on it, had taken him on a tour of the enclosed garden. Adi had been taken aback by this at first, for more than anything now, he knew he needed the kindly wisdom of the Shayk to help him understand his predicament and what he must do next. He waited impatiently at first as the Shayk walked calmly down each path, stopping to smell flowers, to gently touch small growing things, to comment on the wealth of insect and bird life that filled the garden with busy activity. But after a short time, the peace of the garden, the gentleness of its master, began to steal into Adi's spirit, washing away the tension and fear and unhappiness of the last few days. By the time they reemerged from the heart of the garden, to a little rotunda that had been set with all the appertunances for a light meal, he was feeling quite relaxed and almost happy. Though he still worried about the fate of his friends and how he was going to get back to Kotabunga, somehow the experience of being in the Shayk's garden had made him feel almost reconciled to all that had happened. Things could be bad, but they could also be good. He had come to a good place, a place where, at the very least, his bruised spirit could know some peace, some repair.

But his mood began to change again when they came to the rotunda, for Sadik and Ibrahim were both there, waiting. Ibrahim's glance at Adi was no more friendly than it had been earlier—in fact, the suspicion in his eyes seemed to have sharpened. And Sadik—well, the young man was standing there submissively, a towel over his arm, obviously ready to serve not only his beloved master but also his master's guest. This made Adi feel exceedingly uncomfortable, though the Shayk seemed not to notice. Sadik knelt before his master and, taking up a bowl of rosewater, washed and dried the Shayk's hands, then turned to Adi to do the same.

"Please." Adi could not help flinching. "It is not necessary. . . . I . . ."

"You are eating with the Shayk," said Ibrahim gruffly. "You are his guest." Implicit in his glare was not only that Adi was being rude, but that he did not deserve the honor that was being given to him.

But the Shayk smiled and, waving a hand at Sadik, said, "My son, it is not true zeal to embarrass your fellows. Leave it."

"Of course, Master," said Sadik, but his eyes were full of hurt, and Adi felt worse than ever. Meanwhile, a still-suspicious Ibrahim looked daggers at him, his gaze seemingly trying to pierce Adi's very soul. If only the man would go away. If only he could be alone with the Shayk again.

The Shayk seemed to be in no hurry to send either of them away, though. He gestured at the food on the table—exotic preserved fruit such as dates and figs, sweetmeats of various kinds, slices of fresh local fruit—and said, "I am homesick sometimes for my own land, and my people here are kind enough to make sure I am supplied with such things as come from there. Have you ever been to the Great Desert, Adi?"

"No, sir. I have never been."

"Well, this is the next best thing," said the Shayk, picking up a fig and biting it delicately in two. "Ah, the perfume! We have tried to grow figs and dates here, and have had some success, isn't that so, Ibrahim? But they do not taste the same as they do in the desert. Go on, Adi, eat. Tell me if you think the fruits of the desert are better than those of the great green expanses of Jayangan." He winked. "But I presume that as a son of Jayangan, you would not agree?"

Adi, mouth full of sticky fig and date, said indistinctly, "These are good, sir. Very good."

Ibrahim snorted, as if in derision, but the Shayk took no notice. He smiled and handed Adi a slice of fresh mangosteen. "This is from your country. Now you tell me."

Adi felt three pairs of eyes on him. He bit into the mangosteen, and its juicy citrus freshness cleared his mouth. He said uneasily, "Both are good, sir. But different."

"Ah! A good answer, and diplomatic, my son!"

Ibrahim's glare had not changed at all. No matter what I do or say, thought Adi, Ibrahim will not change his mind about me. Does he know I wear the heart symbol? And does he despise me for it, or distrust me? Adi had not told the Shayk he was a Nashranee, but he felt sure it would not matter to that good old man. But I should have told him straightaway, he thought, obscurely discomforted that he hadn't, that he was here on false pretences, that the Shayk was talking to him as if he thought he was a Mujisal like themselves.

"Now, Sadik, where is the tea I ordered? I believe Adi must be thirsty, and we cannot let our friends go from us without quenching their thirst, is that not so?"

"Oh yes, Master," said Sadik, bowing. He went swiftly to a corner of the rotunda, returned with a tray of tea things, and poured fragrant mint tea into small glass cups.

"So, Adi, you wish to leave us so soon and journey to Kotabunga to find your friends?"

"I have to go there," said Adi, flushing at the implication. "But I am most grateful and honored for your hospitality, Shayk Rasheed al-Jabal. I will never forget your kindness."

"It is I who am grateful," said the Shayk, "for what you have told me. It is clear to me the Demons' Army is gaining in strength, and we must all unite to fight it. And so I propose this, if you will allow me: You and I will travel to Kotabunga tomorrow morning, go to the palace of the Sultan, and apprise him of the full situation. His son, the Crown Prince Yanto, is a great supporter of ours and will persuade his father of the truth of all that has happened. When we find your friends, we will tell them this: that they will be welcome here and will be safe from harm, while we all consider, together, what it is best to do. A great conflict is coming, a great battle that will decide once and for all whether the Demons' Army can permanently be routed from the land by the Army of Light."

Adi looked at the old man. His vision misted and he saw the strength of the Shayk, the purity of heart that was symbolized by the whiteness of his clothes and his hair. He whispered, "Oh, Shayk Rasheed, do you remember what I told you in the garden? Do you remember that I told you who our three companions must be—Snow, Fire, and Sword?"

"I remember," said the Shayk with a little smile, "but I remember also that you had not yet found any of them. Is that not so?"

"Oh, Shayk Rasheed al-Jabal," said Adi, turning a gaze full of joy and excitement on the old man, forgetting about Sadik and Ibrahim in his pleasure, "I must dare to put something to you: Could it be . . . could it be that in you, who are so kind and good and brave, I have found one of our greatest companions? That I have found Snow?"

There was a suppressed exclamation from Sadik, and Ibrahim started forward, with a hand to his sword, but the Shayk waved them both away. "You do me great honor," he murmured. "You do me great honor, little son. But how can this be? Was not Snow, Fire,

Sword some talisman of power invoked by the powers of the otherworld, by the Jinn, as my people would call them? Stories have been written of such things before—magic lamps and boxes and rings and so on—and you know these stories are not true. Talismans cannot help to fight the demons, for they are but merely things in stories."

Adi's scalp crept with a mixture of fear and hope. "Your Eminence, Your Greatness," he gabbled, forgetting how to address a Pumujisal chief, "we had thought at first that was so, that we must look for objects. Then we were told they were to be our companions. I believe that they refer to a quality of heart and soul in a person. So Snow could be great purity; and Fire great strength; and Sword great truth."

"Yes," said the Shayk, "there are those who speak of the sword of truth, and the strength of fire, and how the purity of snow can cleanse away sins. I do not know if I can truthfully take this on, for it seems to me sheer arrogance to claim for myself such a thing."

"But it is not you who claim it, sir," said Adi eagerly.

"No, indeed!" The words had burst out from Sadik, and everyone turned to him.

The Shayk said quietly, "What is it, Sadik?"

Sadik blushed fiercely and bent his head. "Forgive me, Master, I spoke out of turn."

"I asked you what it was you wanted to say, Sadik," said the Shayk, still as quietly, but with a little more steel in his voice. "I will be the judge of whether you spoke out of turn."

"Yes, of course, Master." Sadik looked up, wringing his hands. "I was only going to say, Master, that it would seem to me that if ever anyone deserved the appellation of Snow as a symbol of purity of heart, it would be you. We would all say so, all of us here in the Community of Light. And my friend Adi, who is not yet one of us but who I think loves and understands what we do, also believes so. Oh, my master, it seems to me this is a sign, a sign that the great work you have been doing here will be taken to other parts of this unhappy world."

There was a silence, while Sadik bent his head again and shuffled his feet miserably. Ibrahim's face had frozen into utter impassivity. Adi watched the Shayk with wary hope. The latter appeared to be deep in thought. Everything about him suggested calm and repose, except for the fact that he had taken his glasses off and was absentmindedly polishing them on his robe, over and over and over.

After what seemed like an age, the Shayk stopped polishing his glasses and put them back on his nose. He raised his head, and Adi saw that his dark eyes were shining. "Well, Adi," he said at last, "if you truly think that may be so, and if it pleases God that I should help in this task, in whichever way I am destined to, then I will admit that I may well be he whom you are looking for. Please do not overwhelm me with thanks and homage, Adi, Sadik," he went on quickly, "and do not say anything of this to the other people in the community, not yet. It would seem to me that if there is too much fuss and bother and roaring, it will come to the ears of the demons and alert them to the notion that here may be one of the weapons in the fight against them. What we have to do is try to discover the identity of Fire, and of Sword, and thus together may we join forces against the demons. Adi, I shall accompany you to Kotabunga with my two best men, Sadik and Ibrahim. Together we will forge a new destiny for the world, and confound the demons."

"Pray God we will not be too late," growled Ibrahim.

The Shayk smiled at him. "God will protect his true servants," he said. "You should know that, Ibrahim." He looked mischievously at Adi. "Now then, will you not have another date? A fig perhaps? Or do you still prefer the mangosteen?"

SEVENTEEN

HOURS PASSED. Blind, dumb, helpless on the back of the hantumu's bike—Dewi could feel only the sharp wind on her face, as the rest of her bound body had grown numb. She had no idea how Husam was faring. She could hear the roar of the other engines preceding and following her, and could only assume he must still be on another hantumu's bike. She thought they must be going through back roads now, because there were jolts and bumps at irregular intervals. Beyond that, she had no idea where the hantumu were taking them.

Tiredness began to steal over her, softly at first, then more insistently. She resisted it hard, not only because she wanted to have her wits about her when they arrived, but also because she was afraid of falling off. Her eyes kept trying to close, only to jerk open again under the dark blindfold. Disconnected images kept jumping into her brain; it seemed to her she rocked uneasily on an ocean full of dark waves and hidden shoals of rock, suspended over a pit of bottomless darkness. An evil thing waited there, a thing worse than the worst hantumu, worse than the most powerful afreet, a human thing that had no mercy in its heart for the whole wide world, but wished only for power, absolute power. Its eyes were on her as she sped over the dark sea; its evil eyes watched her every move as she rocked toward what would be her death. The eyes grew wider, searching into every nook and cranny of her soul. In her half dreams, she knew she had done a mad, foolish thing. The Sorcerer would take her in, chew her up, spit her out, in a moment. She would be dead, just as the afreet had promised her in the vision in the Water Gardens; she would soon be dead, like poor Anda Mangil.

She jerked fully awake. The air was rushing past her nose in a wild stream; the sound of the bikes' engines had changed. She felt herself falling forward, as the bike plunged down, down a steep slope. She cried out in fear, but the gag swallowed her scream. Then came a bone-shaking thud as the bike came to a sudden stop; and Dewi, caught unawares, slipped half off the bike, her bound arm flung out against the hot engine, burning her through her clothes. Her vision swam red and black, and she screamed again. She felt herself roughly dragged free of the bike, her bonds loosened. There was sand under her body, sand that smelled dank and felt cold. There was another horrible smell—old bones, old blood, as in the den of a carnivore.

She heard the hantumu's voice in her ear. "I will take off your blindfold now, and the gag. But you will be quiet, and not struggle. Do you understand?"

Battered, bruised, weary, and frightened, Dewi could only just barely manage a nod. The gag was the first to go; the suddenness with which it was ripped away made her retch. The hantumu murmured, "Dirty scum." His fingers ripped at her blindfold, scratching her face as they did so. Light burst in on her eyelids; for an instant, it was too painful to look, so long had she been in the blackness. But she cautiously opened one eye, then the other.

She was in a large cave, flickeringly lit by rush lights set against the walls. In the light of the flares, she saw that on one of the cave walls was a huge black painting, extraordinarily vivid, of a twisted, big-bellied beast that looked something like a huge lizard. She trembled.

Where was Husam? At the moment she thought it, two more hantumu came into view, dragging Husam along with them. The poor old man looked half dead;

his blindfold and gag were off, but one eye was half closed over a purpling bruise, there was blood at the corners of his mouth, and his face was the color of ash. Dewi tried to fight down the wild rage that rose in her at the sight. What cowards and brutes these creatures were.

The hantumu flung the unconscious Husam down like a sack of rice in a corner of the cave, not far from Dewi. "The old fool thinks he's still a fighter," one of them remarked.

The first hantumu smiled. "Well, we'll see how he fares later, eh?" They all laughed, a terrible, cold sound without any human sympathy in it whatsoever. These men might not be demons like the afreet, but they had become something less than men, giving over their wills and hearts to the service of evil.

The first hantumu caught her expression. He bent over her and said, very softly, "So, how do you like being in our master's realm, little girl? Does it please you?" He put a hand on her chin, stroking it softly. Dewi felt her very bones creep at the touch. But she looked steadily at his masked face, saying, between clenched teeth, "I do not have to talk to slaves and servants."

He slapped her so hard, her head jerked backward. Jumping up, he said menacingly, "You're caught like a rat. Caught like the dirty, worthless rat you are. You wanted an audience with our master—well, you'll get it right enough. And you'll soon realize just what a fool you were to think you could stand for even one second against him."

He jerked a thumb at his silent, smirking companions. "What are you waiting for? Tell Kerapi she's in such a hurry to meet our master."

The other hantumu laughed uproariously, as if he'd made a wonderful joke, and left. Their leader bent down to her again. "Don't even think you can escape from here. The cave is sealed from the outside world and demons guard its passages." He took a rushlight and followed his companions.

Dewi waited until she was sure he was quite gone, then got gingerly to her feet. First things first. She knelt down beside Husam's body and felt his pulse. He was alive, though still unconscious. Standing, she looked around her. The hantumu had gone out of the cave . . . up that way. She walked over and found the mouth of a narrow, rocky passageway. At the end of it, she could see . . . nothing. Well, the narrowest of chinks of light. She took a rushlight from the wall and walked down the passageway. It wasn't long, and at the end of it there was a narrow exit, but it was completely blocked by a massive boulder. Only the tiniest slivers of light showed around it. Dewi put her shoulder to the stone. Not only did it not move, but her shoulder felt bruised and scraped afterward. They were indeed sealed in.

All at once, she remembered her father's talisman. With a pounding heart, she felt for it in her pocket—how she hoped it hadn't somehow fallen out along the way. But no, here it was. She held it tightly in her hand and closed her eyes. She concentrated hard on conjuring up Bupatihutan's image in her mind. "Open the door for us, Honorable Lord," she murmured, "O great Bupatihutan, help us, help us."

Silence. No tiger-man appeared in her mind. She tried again. "Great Lord of the Harimauroh, help us."

Nothing happened. Bupatihutan was sealed off from her as surely as the cave was sealed off from the outside. She tried hard to quell her growing panic. After all, she had expected this, hadn't she? Kwanyin had warned her. They were in the Sorcerer's power now; the spirits could not help them.

She made her way back into the cave. Husam was still lying down, but he was groaning, a hand to his brow. He lifted his head and tried to smile when he saw her. "Little heart, I am glad it is you. Will you help me sit up?"

Dewi quickly went over to him. She put an arm

around his shoulders and helped him up. He sat propped against a wall of the cave, feeling at his face. "Aaiyee! If I'd been younger, those hantumu would never have . . ." He looked at Dewi, and caught her expression. "Forgive me. Much good was Sword to you this night."

"Don't blame yourself, Husam," said Dewi gently. "It was my fault for bringing us here." She swallowed. "We're trapped, Husam. There's no way out. The only exit is sealed with a huge boulder. The hantumu said we're caught like rats in a trap. And I fear we are."

"You know what rats are like," Husam said lightly. "Cunning creatures. Rarely get caught. Many a trap's been made for rats, but there is a difference between making the trap and catching the rat. There are more rats than traps in this wide world, isn't that so?"

Dewi could not help smiling, even in the midst of her anxiety. "I suppose that is true. Father says rats will survive even the end of the world."

"Maybe that is because they don't wait for others to help them," said Husam. "They always want to survive, so they always help themselves in whatever way they can. Perhaps we should begin to think like them."

"We might soon have to test whether that will do us any good," said Dewi. "The Sorcerer is coming to us. The hantumu said they were going to get Kerapi to tell him."

"Kerapi?" said Husam. "Why, that is . . ." But whatever he had been about to say remained unsaid, for they heard a great rumble, smelled a smell as of burning; and something came whooshing down through the roof to land in front of them. At first, it looked like a dazzling white pillar of flame, then it reassembled itself into a different form, and in less time than it takes to say it, a man stood in front of them: a tall man dressed like a king in gold and purple, with a tall purple turban on his head, and with a face so cruel it made Dewi's flesh shrink. The man's eyes burned with a deep fiery gleam, and when he opened his mouth to speak, they could see that his teeth were all of gold, and filed to sharp points.

"You wanted an audience with me. I am here."

Dewi and Husam could not move or speak. The Sorcerer—for it must be he—glared at them. "Are you tongueless and voiceless? Get up when you are in the presence of your betters!"

Dewi and Husam got shakily to their feet. Dewi glanced at Husam. There was a puzzled expression in the old executioner's eyes, but she had no time to think about it, for the Sorcerer strode over to her. "What did you want to speak to me about? Speak!" he shouted, looming over her.

He smelled awful, like burned flesh. It made her

want to gag. But his eyes drew her. They were large, full of a malevolent power, the long vertical pupils slicing into her like sharp daggers. She wanted to look away but could not. Her limbs felt as if they were dissolving; her head was swimming; her tongue felt like molten lead in her mouth.

"Poor child," said the Sorcerer in a soft voice. "Poor child, you are weary. You have traveled a long way to see me, and now you are struck mute in my presence. Come, child," and he extended a long, thin, taloned hand, dripping with beautiful rings. "Come here to me, and I will forgive your temerity if you will speak to me and tell me all you know."

"No!" Husam shouted, and flung himself between them. "No! You are not the Sorcerer—you are his slave, the afreet!"

The man whirled around. His eyes were so large now, they seemed to be taking over his whole face, eating it, consuming it, turning it to flame. In an instant, the man had vanished, replaced by a small, wizened, twisted creature half like a monkey, half dwarfish man. But the eyes were the same—huge, glowing, and with sharp, vertical pupils.

"Move yourself, Sword," said the afreet in a harsh voice. "It is not you I am concerned with. Get away from the girl."

"No!" yelled Husam. "You will not touch her. I will—" He broke off, the words gurgling in his throat, as the afreet leaped at him, taloned hands reaching to scratch out his eyes. Dewi flung herself forward. "No!" she cried in her turn. "Don't hurt him. Leave him. Hareekshaytin, it is me you want. You said so."

The afreet dropped suddenly from Husam's shoulder to the floor. Husam bent over, choking. "You know my name," growled the afreet threateningly. It was staring up at Dewi, its eyes again seeking to draw her in. She forced herself to look away, and her eyes fell on the painted wall opposite. A long shiver rippled over her. She looked at the sandy floor, trying to stop her teeth from chattering.

She said, "I learned your name from one who knows you."

She nearly screamed then, for the afreet had leaped to her shoulder, its taloned claws digging painfully into her flesh. Its smell was in her nostrils now, very close; it made her feel so sick that she could barely think. But she managed to stammer, "You . . . you . . . are a slave, Hareekshaytin. A slave! I will not speak . . . to a slave!"

A massive pain ripped through her, a pain such as she had never felt before. She doubled over, screaming, the afreet still clinging to her. It came again; it was inside her skull, inside her flesh, her bones, her very being. She fell to the ground. Dimly, she heard Husam's shouts, saw him rush forward, but she could not worry about him as her head felt as if it were exploding. Wild jagged images unspooled in her mind, faster and faster, silent and relentless: houses burning, people in flames running from them, swords red with blood, black-clad men with blank faces slaughtering defenseless people, who ran before them begging for mercy, disemboweled corpses in piles on the side of the road . . . and then . . . and then . . . she saw her village, but horribly changed, destroyed, houses smoking, blackened ruins, her house . . . a pile of rubble, bodies lying flung outside the door. She recognized Jafar, and Wisnu and Ayu, though they were horribly mangled, their faces twisted in a last terror and agony. She screamed again, and heard the afreet's voice in her mind. "This is the future. This will all come to pass."

Dewi shuddered from head to foot. She whispered, "No, no, no, it is just a fear I have in my mind, and you are twisting it, making it seem real."

"Fool! It is real. It will happen," howled the afreet in her mind, "unless you tell me all you know." The nightmares danced and cavorted in her head.

"I do not know anything," whispered Dewi, then wailed as the pain shot into her, more red-hot and violent than before. She couldn't bear it, she couldn't.

She had to save her family, her village, all those people. She opened her mouth, but then Husam's voice rang out.

"Hareekshaytin! That is not what the hantumu call you. Do you want to hear what they call you behind your back, son of dread Iblis?"

The band of iron and blood and fire around Dewi's head loosened abruptly. The visions shattered and were gone. Her senses began returning to her. Her shoulder ached. The afreet had let go and had leaped onto the floor, staring at Husam. A growl was coming from its throat.

"I heard them. They called you Kerapi. And you know what that means. Fire-monkey," said the old executioner calmly, though Dewi could see that his forehead was beaded with sweat.

The afreet stared at Husam, who went on. "O son of Iblis, you have been a slave so long, bending your power to another's will. Shall you ever return to your home, to Jehannem?"

The afreet swelled. Red and black tendrils of hair like snakes twisted out from its head. It growled again, deep in its throat. "I will be freed, once my master is master over all this accursed place," it said at last. "I will return to Jehannem, and to my rightful place."

"Can you be sure, O Hareekshaytin?"

"This has been promised," said the afreet, staring at Husam. "I will no longer be a slave." Its voice changed. "Iblis! I have been cold and lonely for too long in this accursed human world." Its voice was rising, its clawed hands clenching. "In this accursed place do I appear to you like some ugly thing, like some—what is it you say those black scum call me—like a fire-monkey. But in my own land, I was handsome, powerful. I was a true noble Son of the Flame. Long have I paid for my folly in insulting my lord Iblis, long have I paid, but soon will I pay no longer."

"Those men, those hantumu, they are indeed unkind to call you such bad things," said Husam soothingly.

The afreet's eyes burned with a wild light of hatred and fury. "Worse than unkind, they are dead men walking. Before I go, they will know the true nature of the Son of the Flame. They treat me like a thing at their command, like a creature of no consequence, and insult me, though I have helped them so often. They will know, before their eyes melt in their sockets, and their hearts shrivel to cinders inside them, and their flesh runs in puddles of oil on their worthless bones, they will know the truth, and they will be made soulless and mute with the knowledge. Oh, yes, yes! Then I will fling the last of their spirits into Jehannem, and they will be tortured for all eternity for the things they did and said to me."

"A good plan," said Husam gently. "A good plan indeed, Hareekshaytin."

"Who gave you my name?" said the afreet, suddenly whirling on Husam. "Who was it?"

"It is a good name," said Husam quickly, backing away. "It is a name truly of Jehannem, not like that insulting name 'Kerapi' they call you."

The afreet screeched with fury. The very sound of the name seemed to make it wild. "Wait till I get my hands on those men! I will rip their entrails to pieces, I will wrap them around their heads."

"Perhaps you should tell your master," said Husam smoothly. "He might punish the hantumu for it himself."

The afreet yelled, "My master loves those creatures! He has them by his right hand. Me, who have given him so much power, he treats like a beggar; and yet he rewards worthless humans who are not worthy of even being in my presence. Why, he is even more careful of you, who have thwarted him constantly, than he is of me."

"O noble Son of the Flame," Husam said, "just how long has it been since those black spiders and their master have ridden on your power?"

"Too long," said the afreet.

"Oh, I understand how you must—"

"Silence!" shrieked the afreet, its eyes bright red. "You understand nothing, human thing. How can you even begin to?"

Husam shrugged. "I understand you yearn for your home, Hareekshaytin, for your old place in Jehannem, for your position in the world of demons. You have been stripped of all your glory in this place. You are a son of wild Iblis, who never bowed to any man. Yet here you perform the will of inferiors. Why do you not rebel?"

The afreet began to laugh. Its laughter was the same terrifying sound Dewi had heard in the atrium—inhuman peal after peal of wild, desperate, savage laughter. "You can never understand, old man. Never, even if you live for a thousand years. Rebellion is only for those who hope. There is no hope in me—only certainty that one day my master will have to free me, and the sooner I help him to accomplish what he wants, the sooner that will be, because until then, his will to power is too strong for me to resist."

"Is that so?" said Husam. "Why, I had always heard that afreets are the strongest of all of Iblis's children. Why is it not you who hold sway? How can the Sorcerer hold you so?"

"He wears a ring," said the afreet, glowering, and Dewi held her breath, knowing that it was falling into the trap Husam had set. "It is a ring forged in Jehannem by the master blacksmith of Iblis himself. It has as its binding one of the dread names of Iblis. I cannot break free of it, as it was at Iblis's command that I was enslaved."

Suddenly, it crouched down and whimpered. "He is calling me." It froze in a humble, listening posture. Then it fell to the ground, writhing as if in torment, holding its head in its hands, making weirdly awful keening, moaning noises. Dewi could almost feel a strange kind of pity stirring in her. In the next instant that feeling disappeared, for the afreet suddenly rose to its feet, its face filled with an inhuman, cruel joy. "My master has told me much! He promises me much bloodshed, much destruction! Much blood will be spilled this coming day, for we march. We march! It is our time!"

"Oh, then you will need us with you," said Dewi very quickly. "You will need us to tell you what—"

The afreet turned on her, still laughing. "You fool! My master has told me that he understands now, he already has what is needed!"

Dewi's heart pounded. "No, that cannot be, because you don't have Fire—"

The afreet cut in, with a mocking air. "You poor human thing! You strove to thwart my master, but he has been cleverer than you. You gave yourselves willingly into our hands, thinking thus to trick us, but you failed, for you did not realize that my master had anticipated this. And so you are here now in this dungeon, helpless and unable to take part in the final battle when my master will emerge in his full glory and destroy all his enemies."

"Do you think we can be bound by a dungeon, son of Iblis?" growled Husam. "It is our destiny that we will take part, and so it shall be! Otherwise, if your master did not need us, why would he hold us here? Why not kill us?"

The afreet laughed again. "You are a fool, old man." Its eyes slid over to the wall where the huge lizard hunkered. "We do not need to kill you. There is a much better way. The darkest part of the night comes just before dawn, and with it, the reign of the oldest thing of all, who kills without reason. You see this?" he said, pointing to the image on the wall. "This creature comes alive at the darkest part of the night. It is an ancient, wordless evil; there is no use pleading with it. It will devour you. We never stay here at this part of the night—it is too dangerous. But you will be here, in its sacred place. The oldest, most savage spirit of Jayangan will destroy you, and nothing can save you from it. You will die in a much more horrible way than you can imagine." It gave a mocking bow. "So this is a leave-taking, human things. We will not meet again." It gave its wild, savage laugh, jumped up in the air, and turned into a white pillar of flame, which funneled up through the rocky roof and vanished. Husam and Dewi were once more alone in the cave.

EIGHTEEN

ADI SLEPT LIKE a baby that night. No dreams or nightmares troubled him, for his spirit was at peace. He had been given a comfortable corner in Sadik's room, and slept rolled up in a soft blanket. He awoke with a start at first light, with Sadik gently shaking him. "It's time to go, Adi. Best to leave for Kotabunga when it's still cool."

Adi rubbed the sleep from his eyes. Sadik was already up, dressed all in white today, his unruly hair smoothly brushed down. His eyes were shining like stars. "Oh, Adi," he said eagerly, "God blesses the day you came to this place, for you are the path to the world learning about the Shayk. Today the Sultan himself will be convinced."

"Mmm," said Adi, a little disconcerted by such early-morning fervor. All things considered, though he admired the Shayk and what he was trying to achieve, and was glad to have found him, he would be relieved to get out of the community itself. The garden was very nice, but the rest of it—no, it just wasn't his sort of place. It was an earnest place, and he was not an earnest person. He liked to have fun too much. And he was not a farmer, or a religious scholar, or a fighter either, really, but a craftsman. He missed, oh, how he missed, his master and the work they did together. That was what was in his soul.

Empu Wesiagi had told Adi that he had worked so well on the Sultan's kris, followed his directions so well, that next time he could create his own kris, suited to himself. Then, if it was well done, he would be taught the sacred finishing formula, and might be allowed to create a kris for their next client. It had been the proudest moment of Adi's life, and it came back to him now with poignant clarity.

He became aware that Sadik was looking at him questioningly.

"Sorry," he said with a little laugh. "I am a little distracted today, my friend. What is it you wanted to know?"

"I said I think you'd better borrow some of my things," said Sadik, laughing too. "Your clothes are rather rumpled and stained now, nice though they once were. It might be best if I lent you these." He went to the chest in a corner of his room, opened it, and pulled out a plain brown cotton shirt and loose trousers. They weren't beautiful, but they were clean and fresh, and smelled nicely of spices.

Standing in his undershirt and shorts, he looked at his own crumple of clothes on the floor. They did look rather travel worn. "Thank you, Sadik," he said.

A car horn sounded outside. Sadik rushed over to the window and looked out. "They're ready! Come on, hurry up," he shouted. Adi pulled off his sweaty undershirt, laid it on the crumpled pile of clothes, and put on Sadik's shirt. It was when he was pulling up the trousers that he noticed Sadik was staring at him.

"You're a Nashranee! I saw the heart around your neck."

Adi glared defiantly at him and pulled on his shoes. "So what? What does that matter to you?"

"Nothing, nothing," said Sadik uncertainly. "I believe that Nashranees can be saved, if they understand about the Light. And so that is well, is it not? Is that not a good thing?"

"Hmm," said Adi gruffly, not wanting to be drawn into such discussions.

"But I thought you were a . . . I thought you were one of us," said Sadik, earnestly, "or at least that you followed the Book of Light, even if imperfectly, given that you talked about the Queen of the Southern Sea, which is just a story for children who do not understand the truth."

"I never said I was anything at all," snapped Adi. "You just assumed I did. My family is Nashranee, so of course I am too. Your family is Mujisal, yes, so you are Mujisal. That's the way it goes in Jayangan, Sadik. You know that."

"Yes, I do know that," said Sadik, looking troubled, "but one day it will not be so, and we will all follow the same way, for I know the Light is for everyone. It is true that many, many Mujisal do not understand fully what they should do to follow the Light, so how can a Nashranee? It must come from the heart, this change, not by force or rage. Perhaps one day, friend Adi, I might talk to you about it?"

"Perhaps," said Adi coolly, though he fumed inside. "Not now, though, Sadik. They're waiting, remember?"

He wondered briefly if Sadik would mention their little conversation to his teacher. In any case, it would not matter, as the Shayk was a good man. Of course, everyone thought their own way was the right one, but in reality that did not stop different ways from existing at once. Adi himself was not one to fight over it. He was a peaceable person, who loved his work and his family and had been content in his life—till the day his master was kidnapped. Now he found himself in a strange and terrifying world, among unusual allies, and all his old notions had had to change.

"We are friends, you and I, Adi," Sadik said solemnly. "I heard your heart calling to my heart, and I knew we were friends at once. That is what matters, no?"

Adi saw that this was a great effort of understanding for Sadik, and it touched him. He said gently, "It is what matters, Sadik. You are a good person, a worthy disciple of your master."

Sadik beamed shyly. "You are too kind, brother Adi," he stammered. "You do me great honor by these words."

"Not at all," said Adi, and he opened the door and stepped out into the cool gray light of morning, closely followed by the still-beaming Sadik.

"Good morning, Adi. I trust you slept well." The Shayk, dressed in spotless robe and turban, was sitting on the well-padded backseat of the shining big white car parked outside. He smiled when Adi nodded, and patted the seat beside him. "Come and sit beside me, and you too, Sadik."

Adi and Sadik slid in. It was an unusual car, which

had perhaps once done time as a limousine, for the back and front seats were separated by a thick pane of wavy glass, and the side windows were all black-tinted. But Adi could see that Ibrahim was at the wheel, and that two young men whom he had not seen before were sitting on the bench seat beside him.

"It's all right, Adi," said the Shayk, correctly interpreting Adi's startled look. "These are Jamal and Ali. They are good boys. They can be trusted to keep their mouths shut. They are here for our protection."

The young men did not seem curious at all. They had not turned around to look at Adi, who from the luxurious depths of the backseat could see only the backs of their slicked-back longish hair and their rock-like, sturdy necks. They certainly looked like they meant business. Well, he supposed even a holy man like the Shayk would need muscle with him; after all, Sadik had said he had many enemies. Even granted some exaggeration, there were always those who harbored bad feelings toward charismatic men. Besides, it showed that the Shayk was not only an unwordly priest but a realist. He knew evil was abroad in the world, and that you must be prepared to fight it, not wait for it to overwhelm you.

Ibrahim started the engine. The big car pulled away from the house, its engine purring powerfully. This car is even finer than Anda Mangil's, thought Adi. It was newer, for a start, and as big as a small apartment. Well, maybe that was an exaggeration, but it was certainly large, and luxurious. There was enough room in the back for a small refrigerator, a radio and TV, and tables that were folded down at present. The backseat was covered in absolutely spotless white velvet, and the floor was carpeted with exquisite rugs of Al Aksara manufacture.

The Shayk was watching Adi's reaction. "You like it, my friend?"

"Oh, yes, sir!"

"It was offered to me by a wealthy supporter of mine," said the Shayk brightly. "You understand, I could not hurt his feelings by refusing it, though it is not in my nature to crave such things. I have come to know that my own feelings count for nothing in the more important pursuit of our cause, the cause of the Army of Light. This car is not only beautiful, Adi, but it is well protected in other ways. Watch!" He pressed a little button by his side. Immediately, thick steel mesh screens shot up, covering the side and back windows and the glass that separated the front from the backseat. The Shayk smiled at Adi's and Sadik's looks of wide-eyed surprise, and pressed something with his foot. Instantly, the TV swiveled, showing that there was a cupboard behind it, which opened, revealing two big black revolvers.

"They are fully loaded," said the Shayk, rocking gently with the pleasure of the boys' astonishment. "And I know how to shoot precisely." His eyes were sparkling behind their glasses. "Yes, I am afraid, Adi, that a teacher must know more than how to memorize verses, in our dark days. Guns and swords may not work against the demons, but they work against their human allies. And it is my responsibility to know how to defend myself and my community." He smiled reminiscently. "In my young days, in my own homeland, I was reckoned to be quite a crack shot, you know, as well as a good swordsman."

Sadik looked a little troubled at this, and Adi thought he knew why. It was all very well to talk in the abstract of armies and fighting, but when faced with the reality, he shrank away. He'd talked so hotly about how the Shayk had had to fight and then flee from his enemies in the past, but had also spoken of how change must come from the heart, not force or rage. Perhaps he thought the demons could be defeated that way too. Silly naïve one, thought Adi, amused. He didn't understand the world very much, and he obviously had never come across the enemies Adi himself had seen. Adi knew this was a serious battle, a fight to the death. The revelation that he was armed had only made him warm more to the Shayk. He was not just a holy saint in his garden, talking gently of peace; he was a tough man of action. Both were needed in their fight against evil, that was for sure.

"I would very much like to hear about your young days, sir," said Adi respectfully.

The Shayk laughed frankly. "I am afraid my poor Sadik would not approve, Adi. He might become afraid of his old teacher!"

"Oh, no, Master." Sadik looked very unhappy. "Please . . . that is not so. . . ."

"I haven't spoken of it for so long," said the Shayk, ignoring Sadik's stammerings. He pressed on the buttons again, and the gun cupboard swiveled out of sight and the screens shot back down. "But it will help pass the time till we get to Kotabunga. Now, Adi, I was not always as you see me now."

Adi, glancing at Sadik as the Shayk took up his story, saw that the other boy's face bore a look of baffled hurt. He must be wondering why he is being ignored, he thought, while I am drawing out his idolized master. Perhaps he will even end up resenting me, he thought a little uncomfortably. I, who am not even a Mujisal, am being privileged by the holy man he admires above all others. He tried to send Sadik a message with his eyes, to say that he could not help it, that it meant little, that Sadik was the Shayk's true companion while he himself was a mere distraction. But Sadik was not looking at him. He was looking at the Shayk, listening to every word with a humble, hangdog expression on his face. Really, it got on Adi's nerves.

The Shayk's story kept Adi enthralled all the way to Kotabunga. From the time the Shayk was a small child, he had shown a great aptitude not only for wielding the sword but also for learning. He had been able to memorize the holy Book of Light by the time he was seven; was having discussions with teachers three times his age by the time he was ten; and by fifteen, he had already accomplished the great pilgrimage to the holiest city of the Great Desert, where the Messenger of Light had been born. Rasheed had realized very early on that it was his destiny to try to strengthen the Army of Light in their eternal battle with the Demons' Army. His preachings on this were fiery and exciting and full of great insights, and people flocked to hear him. But Rasheed didn't only preach. During his childhood, he also fought battles with raiders, wrestled with a lion and a wolf, bested an afreet, and was saved by an angel from the dagger of an assassin. He grew to manhood respected and loved by all those around him and at the age of sixteen was given the title of Shayk as a mark of respect for his prowess and learning, and married the beautiful daughter of a neighboring chieftain. She presented him with a son and then another a year later.

The demons could not allow the young man's charmed career to go on in this way. They caused dissension in the ranks of his followers, and then they caused open treachery. When the Shayk was on a visit to an oasis city, raiders struck at his home camp in the desert and attempted to carry off his wife and sons. They and his clansmen resisted bravely, and God sent angels to come to beat the raiders off. But the demons were not finished yet. The King of the Desert sent men to arrest him, so he and his wife and sons had to flee to a neighboring country. Only two months after that, the boys died after catching a terrible disease. The Shayk's wife fell into a deep depression. She would not speak or eat, she would not listen to the Shayk's exhortations about trusting to the Light to make things better, and soon she died, heartbroken.

A lesser man would have cursed Heaven for not saving his loved ones, and for favoring the wicked against the good, but not the Shayk. He humbly waited for the darkness to lift; and always in his heart, the Light shone. One day he had a dream that was to change his whole life. He dreamed that he had been carried by flocks of lovely green birds to a beautiful little green island, far far away. An island that knew the Light, but only imperfectly. An island that was at risk of being subverted by rich, immoral foreigners from places beyond the setting sun, like the Rummiyans. An island that needed teachers, that needed the full and true understanding of the greatest Messenger of them all. And that island, of course, was Jayangan. He knew what his mission in life was—he must journey far away and preach to the people of that lovely green island.

With his good friend Ibrahim and other followers he settled not far from Kotabunga, and started a farm and a school. The farm and school thrived; they did good works, teaching and also helping to rescue those in need. Once again, enemies watched and waited. They spread false stories about the Shayk and his companions, and those stories reached the ears of the Sultan at the time. The Sultan, who had begun by being friendly toward the young teacher and his followers, turned against them and ordered his soldiers to arrest them. They escaped only through the good offices of angels, and the kindness of strangers who had heard of their work and loved them for it. They fled to another country and waited till things were better in Jayangan.

Things improved indeed when the old Sultan died and his son, Sunan Tengah, took over. Though Sunan Tengah himself was only a lukewarm follower of the Light, concerning himself more with affairs of state, his eldest son, Crown Prince Yanto, was a fervent follower. He prevailed upon his father to allow the Shayk and his friends to come back. They were allowed to return, and Prince Yanto even gave them some land at Gunungbatu, where they have been ever since, growing in strength and fame.

"And that," said the Shayk, winding up his story, "is a little of how we came to be here. I hope you have not found the time wasted, listening to these old stories."

"Oh, no," said Adi, "it is a tremendous story!"

"And now we come to the next part of our story, Adi," the Shayk said, leaning forward and fixing him with a bright gaze. "You yourself have brought us the next part. I always knew that you—or someone like you—would come to us one day with just such a tale as you have told us. The time has come at last for the battle to begin, for the veil to be ripped from the faces of the Demons' Army. This will be a decisive battle, my son, and you have brought it to us—" He broke off, frowning. "What is that dreadful noise I can hear?" The Shayk tapped on the glass in front of him. "Ibrahim, what is going on?"

Ibrahim stuck his head out of the window. He called back to the Shayk, "It's someone playing some sort of song, a radio on too loud, maybe."

They were in a mean, narrow little street, not far from the great square that led to the palace. The music got louder and louder. Adi knew it at once: It was that ubiquitous song "Beloved." But it wasn't on the radio. Someone was actually singing it, the sound floating from the open doorway of a shop farther down. Whoever the singer was, she had a gorgeous voice, he thought, as the melancholy, joyful, passionate strains of the song came rolling on, sending shivers of delight through him.

He turned to tell the Shayk what it was, but the old man was frowning. "What a vile sound," he said. He glared at Adi. "Cover your ears!"

Startled, Adi obeyed. He glanced over at Sadik, who had also, quickly, guiltily, clapped his hands to his ears, though it was apparent he'd been enjoying the song too. Adi tried to say, "Er, it's only this—"

But the Shayk ignored him. "Go back!" he ordered Ibrahim. "We don't want to go down there." Ibrahim nodded and accelerated backward out of the alley.

The Sultan's palace occupied a vast area of the center of Kotabunga. It was set within a large white square planted with palm trees and frangipani and bougainvillea. Its outer walls were also white and had golden-topped gates set in them every few meters. Guards in brown and white and gold sarongs, jackets and headdresses, with businesslike krises set into the waistbands of their sarongs, stood purposefully before each gate. Others patrolled around the walls.

They parked the car under a frangipani tree. Adi expected that Ibrahim, Jamal, and Ali would stay there with the car, and so it proved to be. But it was a bad moment for him when the Shayk turned to Sadik, handed him some money, and said, "You are to go to the market and buy us some mangosteen. We will need it when we come back."

Sadik's face flushed; his eyes shone with hurt. He gave a quick glance at Adi, then, bowing his head meekly, said, "Yes, Master, I will do it."

"I can go with—"

"You are to come with me, Adi," said the Shayk very sternly. "Do not shirk the destiny you have been given. It is not worthy." And so saying, he turned and marched purposefully toward one of the gates, his straight back expressing righteous indignation. What else could Adi do but stumble after him, in a rather undignified fashion, and beg his pardon?

NINETEEN

FOR A MOMENT, after the afreet had vanished, Dewi and Husam stood rooted to the spot, unable to move. Black despair invaded them both. They had played into the enemy's hands. The battle would be joined, the Sorcerer emerge into the open—and they would not be there.

After a while, Husam growled, "Well, it's time to put on our rat's heads, little heart. We will not stay here. We will escape."

Dewi stared at him. She felt numb. "Oh, Husam, how can we . . ." she began wearily, but he shook his head.

"Don't say it, or you will become as spellbound by despair as the afreet and its master want. Now, let's check that this exit really is blocked."

"It is," said Dewi, but Husam was already limping up the passageway, rushlight in hand. She did not follow him. What was the good of it? She already knew they were sealed into this place that would be their tomb—whether from hunger or thirst, exhaustion, or what the afreet had spoken of, it made little difference. She looked at the painted wall. Was it her imagination, or did the rock bulge out just a little more? Her breath fluttered coldly in her throat. The oldest thing reigns at the darkest part of the night. As she stared, the painted lines of the great lizard began to flex—just a tiny ripple of movement, a slight shudder in the rock, but unmistakable.

She tried to tell herself that any form of dying was as bad as another, though she knew it wasn't so. She held on tightly to her father's talisman. It might not work in this place, but it was a tiny shred of comfort, a faint link to her father and to the world above, which she would never see again. Once more, she tried to call to Bupatihutan in her mind, but there was no answer, no vision, nothing but the tiger's claw lying senseless and nerveless in her hand.

Husam returned. His face was strained but his tone was light: "Well, I tried every name, every magic formula I could think of, and it hasn't budged. I don't think we can get out that way."

Dewi, her voice choked with fear, said, "We can't get out any way, Husam. We're doomed. Forgive me,

Husam, for having dragged you into this. Forgive me. I thought I was doing the right thing. I thought that we had a chance. I'm a fool."

"Ah, don't carry on so—there is nothing to forgive," said Husam just as lightly as before. "Besides, we're getting out. We're survivors, remember?" He began walking around the cave, running his hands carefully, slowly, over the rocky walls.

"I watched a film once," he said conversationally, "and there was a secret entrance to a cave in a wall. There was a kind of hidden lever you could lift, and the whole of the wall opened up."

"A film!" said Dewi, taken aback.

"You could help me, little heart," said Husam. He came over to her and touched her on the shoulder. "Come on, we should try and cover every centimeter of this cave. The lever could be anywhere."

Dewi's heart sank. Husam was clutching at straws. She shot a glance at the painted wall. The powerful strokes of black paint that made up the huge lizard were definitely more fluid, more . . . alive. One of the lizard's eyes opened. Her blood turned to ice; her bones seemed to lose their hardness. She managed to croak, "Husam . . . Husam . . ."

"What is it?" he said, and then he turned, and saw it. His hair stood up on end, sticking out stiffly like bits of wire. The lizard opened its other eye. Those eyes were dark, fathomless, without reflection or shadow, deep and dense as stones. They stared straight at Dewi and Husam.

Dewi felt the power of that stare rushing through her frozen bloodstream, throbbing into her terrified heart. And then it seemed to her that the throbbings became—not words exactly, but something older, more primitive, more elemental. She understood them as you understand words you hear in a dream but could never repeat out loud. "Child," throbbed the wordless voice. "Come. Come, we will help you. Come."

Dewi stared into the black lizard eyes and understood. Awe and hope surged through her. She put out a hand to Husam, who took it in his own. In the other hand, she held the tiger's claw tightly. She made a prayer, deep inside herself. And then she said, very quietly, "We have to come to it, Husam. It is calling us. It will help us. We have to trust it. We must."

Husam was ashy gray, his eyes wide and staring. But he walked forward with Dewi, toward the painted wall, which was now bulging and stretching with the movements of the massive beast. They reached it, and Dewi held out a hand to it. Instantly, the lines of the ancient painting seemed to gather together, as the great lizard burst from the wall and sprang at them. A vast darkness roared at them, an enormous jumble of energy, a huge gathering of force that swept them up, the cave vanishing into a pinprick of light that soon winked out and disappeared.

They were in the dark. The kind of dark you can only find underground: a dark so thick that not only does your hand disappear in front of you, you can hardly imagine it being there at all. Dewi's whole body had vanished from her sight, as had Husam's. It was utterly, utterly silent. She still clutched the tiger's claw in one hand.

"Husam," Dewi whispered, and her voice sounded loud in her ears.

For a moment, there was nothing. Then suddenly his voice came, curiously flat and muffled. "I'm here." She could not tell where it had come from. She groped around, trying to feel if he was near her, but she could feel nothing apart from a smooth, rather leathery surface.

"Dewi, where have you taken us to this time?" His voice, tinged with humor, came to her, suddenly closer.

She started. "I don't know."

"Ah!" he exclaimed, a cry echoed by Dewi. They had found each other's hands.

"Little heart, I am glad to find you." The old executioner's knobbly, scarred fingers gently touched Dewi's soft skin. "Now, what will we do?"

"The lizard-spirit might help us again," said Dewi.

"But we can't see anything, let alone the painting . . . perhaps we're in the picture itself, in the creature's belly?" said Husam.

"You know," said Dewi with a funny little catch in her voice, "perhaps you're right." She groped around, trying to find the soft leathery thing again. She touched a hand to it gently. Nothing happened at first, no throbbing, no hissing; but it seemed to her that in her heart, a rhythm that was not hers began to beat. She bit her lip, trying hard not to be frightened, and concentrated on sending out images from her heart into the darkness around them. Please . . . help . . . light.

No reply. No sound. Yet . . . was the dark growing less dark? Was it graying, softening at the corners? Was that . . . could she begin to see vague shapes, like things seen in a mist? It wasn't her imagination. It was real, it was happening! She saw Husam slowly taking form, then herself. She could see his hand. She could see hers!

"Well, little heart," said Husam rather shakily, "I did begin to wonder if I really existed at all. Bless the

Light! I am glad to see my solid flesh again. I would not like to be a ghost."

"No," said Dewi, laughing a little, relieved and thrilled also to see her own solid self. She had not wanted to say anything, or acknowledge it even to herself, but she had wondered if they were in the blank interspace between life and death—in the shadowlands that Senopati had spoken of.

"It's a tunnel," said Husam, looking around. "We're in a tunnel."

It was a large, rather unpleasant tunnel, with a low roof and an old, musty, unused smell. But it was a tunnel with a definite light at its end, in the distance, a tunnel that must lead out, into the light of day. Dewi could have cried with happiness.

"There are niches here," said Husam, peering into the gloom, "and they have . . . oh . . ." He broke off suddenly, and Dewi, peering in the same direction, felt cold all over. In the niche there was a low white stone shelf, and on that shelf was a person—or rather, the remains of what had once been a person. It was a bag of skin, a boneless mummy, lying on its back with flat, leathery arms drawn up over its chest, its sightless eyes staring up, its legs crossed at the ankles. It was clothed in a brown robe with the remains of fur clinging to the edge. Into its dry, straight hair, which hung down the sides of its dry, dead, boneless face, were woven shells, beads of glass, and delicate strands of gold. And under its back, splaying out from its shoulders, were strange cloth shapes, like wings or sails. These were rather moldy and ragged, but the shapes were still clear enough.

Dewi made a tiny sound and took a step back. Husam said, in a voice full of awe and fear, "She's not alone."

And he was right, as the light slowly revealed to Dewi. There was not one niche, but many. It was a tunnel of the dead, a village of ghosts, the House of Dust itself.

"We were sitting by that one," said Husam, nodding toward the first mummy; and then Dewi realized what it was she had touched when they were in the darkness. A sickness rose up in her throat; a terror and horror washed over her like a great wave. And then the wave had rolled over her and gone, leaving in its place a sensation of sad peace, a feeling such as she had known at Chandi Maya, when she had spoken with Senopati. There was nothing to be afraid of here; this was a place of rest. These people had once lived and breathed like herself.

It was their spirits who had helped her and Husam, she thought. The lizard on the wall in the cave had probably been these people's spirit guide. Perhaps they had worshipped it, down in the depths of the underground, and had come to be buried here, in the tunnel? She had heard about such things at school, about the people who had lived in Jayangan long, long ago, before the island was called that, before Senopati's people had come, before even the forging of the first kris. She looked back at the mummies now and felt gratitude, and gentleness, and even love.

"We thank you, O ancient guardians of the dark," she said quietly, very quietly. "We thank you for your kindness and your protection. We will honor your memory every day."

The throbbing had started again, the gentle purring and humming. And in it, Dewi felt thoughts being sent to her, over the darkness of centuries, the threads of millennia. "Child . . . you good . . . we help you . . . but you not tell . . . not tell . . . child . . . bless child."

"I won't tell," said Dewi, tears in her eyes. "I will never tell anyone of what I have seen here. And neither will my friend. You will stay undisturbed forever. And I thank you for your blessing. I only hope I am worthy of it."

"Of course you are," said Husam, speaking suddenly. "Of course you are—or they would never have helped us." He inclined his head and whispered, "Old

Ones, I am not of your land. But I honor you too."

There was silence in the tunnel. But it was a silence that spoke of quiet gladness; a sigh of peace and waiting, as if a dreamer had turned over in a long sleep.

TWENTY

ADI HAD NEVER been in the palace before, though he had often dreamed of coming here. Wide-eyed, he followed in the Shayk's footsteps as the guard took them through the court-yards. How amazing it was to be here, in the seat of the great Sultan of Jayangan! He only wished it could have been in different circumstances; that it could have been with his beloved master, bearing the kris that had been specially made for the Sultan.

The palace was a series of beautiful white and gold pavilions. There were flower gardens with colored fountains playing; multicolored birds sang in golden cages; and the courtyards were floored with pure white pebbles and sand. Guards in the smart brown and white and gold uniforms of the palace, their ceremo-nial krises at their waistbands, patrolled the grounds, and graceful women with flowers in their buns and elegant dark-blue and gold sarong suits walked busily from pavilion to pavilion, bundles of papers in their hands. In one pavilion, there was a shadow-puppet show playing, and in another, musical instruments had been set up, ready to be played. In other circumstances, Adi would have wanted to linger, but today there was no time, and he trotted breathlessly at the heels of the Shayk, who strode purposefully, without a look to right or left.

They crossed another courtyard and came to a great red and gold door. The guard who had brought them explained rapidly to the guard at the door who Adi and the Shayk were. The man at the door looked at them, his gaze level and not very friendly. "Wait here," he said, pointing to a bench near the door. "I will see if you can be received."

The Shayk smiled thinly. "I think you will find Crown Prince Yanto will not like us to be kept waiting like this, but do your duty, my son."

The man returned look for look, and did not flinch. "I will not be long."

"Well, Adi," said the Shayk when they were alone. "Is it what you expected?"

"Oh yes, sir. And more!"

"You are impressed with this power and wealth, my son?"

"Why, yes, sir! It is so beautiful, and seemly. The Sultans of Jayangan are great rulers. It is an honor to be here."

"But are they devout, Adi? Are they truly devoted to the truth? Or is it just wealth and power they crave? Are they true sons of the Light?"

Adi looked in alarm at the Shayk. He hoped no one from the palace staff was listening. Such talk could land you in great trouble. The Shayk saw his expression. He smiled. "I ask only because if our rulers are not devout sons of the Light, then they might become easy prey for the tricks and wiles of demons and unbelievers."

Adi stammered, "S-sir, I believe our . . . our Sultan is indeed devoted to the truth." He added, in some discomfort, "He must rule for everyone, not just those who follow the Book of Light."

The Shayk gave him a quizzical look from behind his glasses. "Hmmm. That is so in Jayangan, indeed. Yet were we treated well by the servant of the palace?" Adi stared at him.

"But sir, he has to protect—"

The Shayk nodded and smiled benignly. "Don't look so afraid, Adi. God listens to you, as well as men."

Adi said nothing more, but secretly, he was shocked. He thought, No wonder the old Sultan exiled the

Shayk, if that was how he spoke. The Sultan was the Sultan, to be respected and looked up to. It was unworldly to think that a Sultan should not have wealth and power. Wise rulers used both well, knowing that a wicked ruler might well oppress his people but in the end would pay for it, certainly before God, and even before men. The people of Jayangan did not meekly support tyranny. The present Sultan was a man very close to his people; his kindness was well known, as were his energy and his dynamism. Besides, the Sultan's patronage had helped to make great craftsmen like Empu Wesiagi what they were, and hopefully would help to make Adi's own career as well. As to the way the guard had spoken to them—well, it was the job of such a man to protect his masters. He hoped the Shayk would make no rash, stiff-necked Pumujisal statements in the presence of the Sultan or the Crown Prince.

The guard came out again. His manner had changed. Now he was polite, even deferential. "Excuse me for keeping you waiting." He opened the red door. "Please come with me, sirs."

The Shayk, shooting Adi a look of mild triumph, got unhurriedly to his feet. "We excuse you, my son," he said calmly, and they passed through the doorway.

The guard led them down a long corridor, toward

an open door at the far end. The doorway was well guarded by several armed guards, who stood aside to let them pass. Adi could not help giving a gasp as they came through this doorway, for the room they entered was quite the most splendid thing he had ever seen. The walls were of pure white marble, with tracery work in filigree silver and green; the ceiling was made of carved, beaten metal in silver and blue; the floor was carpeted in magnificent ancient rugs; and a long, painted banner depicting a Court pavilion, with a regal-looking woman sitting on a blue dais, was hung on a rod from the back wall. There was little furniture, other than a carved sandalwood chest in one corner and, before the painted banner on a raised dais, two chairs made of carved teakwood, inlaid with silver and blue and green stones. On the chairs sat two men, the Sultan and his son, the Crown Prince.

Adi did not look twice at the occupants of the chairs. He had dropped to his knees, head bent. Beside him, however, the Shayk stood straight, unmoving. No one spoke for a moment; then a low, rich voice broke the silence.

"Welcome, Adi," said the voice. Adi raised his head. To his astonishment, he saw that just behind the Sultan's chair stood a woman. She had a beautiful, ageless face, with deep dark eyes, and silver hair that was held back under a magnificent headdress of blue and green and silver. She was dressed in a shimmering sarong that looked as though it had been dipped in liquid moonlight and sea-foam, and on one of her well-shaped fingers, a great white ring glittered. Adi did not want to stare, but he could not help it. She looked exactly like the woman depicted on the painted banner behind her head. She was . . .

"Queen Rorokidul," he murmured rather uneasily.

Rorokidul gave him a thin smile. "My human husband, the Sultan, has not been mindful of his vows. The time is very near." She vanished, and Adi was left staring stupidly at the spot behind the Sultan's head where she had been.

"You may rise, child," said a kind voice, and, starting, Adi saw that the Sultan himself was beckoning him forward. He scrambled nervously to his feet. The Sultan was a rather small, rather tubby middle-aged man with a thick head of glossy black hair and a round, kind face. He sported smart glasses, behind which his eyes shone with an irrepressible twinkle. The Sultan was clothed not in traditional dress, but in a pale gray business suit and shiny leather shoes. On one of his pudgy fingers glittered a great white ring, exactly like the one the Queen had worn.

Prince Yanto was as short as his father, but as

cadaverously thin as his father was comfortably well-fleshed, and as serious-looking as his father looked cheerful. His eyes burned with the light of dedication and study. He was dressed in a similar style to the Shayk, in a spotless white robe and turban. A thin silver chain, at the end of which hung a small medallion similar to the one Sadik wore, was his only ornament.

"Well, well, child," said Sultan Sunan Tengah. In his cheerful voice there was not a trace of the languid disdain one might have expected of a king of such ancient lineage. "I am glad to see you. Your master, Empu Wesiagi, is a great friend of mine, and I am concerned for his safety." Then he looked directly at the Shayk. "And I have heard a great deal about you, Shayk Rasheed al-Jabal, from my son. He speaks most highly of you." At these words, Prince Yanto smiled.

"I think you will find, Father, that the Shayk is more than worthy of my words." His gaze at the Shayk was not that of a prince to an inferior, Adi noticed, but the humble gaze of a disciple to his master.

"I am most grateful that you have succored my young servant, Adi," continued the Sultan to the Shayk. "This will not be forgotten."

"Your Majesty, you do me too much honor."

Adi breathed an inward sigh of relief. At least the

Shayk knew how to talk to royalty, despite his words in the courtyard.

"Not at all. Credit must be given where credit is due. Besides, my son has often wished me to visit your community; perhaps it is time I did." The Sultan smiled. "I've been told you have achieved real results and don't just turn out preachers. We don't need more tedious preachers, but people who actually get things done."

Prince Yanto's eyes widened. He cast a pleading look at the Shayk, who merely smiled. Adi waited uneasily for the Shayk's reply. The old man merely said, coolly, "You are quite right, Your Majesty. I feel exactly the same myself. And it would be a very great honor to host you, Sire. We will prepare for this most important event, whenever Your Majesty wishes it."

"Good. Now, I wish to hear everything that has happened."

"My Lord," said the Shayk quietly, "what we have to say should not be heard by any ears other than your own and those of His Highness Prince Yanto." He looked meaningfully at the guards.

The Sultan clapped loudly. "Guards! Go, leave us alone. Close the door behind you." He waved at Adi and the Shayk. "Now. Before we begin, there is something I must tell you. Adi, your master, Empu Wesiagi, was not coming here just to give me the kris he had made. He had learned something about the truth behind the terrible things that have been happening in Jayangan." The Sultan's eyes suddenly sharpened. "You see, he had begun to convince me that we have a very serious problem, and so I had entrusted him with the task of finding out more. He had learned much from his contacts with other wise men and women. He was journeying here to lay it all before me, because he did not trust any other way of communicating. It had to look like a normal journey, and yet he was nervous."

"*That* is why we went by back roads and little routes," said Adi.

"Did he manage to tell you anything, Your Majesty, before he disappeared?" said the Shayk.

"No, nothing at all. He only thought it safe to tell me in person. So, now, begin. I want to hear it all. Don't leave out anything."

TWENTY-ONE

DEWI AND HUSAM hurried down the tunnel. The light got brighter and brighter, but it was a curious light that seemed to fall in strips, as if it were partly blocked. It reminded them both of something else—the way the light had fallen back at the mouth of the cave. When they finally reached the end of the tunnel, they realized that this was indeed the case. The mouth was blocked by a large, oddly shaped boulder. It looked immovable, but nevertheless, Husam put an exploratory shoulder to it. He winced. "Just as I thought. It won't budge, little heart."

Dewi's heart sank. To come so far and be blocked by a simple stone! She tried to mind-speak to the guardians of the ancient tombs, but there was only silence. A sense of oppression engulfed Dewi. She had to get back out into the air; she could not stand being underground anymore! She clutched the tiger's claw and spoke aloud. "Please, Lady Kwanyin. Queen Rorokidul. Lord Bupatihutan." Nothing. The spirits were not answering. Her voice rose, ringing with a sudden panic. "Fire! Kareen Amar! Help us! Help us!"

Husam tried to hush her. "You don't know what's beyond there. You . . ." A knocking sound came to their ears, sharp and metallic.

Dewi and Husam looked at each other. Dewi was about to speak when the sound came again, louder and more distinct. It sounded like metal on stone. They looked at each other again. "Oh," said Husam quietly, "I think we should move back."

Again came that sharp sound. And then, quite distinct, a human voice, an old man's voice, filled with terror. "God preserve us from evil spirits. God preserve us, for we have done no wrong."

Throwing caution to the winds, Dewi shouted, "We are not evil spirits! We are prisoners, trapped in here. Help us, please!"

There was silence. Then the voice quavered, "Who are you?"

"Dewi, dukun's daughter, and Husam al-Din," said Dewi, much to Husam's consternation.

"You are the dukun's daughter?" The voice had changed. Now it sounded full of a wild joy. "Wait. Wait! I will be quick!"

"Oh, little heart," said Husam into the silence that followed, "I hope you know what you are doing."

"Not at all," said Dewi, with a forced little laugh, "but we cannot stay here to starve to death, Husam, and there is no other way out."

"No, there isn't, but who knows what we will find out there, and who will greet us, and why they sounded so happy to hear who you were?"

Dewi did not answer, for there was no sense in doing so. The same fears were passing through her mind, the same terror that she had entirely done the wrong thing. Time passed, and still nothing happened. Then all at once, the metallic sounds started again, much louder this time. A low hum, rather like wordless chanting, accompanied them. Then came a deafening crack that made Dewi and Husam jump, a loud screeching and groaning, and suddenly the boulder seemed to turn, to roll away as if on hinges, and Husam and Dewi were pulled out, blinking and blinded and almost deaf, into sunlight. Behind them, the boulder twisted again, and fell back against the entrance of the tunnel with a mighty crash, sealing it shut.

They were in a great quarry, cut into a hill, rocky and bleak. High white and gray walls of stone rose sheerly above them. There were several people clustered in a ring around them. They had heavy chains at their waists, around their ankles, and loosely at their wrists, so they clanked as they moved: the sound Husam and Dewi had heard in the tunnel. They were holding picks they had obviously just been breaking stones with. They were all strangers to Dewi. Except one. And that one, for a paralyzed moment, Dewi could only stare at—for it was her father.

Bapar Wiriyanto's face bore the unmistakable marks of suffering. One eye was shut, puffed and angry-looking; there were bruises and cuts and a deep slash on his cheeks, and his hands were cut and bruised as well. But he was smiling, his eyes filled with immense love and joy. He said nothing, only opened his arms wide. Suddenly unfrozen, Dewi flew into them, tears running down her cheeks. He felt thinner, more fragile; but he was warm, he was real, he was alive! For a few moments, the world seemed to stop around them as they held each other tightly. Then Bapar Wiriyanto gently disengaged himself from Dewi and turned to Husam. "Forgive us, sir."

"Nothing to forgive," said Husam gruffly, with a telltale glitter in his eyes. "Nothing at all."

"Father," said Dewi tenderly, looking into his face, "Father, you are hurt. What have they done to you, Father?"

"Nothing that won't heal," said the dukun with an attempt at lightness. "I am just a little bruised and battered, but still alive for the moment. Unlike too many of our fellows, whose broken bodies have been left to rot where they fell."

Dewi swallowed. "Father, Anda Mangil . . . he . . . he was killed . . . by them."

Her father put a hand to his head. "My poor friend," he said softly. "My poor, innocent Anda Mangil." He looked away, overcome. "We cannot allow him to have died in vain," he said in a muffled voice. "We just cannot."

"That we will not, sir!" said Husam firmly.

The dukun's eyes flicked over to the old executioner.

"Father, this is Husam al-Din. He is a dear friend too," said Dewi. "He saved me from the hantumu."

"Husam al-Din, I am most pleased to meet you, sir. I am Wiriyanto." The two men shook hands. "I thank you greatly, Husam al-Din, for being my daughter's companion and helping her," said the dukun gravely. "I am ashamed that I was taken so easily, and was not able to protect her and Adi as I should. So I am most grateful to you, Husam al-Din."

"It is I who am most grateful," said Husam. "I had been away from the world too long, selfishly enjoying my last years fishing, while Jayangan was attacked by the forces of evil. If I can be of any use in this great task, then I am grateful." He smiled impishly. "Besides, I am finding that I missed the excitement of being in the world."

"Husam," said the dukun thoughtfully. "That is a name from Al Aksara, the Great Desert, isn't it? Having traveled there in my youth, I know a little of your language, sir—surely *Husam* means Sword?"

"Yes," said Husam. Leveling a steady gaze at Wiriyanto, he said, "It was also how I lived my life, sir, by the sword. I was the official executioner to the old Sultan."

"Ah," breathed the dukun, his eyes locking on Husam's. "I see."

"We have found Fire, too," Dewi gabbled. "She is a Jinn, Father."

"A Jinn!" the dukun exclaimed, his eyes shining. "Of course—they are creatures of fire, being made of the smokeless flame."

"Snow we haven't found yet."

"And Adi? Where is he?" said the dukun, seeming to notice the boy's absence for the first time.

"I don't know, Father," said Dewi miserably. "We became separated."

The dukun sighed. "Why were you in that place, the

ancient burial ground of the Old Ones?"

"We were helped by their spirit-guide. The afreet had left us to die." Rapidly, she told him the story, and he nodded.

"Ah. That is a great thing indeed."

"Father," said Dewi, "how did you know to help us? It was you, humming, wasn't it, that caused the boulder to open?"

The dukun nodded. "Bupatihutan came to me," he said. "He told me you were in need. He showed me what I should do."

Dewi, opening her hand, showed her father the tiger's claw. "But I called on him earlier, in the cave, and he didn't answer."

"He could not while you were in there," said her father. "The spirits of the Old Ones are more ancient even than his people, and he cannot command them to do anything. His power does not extend into such places. The Old Ones were good people, though everyone hereabouts has forgotten that, and fears them as evil ghosts. That's why it is safe for them to hold us captive here; the local people are so scared of this place, they would never come looking around. The Sorcerer's servants cannot enter into the burial tunnel of the Old Ones, for it is of very old magical protection, and they cannot break the seal."

"You know quite a lot about it, then, sir?" said Husam.

"Together we have an understanding of this place," said the dukun, "but we cannot escape." He pointed to a hole in the quarry, some distance away. "In there are the stone cages where they keep us at night. We cannot escape; the walls are too steep for a chained man to climb. And the Sorcerer's magic negates our own, so we cannot use it—he has set a shield against it. I was able to help you then only because both Bupatihutan and the spirits of the Old Ones wanted it."

"But why are they holding you, Father? Why haven't they . . ." Her voice broke.

The dukun said gently, "Why they haven't killed us? They kill those who resist too strongly or who have learned too much about the Sorcerer and his plans. The Sorcerer thinks he may learn something from the rest of us, or that he will win us over to his cause. He has already tried to do so, by sweet ways and bitter ones."

"Father, do you know who the Sorcerer is?"

"He is a man, that I know," said the dukun bitterly, "but he has never shown his face to us. He comes veiled and disguised to watch and listen as his servants interrogate and torture us. I have seen him order the execution of those who tried to resist or escape. There is no mercy or compassion in that creature's heart, only a burning desire to remake the world in his own image. That is what we know of him." He paused. "But I am lacking in both manners and courtesy, my friends," he went on, turning to the other prisoners, "for I have not even introduced you. Will you forgive me?"

"Hmph, Wiriyanto, we know you well." A bright-faced man with a pronounced limp who stepped forward, chains rattling, laughed. "We know you find it hard to stop talking. I am Bapar Suyanto," he went on, turning to Dewi and Husam. "I am a musician, from Kotabunga."

So this was the man they were to have met when they first arrived in Kotabunga. "I am very glad to meet you, Bapar Suyanto."

"And I you, Dewi. Your father has told us much about you. You make him proud, Dewi."

Dewi blushed. "Thank you."

"And you, Husam al-Din. I am pleased to meet you."

"And I you," said Husam heartily, and they bowed to each other.

"I am Ibi Timur, bird witch, from Demityangan." A small, fat woman with a broken nose and bright amber-colored eyes gravely stepped forward. "It is an honor to meet you both," she said in a very deep voice. Dewi looked at her in awe; she had heard of the bird witches of the great forest of Demityangan in the east, but never met one before.

"I am Agung, hermit from Priangan," said another woman, as tall and thin as Timur was short and fat. Dewi was startled to see she was blind. "The spirits of the mountain bless you." Priangan was the mystic mountain in the west of Jayangan, home of some of the remotest and shyest of Jayangan spirits. To be blessed by them was a rare honor indeed.

"I am Shayk Abdullah Kitab, teacher, who lives near the Tomb of the Five Saints," said a stooped old man in a quavering voice—the voice they had first heard in the tunnel. "God preserve you, daughter! We are glad you are safe." The Tomb of the Five Saints was a famous pilgrimage site for Mujisals.

"And I am Empu Wesiagi, kris maker, from Jatimur." A big, broad man with the brawny shoulders and forearms of a blacksmith smiled at them. What that smile cost him one could only imagine, for like Bapar Wiriyanto, Empu Wesiagi had evidently been badly treated; his face was a mass of bruises and cuts, and several of his teeth had been broken.

"Oh! You are Adi's master, the great kris-smith," Dewi breathed.

"Well, others say I am great, but I know I am still learning," he said lightly. "I am Adi's master. One day he'll be a very great kris-smith indeed."

Dewi burst out, "I wish he were with me now. He would be glad to know you are alive, sir. He was afraid, very much afraid."

"He was right to be," said the kris maker. "I do not know how much longer they will keep us in life." He looked at Dewi's father, who seemed to take it as his cue.

"Is there any chance—did you go to see the Sultan at all, Dewi?"

"No."

"You and Husam must go to Kotabunga—leave us here, and don't even try to help us escape. We are not important right now. We are sure the Sorcerer is about to strike at the very heart of our country."

"But Father, Father, we cannot leave you."

"Look, my dearest child, if this Sorcerer is not stopped, he will enslave all of Jayangan and destroy everything that is dear to us."

"And he has learned exactly what it is that will be needed to defeat him," put in Shayk Abdullah Kitab earnestly. "He has learned—and so he will seek to use those things against the forces of good. That is why he is so dangerous."

"But does that mean he can use Snow, Fire, and Sword against us?" asked Dewi, casting an anxious look at Husam. "That cannot be so, because Sword is with me, and Fire is safe, and Snow . . . we haven't yet found Snow."

"He will seek to neutralize those forces in some way," said the kris maker. "Or he will attempt to destroy them; or he will turn them in some way, with tricks and deception."

"This is why you must leave at once, and go to the palace of Kotabunga to put everything to the Sultan," said Dewi's father. "If the Sultan is not warned, the Sorcerer will have an advantage of surprise that will be difficult to overcome." He paused and looked deep into his daughter's eyes. "Now listen. The sun is into afternoon, and our guards will be returning to bring us our food very soon. Up there, on the western wall of the pit, Bapar Suyanto's keen eyes have seen a breach you may climb; and behind it, according to the keen ears of Shayk Abdullah, is a stream that you should walk along. This stream will take you to a remote, protected village, as Ibi Timur has seen in a dream; and Agung has pronounced that these people are good people, if a little strange, and will help you, if you follow their lead. Now go, at once, Dewi and

Husam, and don't look back."

"Father, I can't just leave you like this."

"Do not be afraid. You must not worry about us. God willing, we will be safe."

Dewi gulped. She said, "Father, please, I want to give you back your talisman. At least then I'll feel a little better." She held out the tiger's claw. He did not take it, shaking his head. "Please, Father, it's for you and the others. I have Sword, I have Fire, I'll find Snow. Please, you must have this! They might well come and kill you now," she pleaded, almost in tears. She saw a vision of Bupatihutan rising up behind her father, placing a clawed hand lightly on his shoulder. Her father's eyes widened. Wordlessly, he nodded and took the talisman. He looked at her.

"Thank you, my dear child," he whispered. Behind his shoulder, Bupatihutan nodded too, his yellow eyes fixed on Dewi. Then he vanished.

"Now, please, my daughter, you must go. Please. Go!" Her father's eyes filled with tears; then he mastered himself, turned his back deliberately, and said to the others, "We should get back to breaking those stones, before the birds of the air wonder why it is so quiet here and gossip about it too widely."

Husam put a hand on Dewi's shoulder. "Come,

little heart," he said softly. "Your father's courage and honor cannot be cast aside. You must do as he asks you."

And so, heavyhearted, leaden limbed, Dewi turned away from her beloved father and his fellow captives and began the painful slog up the steep rocky wall of the quarry.

TWENTY-TWO

THE SULTAN AND the Prince listened in silence to Adi's story. When he had finished, the Sultan stayed for a while in deep thought, the twinkle in his eye replaced by an uncommon gravity. Then he said, "Yanto, my son, bring out what came for us this morning." The tone in his voice was now steely and determined; it also held an element of fear.

Yanto rose from his chair and went to the sandalwood chest. In the silence that hung expectantly in the room, he reached into the chest and took out something wrapped in silk. He brought it to his father, who, also in silence, unwrapped it.

"Oh, dear God in Heaven," gasped Adi. There, lying on the silk, was the kris he and his master had made together for the Sultan. It had been such a beautiful thing, its blade so finely tempered, its red-gilt hilt and scabbard decorated with the crown of the Sultan. And now it lay in pieces, the blade snapped into three bits, the hilt and scabbard scratched and defaced.

Quite forgetting his awe in front of the Sultan, Adi said, "Who did this? How did it get here?"

It was Prince Yanto who answered. 'One of the guards on duty early this morning said it was delivered by a masked man dressed all in black, riding a motorbike. He vanished before he could be arrested."

"Now, what you have told me, Adi," said the Sultan, "makes me understand: The one who has your master also had this delivered. It is a message to us, see. . . ." And here he beckoned Adi and the Shayk forward. He pointed to a place on the defaced scabbard. "Look at the crown."

Adi's flesh crawled as he saw what had been done to his carving: The crown had a great jagged line running through it, and what were clearly meant to be drops of blood, flowing from the place where it had been cleaved.

"This message is for me and my family," said the Sultan. "I understood it this morning as an insult, an empty threat. Now, after listening to you, I know it is more than that. It is a declaration of war by the master of the hantumu. He must believe he and his henchmen are invulnerable; otherwise, why deliver such a thing in broad daylight? He intends to strike at the very heart of power in this land, at my own family, my own power. I had hoped it was not so. I wanted my reign to be peaceful and prosperous, but now I see such hopes were in vain and that we must confront this threat directly." He turned to his son. "Yanto! You are to make sure that the guard is doubled on all the gates; make sure my elite soldiers are called up too. We do not know yet when the enemy will attack, but we must be ready, for nothing is surer, it seems to me, than that they will attack."

"Your Majesty," said Adi, "what of Snow, Fire, Sword? They were to help us in this task. We have Snow here already, if I am right, so perhaps we should endeavor to find Fire and Sword."

"I do not think we have time," said the Sultan. "We have to gather together as many fighting men as possible. That must be the first thing of all."

"Sire, if I may?" The Shayk spoke quietly, yet with a certain authority. "If I am indeed Snow—and, like Adi, I hope I am—perhaps I could help in this task by gathering together as many of my men as is possible. We knew it would come to this one day, that we would have to fight against the Demons' Army, and my boys have been well trained. May I propose my fighters help you?"

"That is very kind," said the Sultan doubtfully, "but you are a holy teacher, not a trainer of warriors. They are far away, are they not, and—"

"Father, I can vouch for the valor of the Shayk's men," broke in Yanto. "They are God's people, fighting for the truth; they are stern enemies of the demons. The Shayk is a great warrior as well as a great teacher. And if we are swift, they will be here in time. Grant permission, please, for us to take helicopters back to Gunungbatu and fetch the Shayk's fighters."

"Oh, very well. It can't hurt. I thank you, Shayk, for your offer, though I am not at all sure we will need your fighters, my soldiers being very well trained and utterly loyal." He cast a rather mischievous look at his son. "How can they not be, when my son has been overseeing them?"

"Thank you, Father, but I think you will be pleasantly surprised to see how good the Shayk's fighters are."

"Is that so? Good, good. You seem to be a most useful man, Shayk Rasheed. Just what we need in these troubled times."

"The Sultan does me much honor," said the Shayk with a faint smile. "I shall go with the Prince to get my men. I will leave my second-in-command, Ibrahim, here in Kotabunga with you, Sire."

"Do as you wish," said the Sultan. "You are a good and brave man, and I thank you."

Adi thought of the boys and men at the community. Was it true they were good fighters, or was that just what the Shayk and his disciple Yanto believed? Some of them looked surly and aggressive, but had any of them, besides maybe Ibrahim, Jamal, and Ali, looked like they might know how to fight, like real soldiers? He thought of Sadik. He was a nice person, but a word fighter, surely, with no experience? And none of them would have seen the hantumu—they had no idea what terror these things struck in you. How could a gaggle of farmers and disciples, brought up in a peaceful village community, know how to fight such creatures? The Shayk himself was an extraordinary man, no doubt able to hold his own, and so was Ibrahim and perhaps Jamal and Ali. But the rest? He had seen nothing to really convince him.

He started. Everyone was looking at him. It was apparent that the Sultan had said something to him, but he had not heard. "Forgive me, Your Majesty, I did not hear . . ."

"I asked you, Adi, what you were going to do."

"Me, Sire?" This time, he was not going to be protected. He was not going to be trapped in safety while those about him risked their lives. "I will stay here, Sire, with you," he said. "The spirits told us we must find Snow, Fire, and Sword. We now know why: to fight the Sorcerer. How we are to do it we still are not sure, but if the Shayk is Snow in his purity and goodness and whiteness, then his task has been decided by his own heart, and he will bring his men here. Perhaps Sword and Fire cannot be found just by looking for them; they must be recognized, understood, in one's own heart. And so perhaps I can be Sword, if I am given one. I do not know how to use a gun, Sire, but my master has taught me how to use a kris. I can help to protect you from the plots of the Sorcerer. We need only find Fire—and perhaps we have done so already, Sire, in the fire of our own resolve." He caught the Shayk's glance then, and saw surprise and admiration shining there. It warmed him.

"Hmm," said the Sultan. "You are a brave young man. I appreciate . . . er . . . your offer. But you are very young, and . . ."

Adi shook with a nervous excitement. The words flowed from him, direct from his heart: "Sire, we had wondered, Dewi and I, why we were chosen by the spirits for this task. Anda Mangil, a man whose courage I greatly honor, told us it was because we were children of modern Jayangan, and that it is not only the past that is under attack, but the present and future, too. Your Majesty, we are young, and the future will be what we make of it. I love my country. I have seen what this evil man has already done. I do not want him ruling our future. I will do whatever is needful, and will fight to the last breath to protect you, Sire. For you are the Sultan of Jayangan, the heart of law in our land, and if the Sorcerer harms you, he harms all of Jayangan."

There was a long silence. The Sultan stared at Adi. There were tears in the ruler's eyes. Then, suddenly, he smiled. "You are a brave, loyal young man," he said. "I thank you from the bottom of my heart. I will never, ever forget it. How I wish all in Jayangan were as true as you!"

"I have other men here already, with Ibrahim, waiting outside the palace," put in the Shayk smoothly. "They can support Adi. It would be best, Sire, if you kept to quarters that can easily be defended."

"I was brought up to fight too," the Sultan responded quietly. "I do not need your men, Shayk. Ibrahim may stay, to help Adi. The others would be best off going with you, to rally your fighters."

The Shayk smiled and nodded.

"I am not an old woman," the Sultan continued rather crossly, "to crouch behind walls when my kingdom is threatened. Yanto, there is no need to look at me like that. I know what your eyes are saying. I have a responsibility to my people. I must be there for them.

I will stay here, but not cooped up. I am not afraid. I am the commander of my people."

"Of course, Father," said Yanto gently, "but do you give me permission, sir, to go with the Shayk to Gunungbatu to get his men?"

"As you wish," said the Sultan, "but remember your own responsibility. You are my eldest son, the Crown Prince, the future of Jayangan. Don't throw it away in absurd heroics."

"Of course not, Father," said Yanto, bending his head, but not before Adi had seen the same light of excitement and nerves that was in his own eyes. At last! The wait would be over, battle would be joined. Nothing was surer, thought Adi, anxious and thrilled all at once. There was no need to worry anymore about the meaning of what the spirits had said. Snow, Fire, and Sword were what they made of them. They were qualities of heart—true companions. He was doing this for all who had tried to fight and were carried off or killed—for Dewi, for Anda Mangil, for his Empu Wesiagi, for Dewi's father, and for all those people he did not know who were already victims of the Sorcerer's war against the land of Jayangan. He would be fighting for them all. And the thought strengthened his heart, and his soul.

TWENTY-THREE

IT WAS NOT an easy scramble to the top of the pit, avoiding loose rocks and treacherous holes—but what was even harder, for Dewi, was not looking back. Her head was full of the last sight of her father; her heart trembled at the possibility that she might never see him again in this life. Something precious and irreplaceable, perhaps the innocence of childhood, was ripped away from her forever with every painful, stumbling step she took. The other frightening and horrible things that had happened since radical evil came crashing into the lovely, safe little world of Bumi Macan seemed almost as nothing now beside this: She was leaving her father behind her, perhaps to share in the sad fate of Anda Mangil and so many others who had died.

Almost everything in her screamed at her to turn back, to stay with the captives. Yet she knew, deep down, that she could not do that. Her father did not want her to. He had made his choice, and as his loving daughter she must respect that. If she disobeyed, then they would have no hope of saving her father and his friends, and the Sorcerer would win.

With their enemies assuming the spirit-lizard had destroyed them, there was a tiny chance Dewi and Husam might get to Kotabunga in time to prevent or at least affect what was about to happen. They could concentrate only on that. Any other way meant failure, without question. She and Husam must not be taken by the hantumu or the afreet again. They would surely be killed this time.

Husam toiled behind her, staying silent, out of deference to her feelings, or perhaps just from sheer tiredness. Dewi would normally have felt tired too, but she did not at the moment; it was as if she were carried up automatically, like a machine.

When they finally reached the top of the pit, they stopped briefly. They would have to be very careful scrambling down the vertiginous slope on the other side. At the bottom of the bare, rocky hill was a thin silver stream. They started off down the slope without a word, sometimes having to almost crawl down, sometimes stumbling and falling over loose scree that rattled under their feet. Once, Husam fell very heavily indeed, and Dewi had to quickly come to his aid. There was blood on his forearm where he had fallen against sharp rock, and his face looked a little gray as he got shakily to his feet, but he managed to say, "It's nothing . . . nothing . . . we must hurry . . . hurry . . ."

At length, they were at the bottom of the hill, and they saw that a little distance along, the stream had been coaxed into a stone irrigation channel. Ibi Timur was right—the stream must lead to a village. If they followed the channel, they would come to it. After a much-needed drink of the cool, clear water, Dewi looked back once, at the quarried mountain rearing high above them, and shuddered, thinking of the men and women trapped in that strange place.

Dewi and Husam walked precariously along the side of the irrigation channel. For a while, it was the only sign of human habitation; but soon they began to see others. A tiny garden clung to a small green patch by the side of the channel; skinny sheep began to poke curious, yellow-eyed heads from behind rocks; and then they came in sight of a shepherd boy, his back to them, sitting on a rock by the edge of the channel, whittling at something and whistling. Dewi couldn't help stopping when she recognized the tune he was whistling, for it was "Beloved."

The boy must have heard a loose stone or something

under their feet, for he whipped around and stared at them. Before he could speak, though, Dewi came toward him, saying urgently, "Please, don't be afraid. We mean no harm."

"You came from Old Mountain, didn't you?" said the boy, wide-eyed. "Are you ghosts, or demons?"

"We are neither," said Husam. "We need help."

"Oh," said the boy, sighing. "I was hoping I might see the ghosts or the demons people talk of. It would be exciting; nothing ever happens here."

"You don't want to see those sorts of things, believe me," said Husam, catching Dewi's eye.

"Oh, but I do," he went on cheerfully. "Then, if you're not ghosts or demons, I suppose you must be one of them."

"Them?"

"Beloved strangers, of course," said the boy, looking curiously at Husam. "Have you forgotten all the while you've been in the Mountain?"

Dewi and Husam looked at each other, perplexed, but all Dewi said was, "Please, friend, is there a village nearby?"

"Of course. You know that. The Stone Village. That's where my father comes from."

"We have forgotten," said Husam hollowly, "in our long sojourn in the Mountain. Where is it?"

The boy looked at him, something like awestruck fear now merging with his impatient curiosity. "So you are them!" Hurriedly, he went on. "It's just up there," he said, pointing to a little slope of scrubbily forested hill above where he sat. "Through the forest, through the doorway. I can't take you there or my father would skin me alive for leaving the sheep on their own."

"Of course," said Husam. "Thank you, boy."

"Not at all," said the boy, still staring at them; and they could feel his eyes on their backs as they turned away from him and went up the hill.

The forest the boy had spoken of was not much of a forest, but more of a haphazard collection of scabby, twisted trees and stunted bushes. What made it really strange were the stone pillars and boulders lining the narrow path through it. Set at irregular intervals, they loomed above Dewi and Husam like unsteady, giant guards. Dewi could not hide her amazement. She had never seen such things before. When she put her hand on one, she felt that same strange hum she had felt when she had touched the belly of the great lizard in the cave, and when they were in the tunnel. The stones were very old, she thought, old as the dawn of time.

She and Husam walked quietly for a while; Husam, too, seemed taken with a strange, wary awe as he made his way through the crooked line of stones. Then

Husam whispered, "If this village that bird witch saw in her vision was lost to the world, I hope we will not be."

"No," said Dewi, "that boy almost seemed to expect us."

"We'll have to be careful," said Husam. "I'm not sure I like all this. I hope we haven't gone from bad to worse. Who's to know where the Sorcerer really is? And this place—these stones feel sorcerous to me."

Dewi was about to say something in reply when Husam suddenly shouted, "Get down! Get down!" and pulled her flat down on the ground. In the next moment, she understood why, for a throbbing roar filled the sky above them. Several vast shadows passed across the sun, a wind howling behind them, bending the bushes and trees. The roar became louder, the shadows bigger, the wind shrieked; then it all passed, fading into the distance, to be followed seconds later by more roars, more black shadows, and a howling wind.

After a short while, Dewi and Husam crept out of the bushes and looked at each other. "Well," said Husam, "that shepherd boy will either have been startled or excited out of the little wits he had!"

"They were helicopters," Dewi cried. "What were they doing here?"

"The hantumu use motorbikes," said Husam. "Why

not helicopters? Perhaps they're looking for us?"

"Why should they be? They don't know we've escaped," said Dewi, trying to sound more confident than she felt. "Perhaps they've come to rescue the prisoners."

Husam grimaced. "Still, let's keep in the bushes. Afreets can't see well in vegetation, and the stones will also put it and the hantumu off, if they are afraid or wary of the old things. Let's hope this village is close enough, and that someone can take us quickly where we want to go."

They reached the village a few minutes later, without further incident. It was a very small place and quite ordinary, mostly, just a cluster of some ten or fifteen bark-and-stick huts surrounding a central pavilion that was the most cheerful and upright building there. What made it unusual was that the buildings, and the gardens around them, were entirely surrounded by a vast stone circle. Some of the stones were like those on the path, tall or squat single pieces; but there were one or two that looked like gigantic tables—two uprights with a huge slab laid horizontally across. It gave the whole place a very strange atmosphere, the giant stones looming over the humble little houses, once again like giant guards watching speechlessly through uncounted centuries.

There were people working in the gardens—men and women dressed in seamless robes of various pale colors, with sashes around their waists. Their hair was braided, they wore conical hats, and their faces were decorated with various designs in blue and green. They stood up from their work and looked at Husam and Dewi as they drew near. There was an expectancy, a lack of surprise, on their faces that reminded them of the reaction of the shepherd boy. The first words spoken to them only confirmed that.

"Good afternoon, beloved strangers," said a woman standing at the center of the group. Small and stout, she had an air of purpose and determination about her that suggested she was someone of importance and character. "Welcome here once more among us."

Dewi and Husam looked swiftly at each other. Follow their lead, Agung had said. "Er . . . thank you," Husam said at last. "Could you help us, kind lady? We need to get to Kotabunga, to see the Sultan, as soon as possible."

It was the woman's turn to look at her companions. They all wore startled expressions. Then the woman said, "Beloved strangers, we must confer, if you will forgive us."

"Of course," said Dewi, but the woman paid no attention, for she had turned away at once to huddle in confabulation with her companions.

"These are strange people," said Husam under his breath to Dewi. "I do not understand them at all."

Dewi nodded. "It is as if they were expecting us in some sense," she said.

The woman turned back to face them and said, "Beloved strangers! We understand what you are doing. You are testing us in some way, and though we know you could stretch your wings and fly halfway around the world should you so desire it, we know you are conferring on us a great honor by asking us thus to come to your aid." As Dewi and Husam stared at her, stunned, she went on cheerfully. "And so I, Kembang, headwoman of this village, am charged to tell you this: We will indeed offer up the speeda you left behind last time so you can reach Kotabunga." She beamed at them. They could only goggle back at her for a minute. What on earth—or off it—did she think they were? And what was a speeda? There was no car in sight—in fact, no transport of any kind, not even a bicycle.

"Thank you," Dewi managed to say, when the silence had lengthened a little too long and the woman's happy smile was slowly being replaced by the beginnings of an nervous expression. "Thank you. That is very kind."

"We are happy, beloved strangers," said the

headwoman, with a funny little bow. "You have come from our sacred place, from Old Mountain, and we are honored. Please follow me."

As Dewi and Husam followed the swiftly striding woman, they saw that the other people in the gardens had drawn closer together, and that their gazes at the pair were an odd mixture of delight, awe, and anxiety. Dewi whispered to Husam, "They think we've come from that place, that we're from the place of the Old Ones, the people who helped us, who had those strange wings attached to them."

"Yes," Husam whispered back. "See the pillar in the middle of that pavilion, and the flowers on it? That's no Mujisal house of worship, or Nashranee—not even Dharbudsu. That's something I've only heard about, not seen—the old, old faith of Jayangan."

"These are the descendants of the people of that mountain," said Dewi, staring. "They think we're their ancestors, come back to life."

Kembang had stopped before one of the huts. She beckoned to them. "Come, beloved strangers." She looked excited and proud. They hurried over to her, and she led them into the darkness of the little hut.

When their eyes got used to the dimness, they saw that the hut was only one large room, simply furnished, with a table, a couple of chairs, a fireplace, a curtained alcove in a corner, a chest in another, and a tall shelf in yet another. On this shelf, in pride of place, stood a massive, old-fashioned wireless radio, an unexpected sight here. No doubt its presence explained why the shepherd boy, who lived in such a remote place, knew the tune of "Beloved."

The woman disappeared behind the curtain. Thumps and bumps issued from behind it, and Husam and Dewi looked at each other, mystified. Finally, the woman emerged, puffing, proudly dragging out the last thing they expected to see.

It was an ancient, heavy motorbike and sidecar. In the half-light of the hut, it gleamed softly. "Come outside, come, come," said Kembang happily. She bowed to Husam. "See, beloved stranger, we have looked after your speeda well."

Out in the full light, they understood why she called the machine that. The brand name of the company that had made it, and which must have gone out of business long ago, was emblazoned on it: Speeda.

"We always knew that one day you would come back for it," said Kembang. "It has been very kind to us, and we are glad you allowed us to use it for so long." She beamed at them. "But we always knew this speeda must one day return to its own place, so we looked after it for you."

"That is very good of you," said Husam, blinking a little. He looked at Dewi. She understood his glance—he was uncomfortable with this deception, even if it had been an involuntary one. Impulsively, she said, "Kembang, there is something we must tell you," and without stopping to draw breath, she told the head-woman all that had happened, especially what had happened in Old Mountain. Kembang listened intently, not interrupting once. When Dewi had finished, she said, "I see."

"We did not mean to deceive you," said Dewi nervously. "It was just that . . ."

Kembang shook her head. "Do not be concerned." To their surprise, her eyes were shining. "The Old Ones spoke to you? You saw them?"

Dewi nodded. Kembang clasped her hands. "You do not know how glad you make me. Oh, you might not be our beloved strangers, but you are beloved strangers just the same—just like the one who left us this speeda, before I was even born." She touched its gleaming metal affectionately and rather wistfully. "This has been good to us, but we understood it had to be returned one day."

"Kembang," said Husam gravely, "we make you this promise. This speeda is to be part of a great battle, but when that is over, it will be returned to you."

Kembang's eyes lit up, and she stroked the bike again. "Oh, beloved strangers," she said softly, "you speak of a great battle. Is that against the Lord of Shadows, the evil one?"

"Yes, it is," said Husam. "It is indeed."

"Then it is just as it should be, for our prophecies speak of such a battle," said Kembang decisively. She looked at them, her head on one side. "Beloved strangers, where have you taken Snow, Fire, and Sword? You will need them in the battle against the Lord of Shadows."

They stared at her. Then Dewi said, faltering a little, "We have Sword . . . and we know Fire . . . but Snow . . . Snow we haven't found a trace of."

Kembang nodded. "That is what the prophecy says. Snow is hard to find. And that is because Snow is antithetical to Fire. Only with Snow's death, melted by Fire, can life-giving Water be born, which will refresh the land. That is the meaning of Snow, do you see? Only by death can life come."

"How do you know . . . where did you . . ."

Kembang smiled. "We are far from the world, but we hear many things. And our spirits are ancient, very ancient, and know things from before the dawn of time. This battle is an important one. We, too, are a part of it somehow. We must not stand aside this time."

"That is so," said Husam. "No one can stand aside. This must be why the Old Ones helped us, in the mountain."

"That is what I thought." Then she looked worried. "We have survived before by hiding away from the world. We are few, and weak. It is hard to know how we can properly join in this fight without being destroyed."

Suddenly, an idea came to Dewi. She said, "Kembang—the wicked ones whom we are fighting, they are desecrating Old Mountain. They use the wiles and strength of demons to hollow it of its goodness. They held us prisoner in the cave of the Great Lizard, hoping it would devour us. And they are holding good people in the pit on Old Mountain, chained with heavy iron links."

"We heard noises there, but we thought it was demons."

"No, no, they are not demons, but good men and women, who are needed in our fight. Among them is my own father. So . . ."

"So you want us to go to Old Mountain," said the headwoman, with an expression in her eyes that Dewi found difficult to fathom. "You want us to go and free the captives?"

"Yes, and bring them back to your village, where

they can be safe," breathed Dewi. "That could be your part of the fight, if you will agree."

"This is a place where we have not set foot for many, many years," said Kembang. "Many generations ago, our people were numerous, our ways respected and shared by all. Then the changes came, and we were killed, driven out, our ways smudged, obscured, forgotten. Now there is only this village that remains, safe within the stones. We have not gone back to Old Mountain for a long, long time."

"Now is the time to go back," said Dewi.

"Yes," said Kembang, straightening. "You are right. It is time to go back." Her shoulders were squared. She said, "Beloved strangers, you honor us."

"No," said Dewi, "it is you who honor us. It is your honoring of memory that has meant that the demons cannot use Old Mountain as they wish. And your part in this task is a very great one. I would not know how to thank you, if you did this."

"Tchah," said Kembang, coloring and looking away. "There is no need for thanks. We will be glad." She reached into her clothes and brought out an ignition key, which she handed to Husam. He exchanged a questioning look with Dewi—would the bike actually work, would he be able to drive it?—but as if not at all concerned, he sat astride the bike, while Dewi clambered into the sidecar. He put the key in the ignition and started it. To their surprise, but to Kembang's beaming pride, it roared into life.

"My father's sons looked after it well," she said. "They took it sometimes on trips to town so we could sell our vegetables and eggs. This is how they earned money to feed it. They have not taken it for a long time, but I think it will take you quite far." She put out a hand and touched each of them, fleetingly, on the hand. "Good-bye, beloved strangers," she said softly. "We hope you will come back to us one day."

"We plan to," said Dewi heartily, thinking of her father.

Husam added, "And then we'll return the speeda, never fear."

Kembang nodded. "That is well. We will play our part, beloved strangers, for it is right we do." She stood back and, with the other villagers, watched Dewi and Husam trundle rather unsteadily out of the village on the purring machine.

Husam managed to keep the bike going in a more or less straight line, driving very slowly, till they were out of sight of the village, and then, cautiously, upped the speed. Fortunately, the path, though narrow and set between pillars and boulders, was straight and quite well made. Some distance from the village, the road dipped sharply downward, nearly unseating Husam and Dewi, and the pillars and boulders disappeared, as did the trees and bushes. They were now in open country, barren-looking fields on either side of them.

Neither of them spoke for a little while. Then Dewi said, shouting above the roar of the engine, "I wonder who left this motorbike with them?"

"It's an old thing," said Husam, "and Kembang said they acquired it before she was born. Its owner was probably a lost traveler—an intrepid explorer, a madman on a jaunt, who knows? It was ages ago, and he is doubtless long gone from this earth. What matters is that he left his machine there. It served them well; now it serves us. Truly, God is great!"

"Truly," said Dewi gravely.

"What worries me, little heart, is what Kembang said about Snow. If that is true, then we need Snow only to take him or her to their death. Kembang was very matter-of-fact, but I don't like the sound of it at all. Sacrificial lambs may be good bait for wolves, but it does not seem honorable to me. How can we fight evil if we know beforehand that one who is to be our companion will die? And how is it that it is Fire that will do it? Poor Kareen Amar—why should she have to be the death of a stranger?"

“She doesn’t *have* to . . .” began Dewi, but Husam snorted.

“She is of the Jinn. They are a people strongly devoted to fate, and prophecy.”

“Yet they have free will,” said Dewi steadily. “I remember reading that, in a book my father has. They can choose.”

“Well, yes, but Kembang was quite clear. Fire is to be the death of Snow.”

“The afreet is also made of fire,” snapped Dewi. Husam started. The motorbike juddered.

“Oops—sorry. Why, Dewi, you are quite right.”

“Oh, really, I know no more than you. I wish we’d never heard what Kembang said. But we did, and the knowledge can’t be wished away.” Oh, if only she could speak to her father about it right now! And how slow the bike was! “Can’t you go faster, Husam?” she shouted, but he shook his head.

“It’s going just as fast as it can, I think. It’s old, Dewi, like me, you know!”

TWENTY-FOUR

ADI RACED BACK through the corridors and courtyards to the entrance of the palace. Nobody stopped or challenged him, for it was bedlam. So much was going on—guards hurrying from one end of the palace to the other, the Sultan's servants rushing to barricade themselves in their quarters or streaming out of the palace toward the city—that nobody noticed him. This activity was not an impressive sight: not the sight and sound of people preparing themselves for battle, but a panic-stricken rush to find safety.

Adi ran, stomach churning, heart sinking. Despite the Sultan's brave words, it was obvious that nobody was ready for the invasion of the Sorcerer. Nobody knew where to look, what to expect. The Sultan had wasted precious time. At first he had refused to believe there was anything wrong, and even when Empu

Wesiagi had begun to convince him, he had kept it quiet. Perhaps he had thought he could deal with it in secret, behind closed doors. Now, he knew he could not. And so did his people. How they had found out so quickly he was not sure, but it was likely that the guards had been listening at the keyhole and spread the alarm. The country had been at peace for so long, and the palace guards had never experienced an insurrection or real trouble. Perhaps they had become soft.

He reached the palace gate and looked out. The square was a heaving mass of people and all kinds of transport—taxis, cars, trucks, buses, bikes, motorbikes, betchars, even horse-drawn carts, all milling around trying to funnel down the streets that led off the square and into the city. He searched the crowd, trying to see the Shayk's car, which had been parked under one of the trees at the edge of the square. Just then, screams and yells erupted from the crowd as two helicopters flew low above their heads, heading out of the city. There would be even more panic now, Adi thought. He looked wildly around and saw Ibrahim in the car, a little distance away. He had drawn his sword and was waving it out the window, and yelling at people around him, trying to get them to move, to make way so the car could get through. Adi wriggled through the crush of people, making for the fierce figure. But he was jammed in between columns of panicking people, and couldn't move backward or forward. He yelled, very loudly, "Ibrahim! Ibrahim! No, don't go! We have to stay here! The Sultan, the palace!"

Someone grabbed his elbow. It was Sadik. "What's going on, Adi?"

"The battle . . . the Sorcerer . . . it's going to start . . . the Shayk, he's gone with the Prince to fetch people, fetch fighters. He said Ibrahim should stay to help us here, in case the Sultan's attacked before they return."

Sadik's eyes widened. "I'll help too! I'll stay! I'll go and get Ibrahim. Wait." And he was off, elbowing his way through the crowd with remarkable self-possession and swiftness. Adi began to back away, toward the palace gates.

In a very short while, Sadik reappeared with Ibrahim at his side. The big man had moved quickly through the crowd—perhaps a drawn sword cleared people's minds wonderfully. Despite his earlier yelling, he looked quite calm and collected, his eyes shining with a savage glee. He was looking forward to this battle.

Adi explained rapidly what they had to do. Ibrahim looked faintly disgusted that he was just going to be a guard for the Sultan, but he nodded amicably enough, aware that his beloved master wanted it so. Sadik, however, was almost beside himself with excitement, chattering about how this was the greatest day of his life, that everything he had been taught in the community was coming true, that this was a great day for Jayangan, that evil would be defeated finally and the reign of goodness would come, and that the Shayk would be a national hero and honored fully, as he deserved.

"Wait," said Adi, rather disagreeably, into this flow of words. "We're not there yet. Look at the people out there in the city. They're panic-stricken; they're not going to fight. And they'll hamper us just by being there."

"They're panicking because they are afraid. And who wouldn't be?" said Sadik fiercely. "People know about the things that have been happening, and they've heard it's the most evil of all black magicians running those hantumu. They say he has evil spirits under his tutelage too, a whole army of demons!" He paused, and said softly, regretfully, "The Sultan should have done something long ago."

"Ha," said Ibrahim bitterly. "The Sultan cares a great deal for his own position and a peaceful life, and not much else. He has hidden from the truth because he is afraid of the reaction of his own people. And he's afraid of making decisions; he has held things off till it's nearly too late. It would be different if his son were in power. He understands the truth, and always has."

Adi stared at him. Such talk was sheer treason. It annoyed Adi deeply that an arrogant foreigner like Ibrahim should judge the Sultan of Jayangan and find him wanting, and all his pride boiled up at the insult. Yet Adi could find nothing to say to the fierce-eyed swordsman. How could he? Ibrahim looked quite capable of literally knocking his block off. Besides—he gazed despairingly around him at the running, shouting, shoving guards—he could not find it in his heart to wholeheartedly defend the Sultan, who had indeed been too slow in reacting to the signs, and too whimsical at a time of gathering danger.

Ibrahim glared at him. "You people are all the same," he said. "Bound by your foolish respect for human laws, you don't even see the nose in front of your face! You've forgotten what it means to be a warrior of the Light. You think you can make deals with the demons and they'll leave you alone. Well, the Shayk has always known that to be wrong. He was exiled for speaking the truth, and now the truth has come back to bite the complacent people of Jayangan!"

Adi's hand leaped to the kris at his side. He said hotly, "We fought evil in Jayangan long before your people ever deigned to set foot on our soil. How dare you think yourself better than us, just because you are from Al Aksara, as if there had never been any such troubles in your own lands? I have a hunch your master would not like what you are saying, and punish you for it."

Sadik gasped, but Ibrahim smiled thinly. "You are a fool, Jayangan boy, and you will pay dearly for it when this is finished and my master no longer needs you," he said coldly. Turning on his heel, he walked away from Sadik and Adi, toward the courtyard that led to the inner palace. Guards rushing toward the various entrances to the palace streamed around him, but his tall figure easily parted the crowds.

"Adi," said Sadik. "Adi, you shouldn't have said that. Ibrahim will—"

"I don't care," said Adi angrily. "How can you stand there listening to him? You are from Jayangan yourself. Did you like what he said?"

"No . . . no . . . but . . ."

"But nothing! It's all very well for him to criticize the Sultan and what he should or shouldn't have done," hissed Adi. "He didn't know anything himself, before, and neither did the Shayk," he went on, sharply, ignoring Sadik's obvious distress. "We have to be united in this, Sadik, not criticize one another when we are facing a common enemy. The Demon King has always used such dissension to further his own aims. Surely you know that!"

"Why, yes," said Sadik, "but my master—"

"Your master is a good man, but he should not employ people like Ibrahim," said Adi angrily. Ibrahim was the sort of Pumujisal who gave them all a bad name. He thought purity and holiness came from despising others.

"Please," said Sadik, and his eyes shone with tears. He put a timid hand on Adi's arm. "It's quite true what you say, about dissension only furthering the cause of demons, but please, Adi, you're doing that yourself, you're falling into their trap. Let's forget what Ibrahim said—it's not important, not compared to what we have to face. He's a good fighter, absolutely loyal to the Shayk. He's on our side, Adi. You musn't forget that. Please, Adi."

Adi held his gaze for an instant, then looked away. "Very well," he said gruffly. "You're right. It's not important, not right now." But it will be later, a tiny voice inside his head whispered. After all, Ibrahim hadn't liked Adi from the start, had mistrusted him on sight, had insulted him from the very beginning. Adi clenched his fists; then, catching sight of Sadik's anxious expression, he tried to smile. "Sorry, Sadik. You're quite right. Now come on. We'd better make sure that barbarian of an Ibrahim doesn't get run through straightaway by one of the Sultan's guards for speaking like that in public."

Sadik sighed but nodded. He followed Adi silently, dodging guards, who were now carrying armfuls of weapons—machine guns, rifles, pistols, flamethrowers, swords, krises—and positioning themselves at appropriate spots on the walls. A semblance of calm was beginning to return to the palace grounds, though there was still a great deal of tension in the air, and people were scurrying hither and thither. Adi and Sadik passed swiftly through the outer courtyards and into the interior ones and, at the door to the Sultan's quarters, were stopped by two enormous guards with blank, impassive faces, who carried some of the biggest guns Adi had ever seen, or even imagined. But the men had obviously been well briefed, for as soon as the boys told them their names, they nodded and let them pass through.

The Sultan's quarters were in a very large complex that comprised many different rooms, including quarters for the Queen, her female relatives, and the children, audience chambers such as the one Adi had been in earlier, and private rooms for the Sultan himself. There were guards here too, but also soldiers dressed in combat uniforms. Tough-looking, cold-faced men, the soldiers made Adi feel rather better, for they looked as if at least they deserved the Sultan's trust. The boys caught sight of Ibrahim deep in conversation with a couple of the soldiers; he appeared to be explaining something to them, and Adi smiled bitterly to himself, thinking the man was probably telling them how to do their job. He hoped they'd punch the insolent creature on the nose!

The guards took Adi and Sadik to a small room at one end of the complex, where the Sultan sat at a modest desk, writing. When they were announced, he turned around and smiled at them.

"Come in, shut the door." He put his pen down and motioned them to stand before his desk. Adi saw that beside the pen and pile of papers on the desk there was a two-way radio, a kris—a large, splendid weapon, very well sharpened and polished—and also a revolver.

"So the pair of you are to be my guards." The irrepressible smile sweetened the Sultan's round face. "You are so young to be so brave. I must say that though I have to believe in the reality of the threat we are facing, I can scarcely bring myself to realize that these things have actually come to pass." He waved a hand at the papers on his desk. "You cannot imagine the amount of paperwork such a thing consumes.

Decrees for this, licenses to do that. I had hoped never to have to sign such things. I dislike war and violence, utterly. I had hoped other methods . . ." He broke off, smiling tiredly at them. "Forgive me. I am ranting, and should not burden you. You are my guards, not my advisers."

"Oh, Your Majesty," said Adi impulsively, "I am honored that you should trust in us."

"And I," said Sadik. He had been wide-eyed the whole time they had rushed through the palace; here, in front of the Sultan himself, he seemed quite awestruck. Adi knew just how he felt. To be here, talking to the Sultan—well, as a child from a modest family, you never imagined something like this happening to you. And to be here to protect the Sultan himself—that was like something out of a dream, an old story, a legend. He caught Sadik's eye and grinned. Sadik grinned back.

"You are one of the Shayk's boys, aren't you?" said the Sultan to Sadik, who nodded.

"My name is Sadik, Sire," he said, bowing very low.

"Don't bow, don't bow," said the Sultan impatiently. "Only bow before God, that's the ticket, Sadik."

At that moment, there was a loud knock. The Sultan frowned a little and looked at the boys, who immediately positioned themselves near the door. The Sultan winked at them; then he said, loudly and rather haughtily, "Who is it?"

"Sire, it's me, Rahman," came a rather high, panic-stricken voice. The Sultan raised his eyebrows. "The commander of the guard," he whispered to Adi and Sadik. Aloud, he said, in that same haughty voice, "What is it, Rahman?"

"Sire, a message. An urgent message has come. It was delivered to my very quarters, Sire. By a man dressed all in black, with a black mask over his face."

"What!" The Sultan got up so quickly that he knocked his chair over. He strode to the door and pulled it open. "Give it to me, then, Rahman."

The man at the door was tall, fat, well dressed, and sweating. He bowed deeply and handed over a sealed envelope. The Sultan immediately ripped it open. He pulled a sheet of paper out and rapidly scanned its contents. Adi and Sadik saw all the color drain out of his face, making him look old and gray all of a sudden. There was a terrible silence; then the Sultan yelled, "Rahman! Why didn't you detain that man!" He was still gray, but his kindly face transformed instantly into that of a snarling tiger. "You fool!"

Rahman shrank back. "Your Majesty, he vanished so quickly, and I didn't think—"

"You never do! Fool! Yanto was right—I should have

gotten rid of you years ago."

"But Sire . . ." It was Rahman's turn to look gray and old. "I—"

"Go away. Get out of my sight," snarled the Sultan. "This minute."

"Sire . . ." bleated the unfortunate Rahman, but the Sultan closed the door in his face. He stood at the door for a moment, breathing deeply, then rushed over to the radio and twiddled the dials. He picked up the mouthpiece. "Tiger One, come in. Tiger One, come in." The radio crackled fiercely, but no voice came over. "Tiger One, come in." Crackle, crackle. The Sultan sighed despairingly. His face set in deep lines. "Tiger Two, Tiger Two, come in. Come in, Tiger Two." Crackle, crackle. He tried again, but still no change. Slowly, he turned away from the radio.

Adi and Sadik dared not move. Adi's heart was racing. One of the hantumu had been at the palace, right inside it! Fear crept over him.

"My son . . ." said the Sultan harshly, after a long silence. "They . . . they have forced his helicopter down. The . . . the hantumu and their master hold Yanto prisoner. They will kill him unless I agree to meet with this . . . this man . . . today."

"Does he say what he wants, Your Majesty?" said Adi.

"He says I must go to meet him, and that then he will tell me his demands."

"Where does he want you to meet him, Your Majesty?"

"He says I am to go to the Water Gardens, and someone will take me to the Sorcerer."

"Sire, it is a trick," said Adi definitely. "He wants you out of the safety of the palace, in a place where he can—"

The Sultan laughed mirthlessly. "The Water Gardens are as safe as my palace. I am safer in the atrium of my mystical bride, Rorokidul, than I ever would be here," he said. "Though . . ." He broke off, looking rather stricken.

Suddenly, Adi remembered Rorokidul's words. "Sire, Sire, when I first came to see you, with the Shayk, I saw the Queen of the Southern Sea, Rorokidul herself, standing behind your chair."

The Sultan's expression lifted. "Are you sure, Adi?"

"She was definitely there, Sire," he said, ignoring Sadik's look of astonishment. "And she said . . . she said . . . er . . ." He cleared his throat. "Forgive me, Sire, but she said that her human husband had not been mindful of his vows."

"I see," said the Sultan. He looked rather shamefaced. "She's reminding me that I need to renew contact with the spirits. I've been neglecting her of late. I thought perhaps, in our modern world, you know. . . . Besides, Yanto's been on and on at me to move away from too much reliance on the spirit world, because he thinks it's not good religious practice. Ah well! This is good news in a way, Adi. If you saw Rorokidul here, it means she hasn't turned her back on us. Rorokidul has always been closely linked to my family, and it is partly through her protection that my family has flourished. But the palace—why, anyone could get in. After all, the hantumu got into that fool Rahman's quarters to deliver his message, didn't he?"

Unease gripped Adi. "Sire, why would a man who threatens your family and your kingdom ask to meet you in the very place that is a source of your power?"

"You may well be right, Adi, but I cannot take the chance of leaving Yanto at their mercy. They told me in the letter, just to make sure I know they have him, of a birthmark he has on . . . on a part of the body not normally shown in public. No one except my family knows of this. They must already be humiliating him, hurting him." His face twisted. He closed his eyes briefly. "Oh, what an idiot I was to let him go on this fool's errand. I should never have trusted to such a harebrained plan."

Neither Adi nor Sadik mentioned that it was not

only Yanto who was missing but also the Shayk. Yet they both thought it. Adi could see in Sadik's wide, frightened eyes just how afraid he was for his master. As for himself, he felt sorry for the poor, kind, brave old man who had staked his own safety—and the peace of his people—on helping to defend the Sultan's power, no matter what he thought of the Sultan. He had thought the Shayk was Snow—and now Snow was incapacitated, or maybe even dead. Harshly, he said, "Sire, it is too late for regrets. It is time now for decisions."

The Sultan's eyes flashed. "How dare you . . ." he began. Then he broke off sharply. "Forgive me, Adi. You are right. It is time now to act. And so I will go to the Water Gardens to meet the Sorcerer."

"And we will come with you," said Adi, echoed by Sadik, who added, "Sire, we can ask Ibrahim to come with us—he is a good fighter."

"Tell him to come if he likes," said the Sultan, handing Sadik the kris that had been on the desk and tucking the gun into the waistband of his own trousers. "We'll leave by the back; I don't want too many people to see us." He moved like a young man now, briskly, with a sense of purpose that Adi knew would not be blunted anymore.

TWENTY-FIVE

Dewi and Husam rode on through the afternoon. The bike drove smoothly enough, and fortunately there were few bends in the road, so Husam did not have to do much steering, but it was definitely not as fast as a modern motorbike would have been. Dewi cursed it under her breath. She also wondered just how much fuel it had in its tank, and how long it would last. They had just passed a sign to Kotabunga, and it was farther than she had hoped. But there was nothing she could do about it, not even urge Husam to greater speed. The machine wouldn't take it.

She thought of poor Anda Mangil, speaking so cheerfully about how new threats needed new magics and new ideas. Well, she was sure the spirits would think this bike came under the heading of new magics, but it was not much of a comfort. Why couldn't they have been given powerful bikes such as the hantumu used? As to new ideas, she had precisely none in her head. Nor old ones, in fact. Even if the Sultan believed them—which might not be the case—what then? Warning him against a sorcerer whose name nobody knew and whose nature could hardly even be guessed at was surely not a very useful thing.

Her thoughts were jolted out of her head by Husam slamming on the brakes. Dewi sailed gracefully out of the sidecar, onto the dusty road. For a moment, she was utterly winded and could not even speak. Husam immediately jumped off the bike and bent over her, babbling apologies. Desperately worried when she did not respond, he said, urgently, "Dewi, Dewi, speak to me! Are you all right?"

Dewi found her voice. "Not all right, but not badly hurt," she said crossly. "Help me up." As he did so, she said, "Why on earth did you do that?"

"Look," said Husam, pointing. Dewi followed the direction of his finger. There was a cloud moving on the road toward them, a formless shape, far away. "It's people," said Husam quietly. "Lots of people. They're streaming out of Kotabunga."

"The Sorcerer's there already!" said Dewi, scrambling for the bike. "Quick, quick, Husam!"

He hurried to help her.

"Let me drive this time," she said.

"Okay—you can't do much worse than me," said Husam ruefully. Dewi jumped on the bike, while Husam folded himself into the sidecar. Alas, when Dewi tried to kick over the bike to start, it just kept ticking and whirring, but the engine would not start up.

"Oh dear," said Husam even more ruefully. "Looks like we have run out of—" He broke off as a wild sound came to their ears.

"What the—?" He peered ahead. "Dewi, Dewi, quick, get on the side of the road. It's coming straight for us!"

There, emerging out of the formless mass in the distance, a smaller cloud of dust, with a center of fire, was coming toward them, very rapidly indeed. Dewi did not stop to think; she jumped off the bike and painfully into the thornbushes at the side of the road, Husam falling beside her in a most undignified sprawl. Both of them tucked their heads under their arms and curled up tightly, trying to make themselves as small as possible, trying to ignore the pain as the long thorns pricked every centimeter of their exposed flesh.

The blast of sound came again, very loudly this time; then came a grinding crash, a bang, a yell, and some very loud swearing. Dewi's eyes flew open, as did Husam's. They carefully extricated themselves from the thornbushes and came to stand by the side of the road.

"Er . . . Kareen Amar, we are glad to see you," said Dewi in a small voice.

"Funny way of showing it," said the Jinn, very crankily. She kicked out hard at what remained of the speeda—a twisted, half-molten lump of metal. "Why did you leave this thing in the way?"

"It was going to take us to Kotabunga," said Husam quietly, staring at the pitiful remains of Kembang's pride and joy. "Oh dear, Kareen, couldn't you have been more careful?"

"Useless dumb machine," said Kareen Amar loftily. She turned away from them and whistled, very low. A *toot-toot*, as if from a horn, answered her; and in the next moment, an astonished Dewi and Husam saw Anda Mangil's car trundling toward them from its hiding place in the bushes, a short distance away.

"Now, that one is clever," said the Jinn happily. "Anda Mangil does not die while his car lives. Come on, you two," she went on, impatiently beckoning them to get in. "Staring like fish out of water won't help us get to the Sultan, now, will it?"

Dewi looked back once at the twisted heap of blackened metal that had been the prized possession of the Stone Village clan. She felt bad about the state it was now in, despite her earlier unpleasant thoughts about its slowness and clunkiness. It had been of great use to them, and they had promised to bring it back. Glancing at Husam, she saw the same thought in his eyes. But there was nothing they could do right now. They would have to try to repay the villagers. They'd have to get them a new one, somehow.

At least Anda Mangil's car was back to being what it had been before she'd unwisely called on the unfettered power of Fire, thought Dewi as she and Husam climbed into the backseat of the car. In fact, it seemed better than before—everything looked new, spotless, gleaming. Even the pictures of the holy sites had a brand-new look to them; they shimmered three-dimensionally under their glass frames, as if you could truly walk into the heart of each. Dewi touched one of them and all at once heard Anda Mangil's voice in her head, gently teasing. Tears sprang into her eyes. His spirit might well be here, in his beloved car, but oh, how she wished he were there in the driver's seat and would turn his head to smile at her.

But it was Kareen Amar in the driver's seat, Kareen Amar who was chatting volubly over her shoulder as she started up the engine, though for a moment Dewi hardly heard what the Jinn was saying. It was the mention of Adi's name that drew her attention.

"What did you say?"

Kareen Amar turned right around to look reproachfully at her. "Young one, your ears do not always work properly. I was telling all about how Kotabunga has gone mad and people are streaming out of it into the countryside. There are stories running like wildfire among them, that Jehannem has opened and that all the demons of hell are pouring out of it and will destroy Kotabunga in a rain of fire. They say, too, that the army has already been destroyed, that the Crown Prince has flown away in a helicopter, and that the Sultan has been seen leaving the palace, and—"

"No. Adi. Adi—you spoke of Adi!"

"Yes, I saw him in a car, going toward the palace. He was with some people. I sang to him, but he did not come. The car turned a corner and was gone."

"And these stories about Jehannem . . ."

"Are untrue," said Kareen Amar primly. "People are panicked. They will believe anything. Only this is true: The Crown Prince has left by helicopter, and the Sultan is no longer in the palace."

"The helicopters!" said Dewi and Husam in unison. "Was the Sultan in one of the helicopters?" added Dewi.

"No, my informant saw only the Prince and an old man, a stranger, dressed all in snowy white."

Both Dewi and Husam started. "In snowy white!" Dewi echoed. Could it be a sign?

Kareen Amar took no notice of this interruption. "Furthermore, a servant, hiding in one of the back rooms, told me she saw the Sultan and three companions heading out of the palace. Perhaps Adi was one of them."

"Where would they go?" said Dewi despairingly.

"It is in my mind that they will still be in Kotabunga," said Kareen Amar. "The Sultan will not want to leave his capital at such a time. Perhaps, though, he has gone to some other place, safer than his palace, which is in a right old mess. If we knew what that was, then—"

"Wait!" said Dewi. A memory had come back to her, something Ratupohon had said. "There is a place where the Sultan's family have always derived at least part of their power. The Atrium of Rorokidul in the Water Gardens."

Both of them stared at her. "But as we know, the afreet has gained access to that place. It is not safe any longer," said Husam.

Dewi replied, "It wasn't safe for me, but surely Rorokidul would protect the Sultan. It is a pact that was made centuries ago with his family."

Husam sighed. "The trouble is, little heart, that

spirits can be whimsical, especially if they feel themselves slighted," he said. "And I have heard that Sunan Tengah has . . . er . . . neglected some of his ancient duties. Rorokidul might be . . . um . . . slow in responding, if he does call on her help."

"Yet she would surely not allow the Sorcerer to destroy the royal family of Jayangan just because she might be cranky with him," said Dewi definitely. "The spirit world is capricious, but it is not stupid. This Sorcerer threatens the spirit world every bit as much as he threatens ours, or we wouldn't have been helped in the way we have, if they felt no concern. And indeed, Kareen Amar wouldn't be here either."

"That is very true," said the Jinn, beaming. "Kareen Amar is glad you, young one, have learned to understand something." Then her face fell. "The problem is, the Sorcerer is not stupid either. He was able to breach the protection of the Water Gardens before, with the afreet; he may well do so again, differently."

"Whatever may happen, we have to try," said Dewi. "We have to get to them, Kareen Amar. Can you get us there quickly?"

"But of course," said Kareen Amar in a rather offended tone. "I and my friend Car will get you there quickly, you'll see!" So saying, she put both hands on the steering wheel. Her eyes were wide open, blazing;

she hummed a wordless tune under her breath. The car shot forward, not jerkily or clunkily, as the bike had done, but with a great surge of power that propelled them forward so fast, it was like being in a plunging elevator. In record time, they reached the crowds pouring out of Kotabunga. People scattered right and left as the machine came bearing down on them. Looking behind them, a startled Dewi saw that a trail of fire was streaming out of the exhaust like smoke normally did. She closed her eyes. She hoped Kareen Amar knew what she was doing. She hoped that Anda Mangil's car would be not reduced to a smoldering heap of twisted metal, like Kembang's bike. She hoped . . .

There was a grinding crash, a scream of tires; Dewi and Husam were thrown forward. Then the engine died. Kareen Amar said, with great satisfaction undercut with a trace of worry, "The gardens are just around the corner. We will leave the car here, out of sight."

Without a word, a grim-faced Ibrahim followed the Sultan and the boys, sword drawn, as the ruler led them through back corridors, dusty antechambers, and a rather shabby, abandoned-looking back kitchen, emerging at last in an even shabbier yard. Everywhere there were signs of hurried departure, and the Sultan's eyes had a rather sad expression in them. He had pretended everything was okay; he had tried to deal with the growing menace in a way that would not panic his people. But you can't shut off all rumors and stories. People knew things were happening, but because nobody in authority had even admitted it, it had made things twenty times worse. And now the mass panic could only serve to help the Sorcerer. Oh, the man had been clever, fiendishly clever. The unknown enemy, striking unpredictably from the shadows, will always strike more terror into human hearts than the declared one, facing you on the battlefield. Those ruthless and clever enough, who care nothing for the honor of the world or for the normal concerns of humanity, will always know how to use not only real weapons but also the paralyzing one of sheer terror.

Adi brought his heart pendant out from under his clothes and clasped it tightly, breathing a little prayer. He caught Ibrahim looking narrowly at him as he did so. But he cared nothing for what Ibrahim thought of Nashranees or anyone or anything else anymore.

The Sultan came to a small rusty door, which he kicked at impatiently. It fell open. "I used to get out of the palace this way all the time when I was a boy," he said, beckoning them through. "Hurry, there is a shortcut to the Water Gardens from here. Perhaps we can get to them before anyone else arrives."

The others exchanged a look that the Sultan did not see, as he'd already hurried away. It was unlikely they'd arrive before the Sorcerer and his men, who were perhaps already there. They streaked off after the Sultan, who was running down the street as fast as his rather stubby legs would allow.

Ibrahim drew level with Adi. Out of the corner of his mouth, he hissed, "You're a spy, aren't you? I thought as much. Scum!"

"What are you talking about?" Adi spat back.

Sadik, who had also caught up, echoed, "Yes, what?"

Ibrahim jabbed a long finger at Adi's heart symbol.

Sadik said, "He's a Nashranee."

Ibrahim glared at him. "You knew?"

"Yes. So?"

"You knew he was not one of us, yet you brought him into our community!"

"I've never heard it said that we could not bring friends or guests. Fancy calling him a spy. Why would anyone want to spy on us? We're an open community—we're just farmers and seekers. And Adi's a good man. A truehearted one, Ibrahim!" Sadik's eyes were shining with anger. "You can see that for yourself."

"I see," said Ibrahim very unpleasantly. "I see. I

think the Master will want to hear your opinions of Nashranees, Sadik."

"You can tell him yourself, Ibrahim," Sadik said, hotly. "Go right ahead. Yes, see what he says, when you trouble him about such idiocies, when the whole land is in danger from the demons!"

Just ahead, the Sultan stopped and turned to look at them, frowning. "Have you forgotten where we are, and what we're doing?" he said coldly. "What is the meaning of this ridiculous quarrel?"

"Nothing, Sire," said Adi quietly, when no one else spoke.

"Good. I'm glad. I will not have such nonsense when my son is in danger," said the Sultan sharply. "And I hope you did not mean what you said, Ibrahim. I do not like fanatics of any kind. Nashranees are just as much a part of Jayangan as Mujisals, or Dharbudsus, or all those who live in our country. And all of us are bound by that, including you and your master. None of you is above the law. Is that understood?"

Ibrahim stared at him, his eyes flashing. Then, very slowly, he bowed. "Of course, Sire."

"Very well," said the Sultan crossly. "Now, that's that. We need to take this street; the gardens are not far." But Adi's heart was boiling with rage again. For two cents, he'd have challenged the stupid, arrogant desert man to a fight. Didn't he understand that it was precisely such talk, such behavior, that gave the Pumujisals a bad name? Perhaps the Shayk didn't know he thought like that; or perhaps because Ibrahim had been an old and trusted friend, he allowed him too much latitude. It was a pity. Then he caught Sadik's eye and smiled. Sadik had shown himself to be a true friend, and a real disciple of his extraordinary master. The Shayk would be proud of him.

Dewi unfolded herself from the car. She stared at the stone wall that surrounded the gardens. Above the wall could be seen waving date palms, and frangipani, and other trees. A faint sound of trickling water could be heard. Inside, it would be green, scented, lovely. A pulse of nerves was beating under her skin. She remembered all too well being here.

Beside her, Husam said, "There's the door." She jumped. "Are you all right, Dewi?"

"Oh, I'm fine." Dewi walked to the door. "There's nothing to be afraid of. The Sorcerer won't come here again."

She was aware of Kareen Amar and Husam exchanging a look but took no notice. She pushed the door, and it opened easily. She walked into the garden.

The dead plants had been removed, holes in the

ground the only sign they had once stood there. The broken statues still lay where they had fallen. There was silence, the silence of something badly injured, even dying.

"This is not a good place," said Kareen Amar anxiously from behind her.

"It is a good place," Dewi corrected her. "It will try to protect us."

"I can hear someone coming!" hissed Husam. "Quickly, hide!"

And he dived into the green undergrowth, wriggling on his belly. Dewi followed him, then Kareen Amar. As they did so, the green closed around them, hiding them fully from sight, but not closing their hearing.

"Oh, sweet God." The Sultan was thunderstruck. He had seen the open door to the gardens and, before anyone could stop him, had rushed in. Now he stopped in the middle of the path and looked around him, stunned. "What has happened here?"

Even someone unused to the splendors of the gardens could see at once something was wrong. Withered leaves and broken stone were not sights you associated with the most famous garden in all of Jayangan.

"Where are the gardeners?" called the Sultan. "Where are my people?" He swallowed. "And where is the man we should be meeting?"

Adi and Sadik exchanged a glance. They ran back to the open door. But just as they reached it, it slammed shut, so fast and hard that the wind from it nearly knocked them over. Adi and Sadik pushed hard at it. But it would not budge. It was stuck.

"There is another door, just over there," said the Sultan after a moment of paralysis. He was gray-faced again, but strangely, there was no fear in his eyes.

"Let's check it," said Sadik, while Ibrahim stayed where he was, a thin smile on his face. He watched them while they ran to the other door. But it, too, would not open.

"We will go at once to the atrium," said the Sultan. "They cannot have penetrated there; it's impossible—Rorokidul would never let them." And he set off at a zigzagging run through the desecrated gardens, puffing and panting as he went, not looking behind him to see if they were following.

Back in the huddle of bushes, Dewi and the others were struggling to get out, but it wasn't easy; the plants were clinging tightly, unwilling to let them go. Perhaps the plants knew they were in danger and were trying to save them; perhaps the vines had other designs, not so pleasant. Dewi quietly called on Ratupohon, and suddenly, there was the green woman, one finger to her lips. She heard the spirit's voice in her mind, jerkily, brokenly. "You must be careful. Something bad has got into the garden, down there in the atrium. The Sorcerer! I could not stop him. You are in very great danger. You would be better off staying here. My plants will protect you from the—"

"Ratupohon," cried Dewi, "it's too late to stay safe. You must let us go!"

"Very well," said Ratupohon, a little more clearly now, "but I cannot protect you."

"She has us," said the Jinn suddenly. "She has us. I am Fire, green woman; and this is Sword. We have come to accomplish what must be done. Please, let us go."

The vines promptly fell away. Rubbing at the itches that the bushes had left on their skins, they scrambled back onto the path.

"The atrium is that way," said Dewi, pointing. "Come on!"

TWENTY-SIX

HEART IN MOUTH, Adi clattered down the dark spiral staircase after the others. He did not like the feel of this place at all. It was like a well, he thought, from which they could not escape. Sadik must have been feeling nervous too, for he was going down very cautiously indeed. But the other two appeared to have no qualms at all. The Sultan raced down and down and down, toward the soft light, and Ibrahim raced after him, sword drawn.

The light grew strangely brighter and brighter the farther they went, but it was not this that made Adi's skin prickle and feel clammy with a cold sweat. It was not even the idea of the Sorcerer trapping them in the gardens that made him feel scared. A smell of dead sea things permeated the staircase, reminding Adi irresistibly of the dangerous and unpredictable nature of the ocean. How did any of them really know how the

Queen of the Southern Sea felt? The spirits did not always protect those they were supposed to. Whim and anger at perceived insult could easily, and unpredictably, turn them into frightening enemies. And the Sultan had admitted that he had neglected the formidable Rorokidul of late.

Adi held tightly not only to his kris but also to his heart symbol. As a Nashranee, he should not be as fearful of the nature spirits, who were, after all, bound by God's law. But surely no one from Jayangan, whether Nashranee, Mujisal, or Dharbudsu, could really, truthfully, say they *never* feared them.

In front of him, Sadik stopped and whispered, "This is a bad place, Adi. This is a place of evil spirits."

"No, no," Adi whispered back, much more confidently than he felt. "It is just the place where the Queen of the Southern Sea, Rorokidul, comes to meet her human bridegroom, the Sultan of Jayangan."

"Exactly," said Sadik.

"I thought you didn't believe in her existence anyway," hissed Adi, more in an attempt to give himself heart than out of a real desire to taunt Sadik.

"I don't," said Sadik, but his voice trembled and Adi knew at once he was not telling the truth, and that the other boy was in a real agony of apprehension. He said gently, "Sadik, do not be afraid of the spirits. They are of Jayangan and they love this country. Trust to God and you will be fine."

Sadik began, "But I—" Then he broke off abruptly. "What's that?"

Adi stiffened. He, too, had heard it—a soft sliding on stone, which sounded remarkably like stealthy footsteps above. Someone was following them. His heart raced. After motioning to Sadik to keep in the shadows, he climbed quietly back up a few steps, gripping the kris tightly, listening. The sound had stopped, though. He climbed back up a little way, expecting at any moment to be grabbed, but there was nothing and no one. Yet there was a feeling here, a sense of an alien presence suddenly, a whiff of . . . of burned flesh.

Horrific images leaped into his mind: blood, fire, death. Terror gripped him momentarily; then he shook his head angrily. He wasn't going to start imagining things now! Trying to master his fear, he climbed a little higher, and higher, till he could see the light of the gardens up above. No one grabbed him; nothing moved. The only sound was that of his own footsteps. Running as fast as he could, he went back down to Sadik. "Must have been a rat," he said.

Sadik nodded, wanting to be convinced.

"Adi, I think this was all a trick. They haven't got the

Prince at all—they just wanted to bring the Sultan here, and—"

"But that can't be right. You heard the Sultan trying to contact the helicopters," said Adi.

"Yes, but . . ." Sadik gulped. "The Sorcerer is obviously very powerful. Perhaps he was able to jam the helicopters' communications."

"And perhaps he can do anything he likes," said Adi, turning down the stairs. "But perhaps that is his greatest weapon of all—that we think he can do anything."

I wish I really believed that, he thought as he moved resolutely downward, his ears singing with the expectation of being ambushed at any moment. He wished he could be sure that what he'd said wasn't just the biggest load of nonsense that anyone ever spouted. Perhaps the Sorcerer was capable of doing anything he chose to. Perhaps he wasn't human at all, but the Devil himself, come to finally take over the world.

Being in this place again made Dewi remember all too vividly what it had been like last time. She still did not feel safe here; the gardens had the air of a place that had been fatally wounded. She could sense the spirits of the green world all around her as she and her companions moved swiftly toward the atrium, and she sensed about them an air of expectancy, of apprehensive waiting. Husam and Kareen Amar, too, did not seem altogether comfortable. Kareen Amar kept glancing around her, as if she thought she'd surprise someone or something in the act of following her; Husam's face was drawn with something that could not be called fear, not on him, but rather an uncertainty that was more unsettling than mere fear. They were almost at the atrium when Dewi stopped. Ratupohon was standing on the path before them. One finger was to her lips, another beckoning them urgently into a grove of trees and bushes to one side of the path. They didn't argue—and barely had time to run and hide behind the bushes before the hantumu came down the path.

They were not on their motorbikes this time, but on foot, swift and silent as black shadows, heading straight for the atrium. There were more of them than before, a dozen or so, and they were armed with black swords. There was no sign of the afreet. As Dewi and the others watched in breathless silence, the leader of the hantumu peered down the well of the staircase. Then, as if satisfied by something, with a wave of his hand he positioned them at the entrance to the well, where they stayed on guard. It was obvious the protection of the gardens had now been fully breached.

* * *

Adi and Sadik had reached the bottom of the staircase, and stopped so suddenly that they bumped heads. But neither of them noticed the pain.

For the Sultan was kneeling in the shallows at the edge of a large, shining pool. It was Rorokidul's pool, and reputedly bottomless, with treacherous cold waters that would claim any intruders who attempted to wade into its sacred depths. The Sultan was not an intruder, though. He had taken off his shoes, his jacket, and his trousers, and was clad only in his long shirt, which reached almost to his knees. He had taken off his glasses, too. He knelt in a posture of utter humility. By the edge of the pool stood Ibrahim, a sneer on his face but eyes alert, sword drawn, watching every corner of the atrium.

The Sultan was chanting quietly. No words could be distinguished, but with a strange sensation of awe and shame and fear rippling over him, Adi felt he could understand. The Sultan was begging the forgiveness of the Queen of the Southern Sea, his mystical bride. He was asking for her help. No, he was pleading for it.

Adi did not want to look at this. It made him feel sick and cold and sorry, all at the same time. He knew why Ibrahim was sneering. He understood Sadik's look of paralyzed horror. But he also knew that however undignified it looked, the Sultan was doing the only thing he could in the circumstances. A centuries-old link between the Queen of the Southern Sea and the Sultans of Jayangan had been frayed, and it must be repaired, no matter what it cost.

His low chant filled the atrium, but otherwise there was silence. Not a ripple disturbed the surface of the pool, whose skin shone like a bright mirror. Moments passed, and then the Sultan stopped chanting, though he stayed on his knees. The silence lengthened. There was no answer to the Sultan's plea; the spirits were silent, the pool absolutely calm.

After a while, the Sultan slowly got to his feet and waded out of the pool. His back to them, he clambered into the rest of his clothes. Then he turned and, without a word, made his way back to the staircase, brushing past Adi and Sadik without even acknowledging them. His head was bowed, his face was drawn; he seemed to have shrunk inside his clothes. Ibrahim followed the Sultan as he trudged painfully up the same stairs he'd raced down so confidently before.

Sadik looked at Adi. "That's it, then," he said softly.

Adi stared at him, rage spasming inside him. How dare she! How dare Rorokidul simply ignore the desperate pleas of the one she was supposed to protect! She had appeared to him, to Adi, solely for the purpose of seeing the Sultan grovel in front of her. Witch, he thought to himself. Capricious and disloyal witch. What good are you, what good are any of you spirits? And in a paroxysm of fury, he grabbed a stone lying on the floor of the atrium and threw it into the pool, shouting, "Rorokidul! Spirits of Jayangan! Where is your help, where is your protection?" The stone splashed into the water, breaking the surface the way a mirror shatters in a thousand pieces. He went on, "If you have abandoned us, then we have abandoned you too, and good riddance. We will face this alone, free of your interference!" His words echoed in the atrium, bouncing off the walls again and again. And then the whole place lit up, and veiled faces appeared in all the galleries surrounding the atrium, and the air was full of voices and presences, dimly seen and perceived, yet real enough. In the middle of them, the shattered reflections of the pool came together, re-forming into a pillar of light and smoke that rose out of the water. And as Adi and a terrified Sadik stood there without moving, a woman's form began to appear, at first dimly, then clearer and clearer, within the pillar of light. Adi knew her at once, though the calmly beautiful face he'd seen in the Sultan's palace was now distorted with anger. He knew that it was his own challenge that had roused Rorokidul from her vengeful refusal to appear to the Sultan. Now she spoke not a word, but fixed her eyes on Adi and raised her hand high. Sadik gave a little squeak and tugged at Adi. "Let's go, go, go!" he pleaded.

But Adi did not budge. "Queen Rorokidul," he said, head high, "you can turn me to whatever it is you want, but it won't change one thing about what you have done today. You chose your own pique above the fate of Jayangan. You chose to dismiss your bridegroom without even a reason. Kill me or bewitch me, I care not at all. You have done the Sorcerer's work for him. You have left the Sultan without protection. And for that it is the Sorcerer who will thank you oh so dearly, Queen of the Southern Sea. Perhaps you don't care. Perhaps you think he can become your new bridegroom, when he is master of all Jayangan. But he will destroy you, and the sacred places of all your brothers and sisters in the spirit world, for he wants to be master of all. He will turn your world to dust and darkness, Rorokidul, and you will be forgotten."

His voice cut like a whip, and the faces in the gallery rustled and trembled in its wake. But Rorokidul did not move, or speak. She was frozen in the light of the pillar, hand outstretched, her gaze on Adi. And it suddenly seemed to him there was a deep, deep sadness in that gaze, a sadness for something far beyond Adi's reach or understanding. Their eyes locked together for a still moment; then the pillar of light shattered as the surface of the water had done and Rorokidul's image vanished utterly. The light of the pool faded slowly after her, then winked out and disappeared, leaving the atrium in darkness, save for the dim light seeping down the stairwell from the garden above.

Adi turned his back and made his way to the stairs, following Sadik closely. Heavily, he trudged up the first steps, expecting at any moment to be struck by a bolt of light, to be frozen where he stood, to be transformed into a cockroach, to be struck in the heart. But nothing happened. Nothing at all, except that they climbed back up, silently, leaving behind the great Atrium of Rorokidul, where once, over long, long centuries, the links of the ancient spirit world and the human world of Jayangan had been made and remade and taken care of. As he climbed, Adi felt the sadness that had been in the Queen's eyes rise in him like a bitter wave, washing over him with a painful clarity. Nothing would be the same again, he thought. Not for Jayangan, not for the Sultan. Not even for himself. He thought of his master, Empu Wesiagi, who lived and breathed the world of the spirits, who wove their protection into every beautiful thing he made. What good was it now?

How could Adi in all seriousness and honesty truly be a part of the world of his master? He would never be a kris maker, for he would never be able to make a kris wholeheartedly believing in its mystical presence, its link to the spirit world—not when the spirits had shown themselves to be both disloyal and useless. They had told them to find Snow, Fire, and Sword, but they had given them no real help in actually finding them. Everything that had been done had been done by humans.

Sadik reached the top of the stairs. In the next instant, he disappeared from sight, as if he'd been whipped away. Adi, following on his heels, felt, rather than saw, the black figure hurtling toward him. Instinctively, he stabbed upward with his kris and heard a sudden *whoof!* Then something fell past him down the stairs. Glancing down, he saw it was a hantumu, that somehow he had hit it, and that the blade of his kris was red with blood. Bile rushed up in his throat; his heart raced. He took the last couple of stairs at a run and emerged yelling and screaming into the garden, his kris held out in front of him. But he had no chance against their numbers, and in a matter of seconds he was disarmed and thrown facedown. His kris was kicked away from him; a huge masked hantumu sat on his back and another tied his ankles and wrists together with a thin rope that cut cruelly into his flesh. He could see no one else, but he knew they must all have been taken—Sadik, the Sultan, Ibrahim.

"No, no, wait, little heart. It won't do any good. We have to wait. You can't do him any good, not yet." Husam was whispering rapidly, desperately, obviously afraid that Dewi was going to fling herself at once on the hantumu to try to rescue Adi.

"Husam is right," said Kareen Amar. "We must wait. They're not going to kill him. Look, they're binding him—they wouldn't do that if they were just going to kill him now. We can help him better if we wait and see where they take him."

Dewi's whole being was racked with frustration, rage, and fear. Wild thoughts rolled through her head in confusion. She couldn't bear to see Adi trussed up like that, but Kareen Amar was right. The hantumu could have killed him—especially as the splashes of blood on him seemed to show that the hantumu who had leaped down the well had come off the worse—but they hadn't. Why not? It could only be that they were waiting for someone, or something. Perhaps the afreet—or perhaps their master. Why had they trussed up Adi, but not the others who had been with him? And surely—kneeling there, hands tied but head high—that was the

Sultan. She had seen him in photographs many times, smiling down in shops and banks and public buildings. But who were the other two, the boy and the man, whom the hantumu held to one side? The man was as tall as Husam, and dressed like him—he was obviously a desert man. And he had a sword at his side. What was it her father had said—there could be more than one Snow, Fire, and Sword. . . .

She stiffened. Something was coming. Something whose presence made the heart seem to pause for an instant, the nerves to seize. Something familiar that made her mind feel suddenly hot, that made her feel like jumping up and running away. The afreet was near. She made as if to get up, but Kareen Amar's hand shot up and dragged her down. The Jinn pinned her close painfully, whispering, "Quiet, quiet, it doesn't know you're here, don't move!"

And there, suddenly, appearing as if from thin air, was the afreet. It was different—taller, broader, more the size of an ape, and though it was still covered in red and black hairs, and its vertical-pupiled eyes smoldered like burning coals, the features of its face had become finer, the shape of its body slimmer. It fixed its eyes on the Sultan.

"So, you have come as a supplicant," it mocked. "What is it you want from us, O ruler of all Jayangan?"

From his helpless position, lying side down on the grass, Adi felt the humiliation of the Sultan as if it were his own. It even outweighed the fear he felt at the sight of the great demon. The iron of resolve had entered his soul after his confrontation with Rorokidul in the atrium. He would never be as frightened of any spirits ever again, not even ones as ugly and stinking as this.

"My son, cursed demon!" cried the Sultan. He tried to rise, but the hantumu pushed him roughly down. There was a ripple of laughter, and Adi felt rage surge through him.

"Your son?" mused the afreet. "Now I wonder. Could it be you are referring to one of those dead things lying on the mountain in the twisted wreckage of the flying machines? It was fun to pull them down, I assure you. It is long since I have had sport like that, entering into those pilots' minds and giving them such visions of hell that they could not think straight." It stared into the Sultan's eyes. The Sultan gave an involuntary gasp, paled, and turned his face away. Dewi flinched, knowing what the ruler would be seeing in his mind: merciless, horrible visions of his son's fiery death.

The afreet laughed. "O ruler of all Jayangan, I would love to play further with you, but this I am not allowed to do right now. For my master is doing you a great honor. He will see you. You will talk with him."

"Why?" came a hoarse croak from the Sultan. "If my son is dead—"

"Perhaps you shouldn't believe everything you imagine," interrupted the afreet, and it laughed again.

The Sultan raised his head but took care not to look at the afreet's face. He whispered, "Do not play with us. Tell me the truth about my son."

"Enough! Get up," said the leader of the hantumu to the Sultan. When the ruler defiantly stayed put, he motioned to the other hantumu, who unceremoniously hauled the Sultan up onto his feet.

"You will have to learn some manners, little man," the leader of the hantumu snarled. "You are not the king now. Your reign is over. My master's is just beginning. You can't demand anything or command answers anymore. If you behave yourself, we might let you and your family live. Take him down!"

Two hantumu grabbed the Sultan by the arms and led him, struggling, back toward the stairs that led to the atrium. Two others took Sadik and Ibrahim and pushed them along after the Sultan. But it was the afreet itself that bent over Adi, its burning eyes on his face. It chuckled—a low, snarling sound. "Ah, boy," it said, "as you were so kind as to help to destroy the protection of Rorokidul with your rude challenge to her, it is fitting you should see the end of your efforts!" And so saying, with an effortless heave, it hoisted him over its shoulder, so that he dangled down, headfirst. Overcome by its stench of burned flesh, by the blood rushing to his head, the numbness where the rope was biting into his flesh, and by the words of the afreet, Adi fainted dead away.

"Now, Dewi," said Husam sternly, when all was quiet, "we will not go rushing down there, do you understand? It is no use fighting the afreet or the hantumu if we cannot get to their master first. They will just kill us. Let us reflect. What are our weapons? My sword, your resolve, your knowledge of the world of the spirits, and Kareen's fire. We will need to use them wisely and carefully, at the right time."

"Yes," said Kareen Amar eagerly, "that is so. Those others have weapons similar, though many more: the afreet's power fights my own, the hantumu's swords against Husam's, and the resolve of the Sorcerer against yours, Dewi."

"But we have to help Adi."

"We will not abandon him, but first of all we have to deal with the guards at the entrance to the stairwell," said Husam firmly.

"That will be easy enough." Kareen Amar grinned,

and her eyes glowed.

"No, wait," said Husam, but Kareen Amar was already gone, gliding out of her hiding place. She turned around once—and became a long lick of flame, racing over the grass toward the entrance to the stairwell. The two hantumu on guard only just had time to catch a glimpse of the flame before it divided in two and was briskly on them, setting their clothes on fire, nibbling at the edges of their skin, crackling up into their hair. Panic-stricken, the hantumu ripped at their masks, which were melting on their faces, and beat at the flames that were engulfing their clothes, but it was as if doing so excited the fire, for it burned brighter and brighter, faster and faster. The hantumu screamed and rolled on the ground now, trying to put out the flames. The hideous smell of scorching flesh began to waft over the garden. It was too much for Dewi. She raced out of her hiding place, calling softly, "Please, Kareen Amar, that's enough, enough."

The flames paused in their terrible work over the twisting bodies of the hantumu. They seemed to hover in midair, as if reluctant. "Please, Kareen Amar," said Dewi, almost crying. "You've got to stop. It's enough."

The fire gathered itself together. Sulkily, it formed into the familiar shape of Kareen Amar. Husam ran to them.

"What would you have me do?" snapped Kareen Amar. "Ask them nicely to move aside?" She bent down over the hantumu, who had gone still. "They are alive, though they will not be able to fight us again," she said, straightening. "Their flesh will heal. And I am not like the afreet; I have left their hearts and souls intact. Now, if you will stop shedding tears over those wicked ones who would have killed you without a moment's remorse, then we can go on our way." She turned very huffily away from them and glided off down the stairs.

Dewi caught Husam's eye. "She is right, little heart," he said. "If you are not prepared to face . . ."

Dewi nodded without speaking. She went down the stone staircase, her head and heart full of contradictions and confusion. Husam followed.

Kareen Amar stopped abruptly. She put a finger to her lips, pressed against the wall of the stairwell, and vanished. Only a scorch mark showed where she had been.

Husam and Dewi crept down farther. They began to hear the murmur of voices. "Stay here," Husam mouthed at Dewi. "Let me see if there's anywhere we can hide." He drew down his headcloth, so it completely swathed his face, leaving only his eyes showing through a slit. In the darkness of the stairs, he could hardly be seen. Flattening herself against the wall, Dewi watched as he disappeared around a bend of the staircase. There was a little light down there, but not the light she had seen the other day—not a weird, glowing softness, but the thin yellow light of torches.

Husam was back in a very short while. "There's a niche, just above the last few steps," he whispered. "It's wide enough for both of us, I think, and it's in the shadows at the moment. There's a hantumu standing guard at the bottom of the stairs, but he's not watching up here, just what's going on down there. Come on. This is our chance."

TWENTY-SEVEN

ADI SLOWLY CAME to, with an aching head, a swollen tongue, and sore eyes. He was gagged, and his wrists and ankles were still tied together; he could hardly feel his hands and feet now. For a moment, he forgot where he was and thought he was back in the rice paddy, waiting for someone to deliver him from his bonds. Dewi would come soon, he thought, rather deliriously, she will come, and take me to her father. . . . As his eyes became adjusted to the light, though, and his senses fully returned to him, he remembered what had happened. His heart pounded. No one, human or spirit, would come to save him here. He would have to try to get away on his own.

He peered around him to try to make out what was going on. It was not easy: The atrium was only partly illuminated by points of yellow light from flickering torches—and by a red glow in front of the now darkened pool, a light that came from the afreet. It was standing guard over the Sultan, who had been gagged and tied to a chair. There were many hantumu in the atrium, spread out at irregular intervals around the pool. He could not see Ibrahim and Sadik at all. Fear fluttered in his chest. Had they already been killed?

The afreet's words came back to him like a hammer blow. He swallowed, trying not to think about it. Had his rash words down here really caused the place to become wide open to the forces of evil? Surely the spirits were stronger than that.

"Sultan of Jayangan!" The booming, distorted voice burst in on the atrium with the force of a thunderclap. Then came the light: a light soft and gentle at first, but becoming stronger and stronger. It seemed to come from a figure who had stepped out of the shadows beyond the pool. Cloaked and hooded in dusky brown, so its face could not be seen, it held its arms out wide, as if conjuring up that very light.

"Sultan of Jayangan!" came the voice again. "You are welcome here. Are you glad to meet me at last?" The Sultan did not reply, and the figure motioned to a hantumu. "Ungag him so he may speak to me." The man did as he was told. "Now, Sultan, answer me!"

The Sultan raised his head and stared at the hooded figure.

"I do not answer those who are too cowardly even to show their faces," he said, with more than a hint of the steel Adi had heard in the audience chamber in the palace.

The hantumu made as if to strike the Sultan, but the hooded figure held up a hand. "No, no," he said softly. "He does not yet know how he will regret it all. Sultan of Jayangan, your insults have no effect on me. I am here to conduct your trial."

"My trial?" croaked the Sultan. Then he cried softly, "Where is my son?"

"Your son is safe," said the hooded figure. "We are holding him in a safe place. You will have to take my word on that."

The Sultan laughed harshly. Behind him, the afreet stirred, its gaze rolling restlessly around the atrium.

"You do not even ask why you are on trial?" said the hooded figure.

"No," said the Sultan. "I have no interest in your wicked stupidities, Sorcerer. I want you to release my son immediately."

The hooded figure seemed to freeze. Its arms rose, and the light rose with it. "Sorcerer? What is this you have called me?"

"Someone who has evil spirits at his bidding, does evil deeds in the shadows, and runs an army of masked hantumu is, I think, best described as a sorcerer," said the Sultan defiantly, and this time the hantumu struck him, hitting him full on the mouth with a great crack. The Sultan doubled up, spitting blood and teeth, but he managed to say, "What else could you call yourself?"

"I am the Bringer of Light," said the hooded figure waspishly, approaching the Sultan. "Can't you see that? What do I bring to this dark place but light? Look!" And he flung his arms out toward the Sultan, so that the light fell fully on him, drenching him with a blinding dazzle of white. "How can I be a sorcerer when I bring the light of truth into the darkness of superstitious fear?"

"How can you not be a sorcerer when you have an evil spirit like that afreet at your beck and call?" snarled the Sultan. Trapped against the wall, Adi felt a surge of love and pride fill him like a wild flame.

"There are means that must sometimes be used—but I have no call to discuss such things with you. Your time, the time of darkness and alliances with true evil, is over. Our time, the time of Light, the time of the real warrior, is about to begin. You, Sultan, you are nothing anymore. We will have no kings in the new Jayangan—no, not even your son, who will understand that he will have to abdicate. We will have no more doddering fools mumbling words of dotage to evil spirits. We will sweep the entire island clean of all wickedness. Everything will start afresh in Jayangan, through the Light we bring. And Jayangan will not be an end to it, but a beginning. We will bring the Light to the whole world. We will sweep darkness from the face of the earth, and all those peoples and places that have loved darkness for so long, and allowed evil to reign. It is I . . . I . . . who will accomplish all this, and end the reign of the demons forever on earth!"

"You are raving," said the Sultan pityingly, "raving to make yourself feel better, for being in thrall to evil spirits." *Whack!* The hantumu hit him again, in the stomach this time. The Sultan doubled over, but he raised himself up again, raising his head to stare directly at the Sorcerer.

"And you are still coward enough to hide your face," he said, panting hard.

The Sorcerer loomed over him, like a great evil bird of prey. The afreet said, "Master, let me teach him a lesson he won't forget."

"Silence, Hareekshaytin," snapped the Sorcerer. "There will be time enough for that. I will show this stiff-necked fool the truth!" And then, in one movement, he pulled the hood off his face, and the cloak off his shoulders, and stood revealed before them. No one moved or made a sound for a frozen second or two. Then a piercing scream rent the air. "No, no, no!"

It was Sadik, running out from a corner of the atrium, away from the grasp of the hantumu, tears running down his face, kris in hand, toward the Sultan and the Sorcerer. Adi watched horror-struck as the young man reached the Sorcerer and stood before him, trembling, his face wild with uncontrollable emotions. "No! It cannot be you. It cannot be so. Say I am dreaming! Say I—"

"Sadik," said Shayk Rasheed al-Jabal quietly, in his normal voice, "you are a fool. Get back—stay there with Ibrahim. Nothing will happen to you; you are not an enemy but one of us."

"You . . . you said we were . . . we were the Army of Light . . . fighting the demons."

"And so we are," said the Shayk impatiently. "We are the warriors of truth, Sadik, fighting to cleanse Jayangan of its ancient evils, its alliances with unclean spirits. We will create a place worthy of the Light here, Sadik. A place from which all the demons will flee, blinded by the Light. We will establish here the reign of Light on earth!"

"Well, what of . . . him . . . it . . ." said Sadik, jabbing with a thumb in the direction of the afreet, "and them." He indicated the hantumu.

"The afreet is under my command. You do not need to be afraid of it. It was thrown out of Jehannem by Iblis, but I have no dealings with that one. I do not need to. I have a ring, see." And he held up his hand, on which his silver ring glittered. "It is a ring of power, which commands that slave. Sometimes unusual methods have to be employed, but we will have no need of it once the kingdom of Light is established in Jayangan. As to the others, they're my dedicated fighters. You know them, Sadik. They're your comrades." He motioned to a couple of hantumu to take off their masks.

Sadik stared at the faces revealed there. "Ali," he murmured, "Jamal. Then our community . . ."

"It was the nucleus of my army, yes. Not everyone there, oh no, not those like you, Sadik, who I could see were too weak to take part at present." He sighed. "Yet I thought that had changed when you brought me the boy. I thought you had grown up at last, that you could become a fighter too. That's why I took you with us. Sadik, come to me." He held out a hand, smiling, but Sadik shrank away, still clutching the kris.

"Very well," said the Shayk coldly. In his spotless white robes with one of the big black revolvers he'd had in the car at his belt, he looked commanding despite his slightness—and utterly ruthless. Adi, staring from his helpless position, thought, Oh my God, how could I ever have thought this man good? How could I have ever thought that was purity shining from those icy-cold fanatic's eyes? They were the eyes of a man ready to do anything to accomplish his utter will to power, power not only over the life and death of others but also over their souls and thoughts and feelings. His reign would be a terrible one indeed.

And now the memory of his pleasure at hearing the Shayk's life story made his flesh creep. He was a hardened fighter, a watcher in the shadows, an evil deceiver prepared to use anything, even demons, to achieve his single-minded aim.

Adi's attention jerked back to Sadik. He looked ill and was unable to stand straight but staggered, words coming jerkily from him: "Oh, God help me. I thought you so great . . . loved you so . . . trusted in you, O Master, and yet you have killed . . . you have deceived . . . you consort with evil spirits . . ."

"Ibrahim, shut his stupid mouth—he will never understand," said the Shayk wearily, and Ibrahim obediently came forward and fetched the boy a mighty whack with the flat of his sword, catching him on the side of the head. Sadik sank to the ground without a cry. The Shayk made a shooing motion, and Jamal and Ali dragged the unconscious young man to one side of the atrium. Adi cried out under the gag. This was his fault. He had thought the Shayk to be Snow, and now poor, innocent Sadik and the Sultan were paying the price.

The sound he made must have reached the Shayk's ears. He looked over at Adi and a smile creased his unwrinkled, ivory-colored face. "Why, my Nashranee friend, I was almost forgetting you. And yet how useful you have been to us!" Trailed by Ibrahim, and ignoring the Sultan, he strode over to where the boy was lying. "I should offer you the opportunity to be with us. Though you are a dirty little Nashranee, you can change. Do you want to accept the Light into your heart, my son?"

Over his gag, Adi's eyes burned defiantly into the Shayk's. The latter shook his head, ruefully. "I see by that fierce glare that the Light cannot reach your hardened heart. Never mind. I never really thought it would. Well, would you like to know what we have in store for you? We'll be accomplishing that stupid prophecy you brought us, about needing Snow, Fire and Sword to defeat the evil in the land. See, Adi, Fire and Sword are already here." He waved a hand at the afreet and Ibrahim. "Only Snow is missing. I know you thought I was it, but in the language of the spirit world, Snow is actually a sacrifice, for how can Snow survive in the land of the sun? So, Adi, being as you are so fond of the disgusting customs of your native land, I know you will enjoy fulfilling the wishes of the demons you have lived under for so long." He jerked his head to Ibrahim and Jamal. "Take him, and that fool of a Sadik, and throw them both in the pool. We have wasted too much time on these stupid young men already."

"No!" Adi tried to say, under the gag. He looked at Ibrahim, trying to plead with his eyes, to ask for mercy, but Ibrahim merely smiled and roughly picked him up under the shoulders. Jamal stared impassively at him, picking up his feet. Adi struggled, but the men held him in a grip of steel. The Shayk had already turned away, murmuring sadly, "Thus die the evildoers at the hand of—" when all at once, a screaming, yelling girl seemed to appear right out of the shadows, caught him squarely around the middle, and sent him flying backward to land on the ground, thoroughly winded.

Pandemonium erupted. Ibrahim and the others immediately dropped Adi and ran to their master's aid, pulling the girl off him and throwing her so heavily to the ground that her eyes rolled back in her head. But before they could do any more, they were set upon by a whirling, black-robed giant, swinging a massive curved sword above his head. "Back, back, cowards, murderers!" he yelled in a stentorian voice, pushing Ibrahim and his friends away from the fallen girl. "Or are you too scared to fight like men, from spending too much time with a liar and traitor and coward like al-Jabal?"

Howling like a banshee, Jamal threw himself at the swordsman; the curved sword descended, and Jamal's head flew across the room. Ali dropped his sword and backed away, but Ibrahim, with a raucous cry, parried with his own sword, in a lightning movement and a resounding clash of metal on metal. The other hantumu, who had been frozen into immobility by the sight of Jamal's severed head, rushed in to help now, but the black-robed swordsman was fighting hard, his eyes gleaming madly above the cloth that swathed the rest of his face. *Thwack!* He got in a huge hit with the flat of his sword on a man's shoulders, and the man went down without a sound. He whirled around just in time to face another attack from Ibrahim, and at that moment the Shayk rose swiftly from the ground, his hand on his gun. Quick as a striking snake, he took aim and fired straight at Husam—for of course the swordsman was he. There was a huge roar, and a tongue of red and yellow flame enveloped the bullet in a shower of sparks. The hantumu jumped back in alarm as the fiery bullet reversed its course and came speeding back toward the gun. The Shayk only just had time to throw the weapon away from him before it literally exploded, setting the hem of his robe on fire and scorching his eyebrows. The tongue of flame rose and took on the shape of a great red bird, with claws of molten metal, feathers of flame, and eyes that glowed. Just as it was about to swoop on the Shayk's head, he twisted his ring and screamed something, and the afreet abandoned its post behind the Sultan and jumped into the air, its body vanishing. In its place was a great white dragon that flamed with pure, blinding fire all along its sides and back; its eyes were red as hot coals. The white dragon threw itself on the red bird, and for an instant all the other combatants paused, struck by the terrifying sight of fire fighting fire. Then the battle began again in earnest, the Shayk himself picking up Jamal's sword and throwing himself into the fray.

The noise of the battle would have been enough to wake the dead, and it certainly woke up Sadik, who had been forgotten in the melee. For an instant, he stared at the scene before him, then, catching sight of Adi still lying trussed and helpless where he'd been dumped, he slid over to him and pulled the gag from his face. "My kris, over there," whispered Adi. "Quick."

Sadik grabbed the kris and cut Adi's bonds. Adi

winced. His hands and feet tingled and spasmed abominably; they would not obey him. Sadik, picking up a sword from the ground, crawled over to the Sultan as fast as he could to cut his bonds. Biting down on his lip with frustration and rage, Adi managed to bring one of his hands under command, grabbed his kris, and set off as quickly as he could, sliding along the floor, toward Sadik.

But the Shayk had seen what was happening. Twisting his ring, he called for the afreet. The white dragon paused in its battle with the other fire spirit to send a livid, dazzling tongue of flame racing toward Sadik. It struck him full on the forehead, sending him reeling back, his eyes suddenly filling with horror, his arms whirling like windmills as the full force of the afreet's power crashed into his defenseless mind. He stumbled and fell heavily to the ground, striking his head hard on an outcrop of rock, and lay still. The Shayk smiled thinly and turned back to the battle, but Adi, with a roar of rage, sprang up from the floor, his kris gripped tightly now. He couldn't feel or hear anything. There was a great roaring in his head that didn't just have to do with the battle of the two Jinns. He had never felt like this before; he wanted to wipe the Shayk not only off the face of the earth, but from all memory. But as he charged at the old man, one of the hantumu stuck out a foot and sent him crashing down. In the same instant, the Shayk threw himself on the Sultan, pinned his arms to his side, and held a sword to his throat. Then he put a finger on his ring and called, "Hareekshaytin, come to me!"

As he did so, Dewi appeared from under his arm, grabbing for his hand with all her might. "The ring! The ring!" she screamed. "It's the source of his power over the afreet. Without it, he cannot command it. Kareen Amar, help us!"

The white dragon roared. Like an arrow it came flying down from the air toward Dewi, but the red bird was on its tail, singing a long, wild, wordless song, its claws outstretched to rip at the dragon's form. The dragon was not hurt, but it was hindered, halted long enough for Adi to tear up from the ground, raise his kris, and stab blindly, connecting with flesh. He stumbled back as the Shayk, with a piercing scream, dropped his sword and clutched at the bloody wound where his ring finger had once been. Everything stilled around them for an instant. But the old warrior was not yet done. His face pale as death, and contorted with fury and pain, he dived for his own severed finger on the floor, pulled off the bloody ring, threw it in the air, and yelled, "Son of the Flame, I set you free! Remember that for this you owe me one last thing—I command you to unleash your full power against all my enemies!"

At once, the ring vanished in a shower of sparks. The white dragon shivered. Flames shot out from it, and the usual form of the afreet emerged like a form from molten glass. It put its head back and gave a most peculiar call that threw ice into the spines of all there and rooted them to the spot, thoughts of battle forgotten for the moment. "I am the Son of the Flame! I am Hareekshaytin! I am the vizier of dread Iblis, Lord of Jehannem!" bellowed the afreet, and as they watched, it grew bigger and bigger and bigger, till it towered above them. "Your ring has gone, and you cannot command me anymore, old man. I bow only to Lord Iblis now." It vanished in a thunderclap, and as the echoes of the thunderclap died away, a terrible smell filled the atrium and two huge eyes—white-hot, inhuman—appeared. Someone screamed, "It is dread Iblis himself, come in place of his vizier!" and in that instant an enormous wall of roaring white flame appeared, cutting the atrium in two. A couple of hantumu, caught near the wall, were immediately enveloped in flames and writhed, screaming, while the other combatants fell over each other in their rush to get away. Adi and Dewi were thrown across the chamber and lay stunned. The Shayk, however, had seized his chance. He was escaping up the stairs, safe behind the wall of flame. But all at once a song was heard—a song high and sad and beautiful and strong in its longing—and the red bird shot through the wall of flame and disappeared. Clearly, they heard a scream from the Shayk. "Iblis! I command you! Kill the Jinn, and the others!"

The wall of flame wavered; then a wild howl of rage echoed around the chamber. It was Iblis's voice—the voice of the dread Lord of Jehannem, the voice that would come to them in their nightmares for years on end. "You dare command me! You dare! I bow to no man!" The wall of flame wavered, then shot upward and whooshed out of the atrium, straight up the stairwell, enveloping the Shayk in a ghastly dazzle of blinding light, which shattered and was instantly gone. The Shayk vanished into thin air.

The chamber was suddenly plunged into complete darkness. A terrified silence held for a heartbeat; then confused shouts and yells erupted. Adi had no idea what was happening; he could hear the sound of running feet, screams, a splash, yells. Someone trod heavily on one of his hands, and he heard Ibrahim's angry voice. "The boy, Adi, find him. Stop, you cowards. Stop!"

Adi slid quietly along the floor, away from the voice,

knowing Ibrahim would be as blind and confused as he was; the combination of the terrible dazzling flame followed by the utter darkness made it impossible to see anything at all. But he rather thought that the hantumu, thrown into utter panic by what had just happened, were not listening to Ibrahim, just trying to escape as quickly as they could.

He tried to peer into the darkness. Where was the black-robed swordsman? And where was Dewi? Last he'd seen of her, she'd been sent flying. Where had she fallen? By the pool? Where was the pool? He crawled across the ground, trying to stay as quiet as he could. Then his groping hands found a body, a face, a pulse that was still beating, though faintly. Not Dewi, but . . .

"Oh, Sadik," whispered Adi in the other boy's ear. "Wait, we will get help. We will find healers who—"

There was a gurgle in Sadik's throat.

"Don't try to speak, Sadik." Adi held one of the young man's hands. "Don't speak. You will only become weaker."

"Fool," came Ibrahim's voice. "Fool, now you will die." Adi rolled away, but not quite in time. A stinging pain jolted through him as Ibrahim stabbed him hard in the arm. Clutching his arm, he continued rolling away as swiftly as he could. He heard Ibrahim coming after him, not quickly, because he couldn't see, but relentlessly. Adi felt his way as fast as he could. Where were the stairs? Where was Dewi?

Dizzy now with loss of blood, he stretched out a hand cautiously. He felt something wet. Water! He must be by the pool. He groped a bit farther, away from the water, trying to find Dewi—and nearly screamed as something brushed his ear and someone whispered, "Quiet. Beware. Do not move, my son." It was the Sultan's voice. "Wait until he gets close."

They waited. They could hear Ibrahim moving around, somewhere not very far away. Then all of a sudden, Adi's skin crawled. He could see a small light, faint, like a tiny candle. In that faint light, he could see what looked like a long finger, and on it, a ring set with a glittering white stone. Adi could not speak. The finger gently touched his wound, and he could feel the pain easing, then disappearing. Blood ceased to pump from the gash; his head began to clear.

A voice said softly but clearly into his mind, "My child, you have been angry with me."

"Queen Rorokidul, I am sorry," began Adi nervously.

"No, do not excuse yourself. There is no need to. You did as you thought best—and you could not know how helpless I felt, how angry I was that I and my fellow spirits could not help you more, how powerless we felt. You see, Adi, we spirits could not see the Sorcerer's face because he is not like other Sorcerers, who at least know that they are driven by their own lust for power. This man lied not only to everyone else but even to himself. He said he was in the service of the Light, but he was only in the service of the unholy fire that burned in him. Fire and Sword could fight him, but only Snow could make him show his true face to all. The evil has lifted from Jayangan now because of your bravery, and that of your friends—and the sacrifice of Snow. And so the healing water can flow again in this land."

Adi said, his throat choked with emotion, "Will you, my Lady, heal my friend Sadik, who, in his purity of heart, was Snow?"

Rorokidul's voice was regretful. "My child, I cannot save him. He is dying; his wound is far greater than yours, for he has been struck in his heart and his mind. I cannot undo what the afreet has done, just as I could not undo what it did to my friend Anda Mangil. I wish it were otherwise, but it cannot be. And so it is accomplished."

Before Adi could reply, Ibrahim's rough voice broke in, very close now. "Talking to demons, are you, boy?" And all at once, in the growing light that was pooling around the risen Queen of the Southern Sea, Adi saw the man's face: streaked with blood and sweat, viciously twisted with hatred and rage. Ibrahim's sword flashed—but it never came down, for Rorokidul's finger shot into the air and he fell with a great gurgling cry, right into the pool behind him. Then Adi heard a sound that he would never forget, a sound that would occasionally wake him up at night, sweating, in years to come. It was a sound as if of a great maw, crunching, grinding, cutting short Ibrahim's terrified scream, as the water devoured him whole.

"Thus die the evildoers," said the Sultan with satisfaction. But Adi had had enough. He stood up and walked away from the pool. And there was Dewi, disheveled and bruised, but unmistakably whole and alive.

He had no words to say to her—he could not speak, he had such a lump in his throat—but he walked over to her, held her tightly for a heartbeat, then released her. She colored slightly and murmured, "Oh, Adi, I am so glad you are here."

"And I you," he managed to say. "You . . . you saved my life back there, Dewi, when they were going to throw me into the . . ." He gulped and looked over his shoulder. The Sultan was still sitting by the pool, looking into it, but Rorokidul was gone.

"And you saved me," said Dewi. "The Sorcerer

would have killed me if it hadn't been for you springing up with your kris." Adi gripped Dewi's hands without speaking, feeling the warmth of them in his own cold ones. Their eyes met; then they turned away and saw a man coming toward them: a tall, black-garbed old man with the face of a hawk, holding a bloody sword.

"You must be Adi," he said quietly. "And I am Husam al-Din."

Sword, thought Adi dully, and he acknowledged Husam's greeting courteously. The four of them were alone now; all the surviving hantumu had fled, and only the dead remained. And Sadik. Sadik, the purest of heart of all, the true Snow, who was dying.

Adi left Dewi and Husam and returned to his friend's side, to kneel by him and hold his hand. It would be lonely for poor Sadik, setting off into the night without anyone he loved. No parents, no siblings, no family, no members of his beloved community. And his master gone forever, lost to him, lost to the world, lost to God Himself. Oh, how bitter it must be, to set out like this to the House of Dust, knowing everything you had thought and believed in and loved was a terrible, terrible lie. Tears rolled unchecked down Adi's face and onto the young man's skin.

Sadik's eyes were closed but he still breathed, very

faintly. Dewi and Husam and the Sultan came to sit by him too, sorrow written on all their faces. No one spoke for a moment. Then Adi said, very softly, "She said it was accomplished, as if that should be enough, when he lies dying. She said . . ."

He could not continue. Dewi said, "We know, Adi. We know. And it is a bitter, bitter thing to say, that the spirits know some have to die so their sacrifice can save others. But they choose their path, Adi, and freely. The spirits cannot force them into it. Snow is the path of the pure, truthful heart. Those who choose that path know the truth when they see it; they are not afraid of it; and they act for it, even if it costs them their lives." She paused, and added with tears in her voice, "Sadik, Anda Mangil, and too many others die not because of any foretelling of spirits, but because of those fanatical killers who say they follow the Light, yet who in their blind, cruel arrogance mistake the livid flames of Jehannem for the gentle glow of Heaven."

Adi nodded without speaking. Dewi placed her hand on Adi's, which held Sadik's; and then Husam quietly placed his hand on hers. Sadik suddenly opened his eyes and said, very distinctly, "I am glad you are with me, my friends." He looked at Adi. "We are friends of the heart, aren't we, Adi? I always knew we would be. And such friends never forget each other, no matter where they are." Adi could not speak, he was crying too hard. "Don't weep, Adi. I can see such a light coming, such a beautiful country, just beyond the edge of my vision. And there is so much love there, so much peace. Oh, it would delight you to see it! There is just one thing, before I go. Do any of you know the words for the dying, in the Mujisal way? I would like to go to meet God with the right preparation."

"Yes, my friend," said Husam, with much emotion, and Dewi and the Sultan echoed him. Together, the three of them began to murmur the sacred words of farewell, the words before death, that might lead a flying soul on the path to Paradise. As the ancient words washed gently over Sadik, his eyes closed again. There was a smile of mixed joy and melancholy on his face, the smile of someone who saw a new life both wondrous and beautiful opening before him, but who was also taking leave of his old life and friends. The breath left his body as he smiled, and so gentle was his soul's leave-taking of earth that they did not even know the precise moment when he died.

TWENTY-EIGHT

"IT IS NOT over yet," said the Sultan, a while later. He, Husam, and Dewi were conferring in low voices, while Adi sat quietly beside the body of his friend Sadik. "The Shayk still holds my son."

"I do not think the Shayk holds anyone anymore," said Husam. "Not after what happened in this place."

"His men will be running for their lives now. And I know where your son is likely to have been held, Sire," said Dewi. "A pit, near Old Mountain."

"Old Mountain! That is the other side of the country, around Gunungbatu," said the Sultan, brightening. "Of course, that is where the Shayk had his wretched community. Once Yanto is safe, I will destroy the whole place!"

"No," said Adi, coming up to them at that moment. "I mean, please, no, Your Majesty. Good people live there, as well as bad ones. They should be given a chance to do good work. There is much need in our country, Sire."

The Sultan raised an eyebrow. "Well, we'll see. We'll clean the place out anyway, get rid of the fanatics. And we'll hunt down all those hantumu and put them on trial. Now then, I need to get back to the palace at once, send a rescue team to Old Mountain." He started off up the stairs, then stopped and turned back to face them. "Thank you very dearly, my friends. You have saved us all. I will never forget what you have done. Never. You will be given every honor and every reward you might want to ask for. The Sultan of Jayangan always keeps his word."

"Sire," said Dewi, "there is one thing that must be done: When the rescue team is sent to Old Mountain, please make sure enough food and drink and transport is sent for many men and women, not just one."

"Ah, your father, Dewi, and your master, Adi, are there too, are they not? Of course it shall be done. Of course. And when all are well and recovered, we will hold great ceremonies on Old Mountain and in this very atrium, to heal the land, and thank God for our deliverance, and repair all our links to the world of the spirits. And the ones who will conduct those ceremonies will be all those great and wise men and women whom the Shayk sought to destroy. The fool!

Perhaps it was because he was a foreigner that he thought my country would fall at his wicked feet."

Husam replied, "It is not his foreign blood but his nature, Sire, which matters in the case of Rasheed al-Jabal. Evil calls to evil, wherever in the world it is found, and he found enough free men here happy enough to carry out his tasks, as well as the enslaved afreet. Shayk Rasheed al-Jabal always thought himself so clever, Sire. And he was a master deceiver and a clever trickster indeed. He may well have spun his last deception and played his last trick, but still, he's not the only one of his kind."

Dewi looked quickly at him. There had been an uncertainty in his voice that chilled her momentarily. Surely no one could escape from Iblis? Surely Jehannem was not a place that had an exit? Of course, there were others—others who had heard him, who had become emmeshed in his seductive lies, and who were now at large. Nothing compared to the Shayk, but their power could grow, if they were not found and stopped.

"Did you know him before?" the Sultan said.

Husam nodded. "Not long after your father the Sultan employed me, there was talk of this man, who had recently arrived in Jayangan. In my home country of Al Aksara, he had stirred up a great deal of trouble; he was known as a dangerous manipulator and deceiver, though he had always managed to avoid justice. I advised your father of his true nature and that he should get rid of him. Indeed, I thought it best to imprison or execute him, but your father was as kind as yourself and thought it wrong not to give a man a chance. After all, he said, no witnesses had dared to implicate Rasheed al-Jabal, and his crimes had been committed in a far-off country long ago. I said the tiger never changes his stripes, but of course I accepted your father's ruling, Sire. Besides, al-Jabal was banished, and we were well rid of him for a time. I had not heard he had come back."

"Oh," said the Sultan, looking rather embarassed. "My father never said why the man was banished, and so when my son petitioned me to—"

"Yes," said Husam. "Your father, Sire, had wanted to give the man a chance. Fair enough. Most people deserve a chance. But some—well, they don't. You can't believe a word they say."

The Sultan sighed. "I wish I had known this, Husam. Well! Now it is done. And it is time we should go." Briskly, he started up the stairs.

"We cannot leave Sadik here," said Adi. "We will

need to carry him out into the sunlight."

"Of course," said Husam and Dewi, and together, the three of them carried Sadik's body gently between them, making their way up the stone staircase, their steps heavy and respectful.

When they got to the top of the stairs, they stepped into a transfigured garden. New flowers and leaves had sprouted on every tree and bush, and from them came the murmur of many voices. Dewi, looking down the path toward the garden wall, saw, in the blink of an eye, forms made of twilight and shadow and patches of sun, faces she recognized: a tall green woman; a lovely old Radenteng lady with an agelessly beautiful face; a silver-haired woman with stormy dark eyes; a yellow-eyed tiger-man with a white turban; and many, many more. But no flame-haired Jinn, no Kareen Amar. The faces were all smiling. She looked at them, then at Adi and Husam, and a mixture of tears and joy came welling up into her throat. She could not know yet if the price so many had paid would not be in vain, if evil had been dealt a decisive blow, and if the forces of dharma, of good, had now fully regained the upper hand. All she knew for sure was that her world had changed, both for good and for ill, and nothing would turn the clock back. She had passed from childhood into knowledge—knowledge of things she had never even imagined before, not in her sweetest dream or worst nightmare. She would have to pass on that knowledge, not just to her family, or even her country, but in all places in the world where it might be needed.

She looked across at Adi. The young Nashranee's eyes were heavy lidded with grief. Adi, too, was no longer the same; his whole life had been turned off its course. What it would turn into, what her own life would turn into, she had no real idea, but she knew that fear and hope, sorrow and happiness, lay ahead. And friendship, deep and strong, with Adi and Husam. Only of that could she be sure.

They were nearly at the gate when into the solemn, golden stillness came a long blast on a car horn, then the *thump thump thump* of a car radio. And in the gateway appeared a big, beautiful dark-red car, which trundled sedately into the garden and right up to the mourners, while all the plants bent back to let it pass.

A familiar face was peering anxiously through the driver's windshield—a red-and-white, blotchy face with red hair a little the worse for wear, scorched and scraped bald in places, but still bright as flame. When Kareen Amar saw them, she beamed, waved, and wound the side window all the way down. The haunting strains of "Beloved" wafted softly through into the evening garden, surrounding Sadik's body, his friends, and the green beauty around them with the joy and sadness, the passing and the immortality, of love itself.

GLOSSARY

adhubilah—a sacred formula in the language of Al Aksara giving protection against evil spirits such as afreets. Usually written above doors.

afreet—a powerful evil Jinn, usually living in Jehannem under the rule of Iblis. May also be enslaved by human sorcerers and used to accomplish difficult tasks.

Al Aksara—the Great Desert, far away across the sea, west of Jayangan. The Mujisal religion began in Al Aksara, and its holiest shrine is the House of Light, deep in the desert. It is the spiritual center of Dawtarn el 'Jisal, the Lands of the Mujisal.

Balian Besakih—the island kingdom to the east of Jayangan. Dominated by the Dharbudsu religion.

Bapar—an honorific title meaning "Mister" and also "Father" in Jayanganese.

Baratja—the western province of Jayangan.

betchar—a vehicle comprising a bicycle attached behind a two-wheeled carriage.

Bumi Macan—Dewi's home village.

Chandi Maya—an ancient complex of Dharbudsu temples not far from Kotabunga. Was once the major temple complex of Jayangan.

Demityangan—the mysterious mountain forest in the east of Jayangan, home of forest spirits and bird witches.

Dharbudsu—one of the three main religions of Jayangan. Was once the majority religion, until the advent of the Mujisal faith. Still has many adherents in Jayangan, and is the majority religion in the island kingdom of Balian Besakih. Its sacred writings are contained within the Book of Life. Some countries in the world are still dominated by the Dharbudsu religion; these are known collectively as Dawtarn el 'Budsu, or Lands of Dharbudsu.

dukun—a traditional village healer/magician/shaman.

Empu—an honorific title meaning "Master" in Jayanganese.

Gunungbatu—the rocky, infertile region to the south of Kotabunga.

hantumu—in modern times, the hantumu are masked, black-clad human assassins, mounted on motorbikes and carrying long swords. In the past, the hantumu were heard of only in stories; they were described as shadowy evil spirits who preyed on lone villagers and stragglers on roads.

Harimauroh—the tiger-people, spirits who live in the forest near Bumi Macan.

Iblis—the Demon King, Lord of the evil Jinn. His

realm is Jehannem.

Jatimur—the eastern province of Jayangan.

Jayangan—the island where this book is set. In Jayanganese, the name of the island means "Dwelling Place of the Gods."

Jehannem—the realm of Iblis, Demon King and Lord of the evil Jinn.

Jinn—one of the Hidden People or spirit people of Al Aksara and many other places in the Dawtarn el 'Jisal. Jinns can be good or bad or in between, male or female in appearance, or even present as animals. They can metamorphose at will and have various magical powers. They were created from fire and are immortal. Some live in tribes and clans, others are lone spirits.

Kejawen—the central province of Jayangan. Kotabunga, the capital of Jayangan and seat of the Sultan of Jayangan, is there.

Kotabunga—the "City of Flowers," the capital city of Jayangan and seat of the Sultan.

kris—a sword or long dagger with a wiggly-shaped blade. It is not only a weapon but also an important symbol for people in Jayangan.

Mujisal—the majority religion of Jayangan and many other places in the world, including Al Aksara, where it originated. Its sacred writings are contained in the Book of Light. A small segment of the Mujisal population practices the Pumujisal variety of the religion, which is much stricter than the general variety. The countries in the world that have a majority Mujisal population are known collectively as Dawtarn el 'Jisal, or Lands of the Mujisals.

Nashranee—one of the minority religions of Jayangan. Came to the island after the Dharbudsu and Mujisal religions. Though it is a minority religion in Jayangan and other countries of the Dawtarn el 'Jisal, it is a majority religion in many other places, which are collectively known as Dawtarn el 'Ranee, or Lands of the Nashranees. Its sacred writings are contained in the Book of Love.

Priangan—the sacred mountain in the far west of Baratja.

Pumujisal—a small, strict sect of the Mujisal religion. Frowns on pleasure of all sorts, believes in work and study only. Its adherents usually dress in pure white, and are often opposed to other religions.

Radenteng—one of the minority races in Jayangan, who are descended from traders and explorers who came to Jayangan from the great Radentengan Empire, far to the northeast of Jayangan.

Rummiyans—the Nashranee countries that lie far to the west of Al Aksara.

Shayk—an honorific title, coming from Al Aksara and meaning "Lord."

Siluman—the portal to the ocean realm of Rorokidul, the Queen of the Southern Sea, and a beach south of Kotabunga.

Sultan—the king of Jayangan.

Tomb of the Five Saints—a sacred Mujisal site in the ancient city of Jaksa.

Tuan—an honorific title meaning "Lord" in Jayanganese.

Water Gardens of Kotabunga—one of the sacred sites of Kejawen. Contains the Atrium of Rorokidul.

zummiyah water—water taken from the sacred well near the House of Light in Al Aksara. Can protect against evil spirits.

ABOUT THE AUTHOR

Sophie Masson was born in Indonesia of French parents and was brought up mainly in Australia. A bilingual French and English speaker, she has a master's degree in French and English literature. Sophie is the prolific author of numerous young adult fantasy novels as well as several adult novels. She lives in Armidale, New South Wales, Australia, with her husband and children.

9/04
MLib